THE MAN  ES

THE CARPENTER'S CHILDREN

J. ROTCHELL

Copyright © 2024 by J. Rotchell

ISBN - 9798870278872

All rights reserved.
No part of this publication may be reproduced, distributed, or transmitted in any form or by any means, including photocopying, recording, or other electronic or mechanical methods, without the prior written permission of the publisher.

The story, names, characters, and incidents portrayed in this production are fictitious or, in the case of certain names, are used fictitiously and are not intended to be a true representation of such persons.

Book cover and Illustrations by Meriel Puttick

FOR ELIZA & FLYNN

NEVER STOP EXPLORING

LOVE DAD
X

TRANSLATIONS & PRONUNCIATIONS

The Old Tongue (MANX)	Pronunciation	The New Tongue (ENGLISH)
Ealish	**Ay-lish**	Alice
Ashlishyn	**Azh**-lish-urn	Visions
Traa Dy Liooar	**Trair** the **L'yew**er	Time Enough
Eayst Folley	Ais **Foll**er	Blood Moon
Dragane ta giu	Dra**gaan** ta **giu**	Drinking Dragane
Dreamallyn	**Dray**-mull-urn	Dreams
Tromlhieyn	Trum-**lie**-urn	Nightmares
Guinn Y Vaaish	**Gun** uh **Vaash**	Pain of Death
Roddanyn Doo	**Rod**-than-urn Doo	Black Rats
Volcaan	Vol**caan**	Volcano
Balley Chashtal	**Bal'**yer **Khash**-chul	Place of the castle (Castletown)
Boaldyn	**Bawld**ern	Manx summer festival
Mollaght obbee	**Moll**akh **obb**ee	Magical curse
Droghad ny Ferrishyn	**Drok**had nuh **Ferr**ish-urn	Faerie Bridge
Oie Houney	Ee **How**ner	Manx winter festival
Slieau	Sl'**yew**	Mountain
Ellan	**Ell'**yan	Island
Jiass	Jass	South
Hiar	H'yar	East
Heear	Heer	West

Twoaie	**Too**-ee	North
Shenn	Shen/Shan	Ancient
Jarroodit	Jer**rood**it	Forgotten
Moddey Doo	**Maw**ther **Doo**	Black Dog
Cashtal ny Raunyn	**Cash**tul nuh **Roan**-ern	Castle of the Seal
Moanee	**Moh**-nee	Moorland
Kibbin	**K'yivv**in	Spike
Clagh foalsey	Clakh fawlser	Fake rock
Wiggynnee	**Wigg**er-nee	Vikings

PROLOGUE

A full, red moon rises against the black canvas of the night sky.

No stars are visible, just the deep, sanguine glow of the moon.

A blur of movement is briefly silhouetted against the face of the moon - fast, but not so fast that the discernible shape of a pair of wings aren't visible for a brief moment.

In the distance, the cry of a baby; faint, distinct, desperate – never growing louder, constant.

A tree appears in the foreground, unmistakeable in its shadowy outline.

A further flurry of movement crosses the moon's face.

This time the movement is less panicked. Determined.

A creature hangs temporarily in suspended flight across the lunar glow. An ear-splitting roar silences the baby's cries, a bolt of lightning thrown from the creature's throat strikes The Tree – an instant explosion of light that fades as quickly as it arrived.

The Tree remains steadfast, just a single bough falling silently to the ground.

The moon sinks in the sky and rests on the horizon over the sea, casting a blood red path of light across the rippling surface.

A drum begins to beat. Steady, increasing in volume but maintaining rhythm. A boat cuts through the path of light dispersing it across the surface, turning the entire sea to blood.

The ship is gone, the drum beat fades and the creature passes once more across the moon as it rises in the sky.

The crest of a hill rises toward the moon and takes a bite from it, ruining its perfect shape.

On top of the hill a figure appears in outline, featureless but clearly a warrior – a spear in the warrior's left hand is hoisted aloft and thrown into the dark.

Not into the dark.

Into the flight path of the creature.

The weapon finds its mark and the creature falls from the sky without a sound.

The cry of the baby returns as the moon turns its face from the scene it has just witnessed.

All is black.

All is quiet.

-1-
NANE

Flax woke, his body immobile but his mind racing, thinking, taking in as much information as he could.

Then he turned to his side and picked up the parchment and writing stick that he always kept next to his bed.

He emptied his mind onto the parchment as he had done innumerable times before.

He stopped and looked over his markings, double checking what he had written against his own memory.

This dream had tormented him as long as he could remember and still, he could make no sense of it.

He had always kept it to himself, not knowing what others would say if he shared it with them. He placed the parchment with countless others – knowing they all contained the same information – give or take the odd detail.

Flax had heard tales of the *Eayst Folley* – a full moon with a face as red as blood but had never witnessed it himself except in his dreams and had no idea what caused it.

Of course the Islanders all had their own ideas, however the truth was that nobody could really be sure. It was documented in the Island archives that they had been witnessed by many but there did not appear to be any pattern as to when they would occur. Past experience led Islanders to believe that the blood moon signalled great change. This was not always a positive thing.

Flax focused his mind on the first shadowy movement across the moon "… definitely wings…" he said to himself, "… but definitely different wings to the flying creature."

The flying creature was a winged lizard, he was sure of that – a *Dragane* - he had heard them called in the old language. But Draganes, according to Island lore, breathed fire not lightning. In any case, no living person had ever seen such a beast. The closest anybody had ever come to one was the rock formation in the sea to the south of the Island that from a certain angle vaguely resembled what people believed a Dragane to look like, its neck bent with its head toward the water. Hence it had adopted the name *Dragane ta giu* or in the new tongue - *The Drinking Dragane.*

There was nothing particularly memorable about the boat in the dream, it was only outlined briefly against the moonlight. But its presence significantly changed the environment; it turned the sea to blood. *That cannot be a good omen*, he thought to himself.

The warrior? - Flax had no idea who it could be. The Islanders did not use spears – their weapons of choice were fighting staffs, bows and slingshots. Even then those weapons were only used for training and hunting. Whoever this warrior was, he was clearly not an Islander.

Then the baby's cry.

Flax closed his eyes and lay back on his bed concentrating, focusing in on the details that he had remembered – not only on this occasion but on every previous occasion he had woken from this dream.

What does it all mean? He asked himself silently, then paused to concentrate once more.

"Maybe it means nothing," he spoke aloud, opening his eyes, "maybe it's a collection of thoughts or fantasies and it means absolutely nothing." Flax had tried to persuade himself of this before, however he'd never convinced himself enough to commit to the idea.

Islanders had a history of *dreamallyn* and *tromlhieyn* – literally dreams and nightmares in the old language – that either came true or had an impact on the Island in some way. More commonly these were referred to as *ashlishyn* or visions.

Many of the Island eldership would tell stories of when *ashlishyn* had proved vital to the survival of the Island by either foretelling events to come or reminding of lessons learnt in seasons past.

Flax knew in his heart and head that his dream, or his nightmare, was an *ashlishyn*. What he didn't know was what it meant. He didn't even know whether it was something that was yet to happen or something that had happened before his time.

The one thing Flax recognised and could be absolutely sure about in the vision was The Tree.

The Tree stood on the Island. In fact, the village was built around The Tree. Island lore recorded that when the first settlers arrived on the Island they used this tree for shelter. This tree was like no other on the Island. It bore no fruit. During the autumn its leaves would turn a brilliant gold colour.

When winter crept in its leaves would turn silver and curl in on themselves so tightly they would look like the needles of a pine tree, but they would hold steadfast on the branches throughout the harsh weather extremes that the Island endured.

In spring the leaves would unfurl and turn a rich green.

Come summer it would bloom for the entire season, then its flowers would close back into their buds at the turn of the autumn and flower again at the start of the next summer season— only the flowers would be a different colour each year.

Not once had a leaf or a petal ever fallen from The Tree, despite the severe weather extremes it was exposed to. There was certainly no other tree like it on the Island – nobody even knew what species it was – that is why it was simply referred to as *The Tree*. Other trees on the Island suffered as would be expected in the environment. As such they were grown by the Islanders in managed plantations in more sheltered areas to prevent damage from the biting sea winds. Not The Tree though, it remained steadfast and immovable.

Records suggested that the first Islanders had tried to harvest wood from The Tree for shelters and making tools and weapons. Only, when they had struck the boughs with their sharpened axes not a mark was made on the bark of The Tree. The Islanders had then used fire on The Tree in an attempt to fell it. The fire had simply not taken to the wood. The Tree seemed to possess some form of invisible magical protection.

Since that time no Islander had dared to even attempt to harm or damage The Tree, it was considered sacred and was a great talking point with any visitor to the Island.

The Islanders even used The Tree as their living calendar, it is how they kept records of time and age.

No matter when an Islander had been born, they would all celebrate a birthday on the first night after The Tree bloomed. A great festival would be held during which gifts were exchanged and everyone feasted together then danced and sang late into the night.

Islanders recorded their number of years alive as blooms – Flax was approaching sixteen blooms of age.

The fact that this tree appeared in Flax's *ashlishyn* was one of the reasons that he dared not mention it to anyone. The idea that something could damage The Tree was not one that he liked to think of. The Tree was a pivotal part of Island life – what would people think if they knew that there was even a chance The Tree could or would be damaged?

-2-
JEES

He stood and stretched out his limbs one by one. Then closed his eyes once more, concentrating on his dream until a familiar scent of freshly baked bread took his attention, he opened his eyes and blinked away the image of The Tree with the falling bough that felt as if it was etched into his vision. After dressing himself he ran his hands through his wavy golden hair. Flax looked at his reflection in a bowl of cold water that he kept in his room. His green-brown eyes stared back examining his face and his unruly hair. With a final attempt to make it look acceptable he ran his hands through it again and then headed out of his room.

Walking into the kitchen he was greeted by his mother who had wrapped some of the freshly baked bread along with some cheese for him to take whilst he carried out his morning jobs.

Flax said goodbye to her, kissing the top of her head as she had always done to him before he grew taller than her. Then collecting his axe and spade, he headed through the village.

Spring was nearly at an end and the anticipation in the village that was palpable. Everyone knew Bloom Day would soon be here and preparations for the festival were in full swing. A large part of the excitement of Bloom Day was that nobody ever knew exactly when it would arrive. Of course, some claimed to know when it would occur and how to calculate this, but on the odd occasion that anybody was ever correct it was attributed more to blind luck than scientific reason.

Looking ahead, Flax could see The Tree standing proud above the village with its many branches reaching out in every direction, leaves and buds moving gently in the morning breeze. Despite the early hour, Flax could already see a familiar figure laid at the base of the trunk taking refuge from the rising sun in the cool shadows beneath.

He shook his head and muttered to himself before turning left and heading out of the village. His intended destination was one of the many small plantations of trees that he managed as part of his job on the Island. It wasn't a job in the sense that he was paid anything for doing it – in fact there was no real need for money on the Island – everybody had their roles and they carried them out. People traded items and food stuffs with each other but there was no need for the items known as coins that visitors would often talk about or offer in trade.

Flax's job was to manage the woodland areas and this included hunting within them – only enough to provide what was necessary for food though. He also felled and chopped the trees for wood, some of which was used for fuel for the fires and the remainder went to his father's workshop. Flax's father was one of the Island elders. He was also the master carpenter.

As Flax had grown he'd often thought to himself there was nothing his Dad couldn't make from wood – tools, weapons, furniture even boats were common objects made by him. From time-to-time Flax had tried to assist his father or take on small projects of his own. Whenever he made a mistake he would throw his tools down in an act of frustration and ask, "When will I become as skilled you?"

Every time his father would affectionately ruffle his messy golden hair and reply "*Traa dy liooar* my son…time enough."

Remembering his father's words, Flax smiled to himself and continued hiking up the hill to the west of the village on the way to the first plantation. His intended plan for the morning was to plant some seedlings in an area that he had cleared last autumn before heading on to the next plantation.

Flax looked back toward the village and saw more of the Islanders starting to move about on their daily chores – the same figure reclining under The Tree whilst others busied themselves. To his right he could see the sun seemed to have paused above The Drinking Dragane, a ball of golden fire above its head. Further still past The Drinking Dragane Flax could see the lighthouse that marked the most southerly known point of land to the Islanders.

The lighthouse rose out of the water, a lone watchful sentinel climbing out of a sea so still it could be mistaken for a sheet of ice. On a calm day like today there seemed to be a no more peaceful place that somebody could be. This was a fragile deception as Flax well knew. He had seen first-hand the onslaught of waves that a cruel southern wind would bring upon the lighthouse during storms. Being responsible for keeping the flame burning in such situations was certainly no enviable task, and a lonely one too.

He looked left to the north and saw the strait of water known as The Sound. He had always thought this to be a very peculiar name and nobody seemed to know the origin of it. What they did know was that at a certain tide the top and under currents pulled hard in opposite directions creating a seemingly smooth surface that masked the deadly conditions beneath. So dangerous was this strip of water that it was forbidden for Islanders to attempt to cross it until they were at least eighteen blooms of age – even then it could only be done at certain tides. A small uninhabited stretch of land known as the Kitterland ran from east to west in the middle of the channel. Whether it was an optical illusion or real, the water seemed to flow in different directions on either side of the Kitterland and on every rocky edge of it the waves beat it relentlessly.

Many Islanders were known to have lost their lives in The Sound - often their bodies swept out to sea never to be seen again. Even in Flax's lifetime a boy from the village, not much older than himself, had been killed trying to cross. Swept away, his body never found.

Flax longed to be old enough to cross The Sound, *why?* – because on the other side of The Sound lay the land - or Mannin as it was known in the old tongue.

Mannin was itself an island – many hundreds of times larger than his Island. It lay so close but to Flax it seemed so inaccessible it may as well have been on the moon. He loved to hear stories told by travellers or by returning villagers (who of course were at least eighteen blooms of age) who had been on trade runs to Mannin.

There were all kinds of stories of magical beings such as Faeries, goat men who lived in the mountains, cats with no tails, rat like people who lived on a smaller fortified island to the east, a black ghostly dog known as the Moddey Doo – these were but to name a few. Flax never knew what was true or not and he longed to see for himself, so he could make up his own mind.

He took a final look at The Sound and in the early morning light he could see the seals basking on the rocks near the water's edge – he could have sworn that he saw one of them looking back directly at him. He blinked a few times to try and clear the reflected light from his vision, but once he regained focus the seal had gone, the only sign of its presence was a rippling wave of circles on the water where it had entered and slipped beneath the surface.

Arriving at the first plantation Flax collected the seedlings that he had been nurturing. In each of his allotted plantations he had built small U-shaped walls from stone blocks that created enough shelter to protect the young trees from the wind, but not so much that they didn't get the required amount of light and water.

As he walked through the plantation he listened to the birds singing to each other and was momentarily lost in his own thoughts wondering if they actually knew what the other was saying.

In a small clearing on the north side of the plantation, he put down his axe and using his spade began to dig out holes ready to accept the seedlings.

He stopped digging. Even above the noise of his activity he became aware that the birds had stopped singing. He sensed movement in the trees to his right, his hand instinctively moved to the small pouch on his belt that held a leather sling and five small stones at all times. He practiced with his sling daily and could hit a moving target at a fair distance nine times out of ten.

Without moving his head, he directed his eyes toward the tree line whilst simultaneously taking out his sling with a stone preloaded in the cradle.

A further blur of movement in the shadows.

He turned his body quickly to face the unknown threat as he raised the sling in his right hand – already rotating, ready to release the stone with force and accuracy. He located the source of the movement and relaxed as a large brown rabbit loped into view from behind a small shrub, it stopped and faced Flax, but seemed to be looking past him. It was at this point that Flax realised the rabbit was not enough to stop the birds from singing – he turned quickly on his heel to face the threat behind him, just in time to see the arrow flying straight towards him.

-3-
TREE

The arrow struck its mark.

It had sailed dangerously close to Flax's head, passing him by and striking the rabbit in the neck killing it instantly. The shooter had a clear view from their elevated position crouched on a low hanging branch of one of the trees.

"You could have killed me!" yelled Flax angrily.

"You were never in danger Flaxney, when have you known me to miss?"

This was true, Flax could not remember a time when he had witnessed a miss. But still, he was angry – truth be told it was more at himself for allowing the archer's presence to go unnoticed. That and being teasingly called by his full name, everyone called him Flax, it was only his mother who regularly called him Flaxney. He raised the sling and swung it with force, releasing the stone in the general direction of the archer. It hit the tree on which they stood and then bounced harmlessly into the undergrowth.

"Temper, temper. You on the other hand have been known to miss brother so I would ask you not to flick pebbles in my direction."

Ealish jumped down from her elevated position landing almost silently on the ground as Flax stooped to select an appropriate stone to replace the one he had used in anger.

He watched as his sister approached the fallen rabbit. She was tall for a female, easily as tall as Flax if not slightly taller. Her frame was slim but lean and her hair was the same golden colour as his – naturally wavy but worn in a plait today. She was approaching her eighteenth bloom but in reality she was nearly nineteen having been born the day after Bloom Day – a fact that Flax did not easily let her forget.

Ealish drew the arrow from the rabbit's neck, wiped off the blood on the mossy side of a tree and replaced it in the quiver that she had adapted to wear on her hip. Next, she drew a small knife with a carved wooden grip and proceeded to gut the animal there on the floor. She seemed to make easy work of preparing the carcass. Flax knew how sharp the blade was as he carried an identical one on his belt – the handles having been lovingly carved by their father.

"Do you have to do that there? And what are you even doing here? Last I saw you, you were snoozing under The Tree. How did you even get up here so fast?"

"So many questions," she replied. "Firstly, why shouldn't I do it here? I am sure that the innards are good for the soil." She said with a smile, using her knife to chop at the remains that were now on the floor. "Secondly, hunting." She held the lifeless rabbit next to her face and grinned idiotically, Flax had to stifle a laugh to maintain his outward annoyance at the intrusion, his sister could pull the strangest faces that could bring humour at the worst of times.

"And thirdly, you know me Flaxney. I am like the wind." At this Ealish leapt towards him and put her hand around his shoulder giving him a one-handed hug before wiping her other bloodied hand across his cheek leaving a smear of blood across it.

"Thanks for that," Flax replied sarcastically, pushing his sister away half-playfully half-angrily before he pulled some moss from a tree and used it to clean his face. She was right though, and Flax knew it. His sister was fast, and silent to go with it. She had spent years honing her skills by practising sneaking up on him and their parents, or generally just anybody she could.

"And I wasn't snoozing – I was observing," she paused for a second thoughtfully as if wanting to say something then added, "you wouldn't understand."

"I saw you daydreaming at The Sound again," she said accusingly. "You know mum and dad won't let you go to Mannin?"

Flax ignored the weighted question and made a targeted comment of his own knowing that it would disgruntle his sister.

"The birds gave you away you know." As the statement landed he could see the annoyance on her face and he couldn't help but feel a little happy with himself.

"They may have given away my presence but you still didn't see me or know where I was, I can live with the birds giving me away, for now…" her voice faded off towards the end of this remark and she seemed to be concentrating on something unseen to Flax.

"What do you mean for now?"

"Never mind… it just means I need to keep practicing my stalking," and with this final comment she placed the rabbit carcass in a bag she carried over her shoulder and took off into the plantation with enviable speed and near impossible silence. Flax strained his ears to listen for any evidence of her movement, a foot landing on dry bracken or a fallen twig breaking under her weight, but there was none.

What was she observing? He thought to himself for a long moment as he replaced the pre-loaded sling into the pouch on his belt without even looking down at it.

He picked up his spade and used it to dig the innards of the gutted rabbit into the soil to help them decompose faster – much as he hated to admit it his sister was right. It would be good for the soil as they would attract all manner of insects and worms to help break them down and release nutrients back into it.

He finished planting the seedlings, picked up his axe and headed south cresting a small hill on his way to the next plantation. Looking to the west he could see his sister moving gracefully across the moorland never having to break her stride despite the rocks and gorse bushes that lay in her intended path.

Flax looked towards his next plantation and smiled when he saw a familiar figure sat on the wall, he knew she was waiting for him.

-4-
KIARE

Ealish was in her element.

She could feel the warm morning sun on her face, there was a slight breeze blowing in from the sea and on it she could taste and smell the ocean. Her golden plaited hair blew behind her. Her custom-made leather quiver of arrows hung from her left hip but never impeded her stride. Her bow was slung diagonally across her back – it clung to her naturally as she ran without the need of any additional belt or sling to hold it in place.

She loved to run, she did it daily, she couldn't remember many days when she had not been out running on the hills and moors of the Island.

She always pushed herself hard, always trying to increase her speed whilst at the same time being mindful of the need to be silent – speed and stealth, stealth and speed.

As she ran she mapped out the path ahead of her, her mind always six steps ahead of her feet looking for the most efficient and silent path possible. Making calculated decisions on where to place each foot as she ran and in which direction she should then push herself with that leg. As she ran in the early morning sun she allowed her mind to wander.

She remembered being a young child of only four or five blooms and being told by her parents that she needed to be quiet so as not to wake her younger brother who went to bed earlier than she did. From that time, she had learnt to move as silently as possible – she knew which floorboard would creak if she stood on it and she still avoided them to this day. She soon transferred her skills outdoors, whilst the other children played games, she would be practicing. At first she found that she had to move very slowly to minimise her noise, carefully placing footsteps here and there using the ground to her benefit. Stepping on soft grass or a large flat rock would make less noise than the loose rocks or pebbles. Seasons of methodical practice proved beneficial and over time she found that she could move faster and faster whilst maintaining a barely audible trace of her presence.

She then became interested in other signs of her presence, footprints for example. It was all well and good being able to move quietly but if she left a big wet footprint on a rock then her presence could just as easily be announced – *to who? Well, to anybody.* Ealish had no ultimate goal, no endgame in mind with regards to why she wanted to be able to move around undetected – apart from the obvious reason of being able to sneak up on her brother to scare him.

However, over time she found her younger brother too easy, so she turned her attention to the wildlife of the Island. Rabbits, hares and even sometimes deer could be found in the early morning or evening, and she found they had much more acute senses than her brother. When stalking such animals, she had to consider not only noise but her scent, her approach to her target with regards wind direction. It truly fascinated her to see how close she could get to an animal without her presence being noticed. Birds were a different matter due to their higher vantage point in the trees, but they were still a work in progress.

One day when her father had been gathering wood for his carpentry, he observed Ealish stalking a rabbit, she would have been only eight or nine blooms. She got within an arm's length of the creature and then just paused observing the animal as it ate for what seemed an eternity. Eventually the animal finished its meal and loped away completely undisturbed by her presence.

That evening he took Ealish back to his workshop with him and produced a bow and a small quiver of arrows. The bow, whilst made intentionally smaller than usual, was still slightly too big for Ealish at her young age. They hiked up to a nearby plantation and chose a nice wide trunked tree as a target.

Ealish had watched closely and with fascination as her father gripped his own handmade bow in his left hand and with his right he chose an arrow from his quiver and nocked it on the waxed string. Standing side on to the target tree he had extended the bow in his left arm and drawn back with the right until the string almost touched his face. He'd drawn in a breath and held it for a moment. Time seemed to slow down. Then he'd exhaled slowly and released the string allowing the arrow to fly forward toward the tree.

Ealish had watched in awe as the arrow struck the tree, slightly off centre so that the arrowhead was unable to bury itself in the wood, causing it to spin off and collide with the tree next to it. "I was never the best shot, but you get the gist," he'd grinned at his daughter, who was still stood riveted to the spot unable to contain her excitement at what she had seen.

"Now, it's your turn," her father said encouragingly, helping her remove the slightly oversized bow from over her back.

And so she'd gripped the bow just as she had watched her father do – he had halved the distance between her and the tree compared to where he had shot from. She'd selected an arrow and with help from her father was able to nock it on the string. She had copied his every move – drawn back the string, taken a deep breath in and held it momentarily. She'd felt her father's presence close behind her. She'd looked down the length of the arrow towards the tree. Just before the stage where she'd felt like her arms may start to wobble from the exertion she had slowly exhaled and released the string loosing the arrow towards the target.

It had fallen pitifully to the ground at her feet, the arrowhead burying itself in the dirt due to nothing more than sheer fluke as there'd been no power behind the arrow from the string, it had simply just fallen from the bow.

"Ealish," her father had said in a soft voice. She had hung her head towards her chest in obvious disappointment. She did not cope well with failure and was always very self-critical of her own performance. "Ealish," he'd said again, she still had not responded. "Ealish." A third time he'd spoken, this time she had sensed a slight tone of amusement in her father's voice.

Without raising her head, she had replied, "Stop laughing! It is not funny!"

"Ealish!" he'd said, more sternly this time – she'd raised her head to look at him. He had crouched down so that his head was at her height. Each of their blue eyes reflecting in the others. There had been a slight smirk on his face and his eyes twinkled. She'd felt him take hold of the bow in her hand and reluctantly released her grip on it accepting that she had let him down. In a softer tone her father had spoken four words as he took the bow from her hand, "You are left-handed."

Ealish had looked up at her father's smiling face whilst maintaining the best grumpy face she could manage. She'd held his gaze but eventually caved and began to laugh. She had been so keen to learn that she had mirrored her father's every move, including taking the bow in her left hand and the string in her right. *No wonder it felt so unnatural,* she'd thought to herself.

"Try again sweetheart," he had said, kissing her on the forehead as he'd handed her back the bow before picking the arrow from the ground for her.

This time, Ealish had gripped the bow in her right hand and so had been able to nock the arrow on the string herself using her much more competent left hand. She'd focused on her target, drawn in a breath and held it as she pulled back the string. She'd released the arrow as she slowly exhaled, just as she had seen her father do. This time the arrow flew straight and true striking the centre of the trunk just above the ground.

"You have the accuracy. The power will come with time and practice my love, *Traa dy liooar.*"

And so it did, Ealish became as obsessed with her bow skill as she had with her stalking. She started with static targets like trees or other items that she could place on a wall or a branch. She soon mastered this with ease and progressed onto hitting targets whilst she was on the move. She would move quietly through a plantation or along a hillside and whilst doing so strike multiple targets with deadly accuracy, she very rarely missed. If she did miss, she would take the same shot repeatedly until she hit it five times in a row.

As she grew older and stronger it was clear to her parents that with her self-taught skills her role amongst the Islanders would be to hunt for food. This was a whole new challenge for her as her targets now moved – the prospect of this thrilled Ealish. She quickly developed her skill with the bow to a point where she could hit a moving hare whilst she herself was moving – this was no mean feat. The Islanders had strict rules on what they would hunt and how often, the main source of hunting was rabbits and hares – they were in abundance all over the Island and seemed to repopulate faster than the hunters could claim them. Even so, Ealish was taught from a young age that she should only ever shoot at an animal if it was required for food for the Islanders or if killing it would be considered a kindness due to injury or illness. There were certain birds that the Islanders would consider as viable sources of food but mainly they would use the chickens which were bred and looked after in the village. There was also the food offered by the sea – many types of fish, crustaceans and molluscs – none of which could be hunted with the bow.

What Ealish truly loved to hunt were the wild deer and pigs that roamed the Island and took shelter in and amongst the many scattered plantations. She found, even now, that they could offer her a real challenge. Being far more suspicious of sounds and scents than the rabbits and hares were, meant and to get close enough to kill one would often take all of Ealish's skill and a full day of hunting. She would often stalk these creatures for half a day before even considering drawing her bow from her back to take a shot.

Both species had been introduced to the Island many generations before and had been left to breed and multiply. It was an unwritten law on the Island that the large game such as the deer and the pigs would only be hunted in very limited numbers and for limited occasions such as Bloom Day. This allowed the natural population of them to be maintained and ensured there was always a sufficient supply of meat when needed.

Even though Ealish was responsible for killing animals she had a deep affinity for them and hated to see an animal mistreated or suffer. She took no joy in killing them when she did, instead she saw it as a necessity for survival of the Islanders. She longed to have a pet of her own but the closest she had got was the donkey that her brother and father would use to assist them carrying wood. Ealish always made sure to bring home a handful of dandelions for the animal as a treat whenever she had been out hunting.

With a final few carefully placed footsteps over the heather Ealish reached her intended destination. One of the smaller plantations on the western side of the Island. She climbed a tree and sat on a branch taking her bow from around her back and placing it carefully next to her. Taking an apple her bag she cut it in half with her knife, dropped one half to the floor and proceeded to eat the other. Once finished with her snack, she sat back and patiently waited.

-5-
QUIEG

Flea sat on the stone wall, her feet swinging freely above the ground, a huge smile on her face as Flax approached.

Flax smiled back at her. Of course, Flea wasn't her real name.

The origin of the nickname went back further than Flax could remember but he was unintentionally responsible for it. It was considered a good omen amongst the Islanders for the first word that a child spoke to be their own name. They believed that this was a sign of strength and good fortune for the future. So as soon as Flax started to make noises as a young child his parents would constantly encourage him to say his name, they would spend entire mornings with him repeating it over and over again or just making the *fluh* sound – which is not the easiest sound to form for a first word. But sure enough, prior to his second Bloom Day he was able to say his first word, *Flax,* in a half audible fashion as least. This brought great joy to his parents given the difficulty of the name. However, for seasons after this event Flax would mispronounce all manner of words by starting them with the *fluh*. So, the donkey became a flonkey, a rabbit a flabbit and so on. Due to this temporary speech impediment in his youth Breesha, or Bree as she was more commonly called, naturally became Fleesha or Flea.

The name had stuck to this day. Flea was also approaching her sixteenth bloom but she was younger than Flax by a season or two. He knew this as she had been born on Bloom Day itself – a prestigious honour and another good omen amongst the Islanders – one of the many reasons that Flax often teased his older sister for having been born the day after Bloom Day. Any baby born on Bloom Day was immediately considered to be one bloom of age.

Flea was not as tall as Flax. Her head came roughly to the top of his shoulder. Her dark brown hair blew around her face in the gentle breeze, her smooth skin was a darker tone than most of the Islanders and her eyes were a deep brown colour. She and Flax had grown up together and had been inseparable during their early years. They still spent as much time together as possible but often their jobs had to take priority.

"You should be at work!" Flax called whilst still some distance away in a mock accusatory tone.

"I am!" came the mock defensive reply. "Dad sent me to put an order into you for extra wood for his furnace." Flea's father was the blacksmith on the Island and was also one of the elders on the council. Understandably he would use a lot of wood to keep the furnace burning hot when needed and as such he was one of Flax's biggest customers

"Bloom Day will be here soon and his orders are stacking up, as are mine." Flea's official job was blacksmiths assistant but her real skill lay with intricate metal work and she made jewellery and other ornate items with precious metals for the Islanders. As Flax neared her, he noticed that hanging around her neck on a thin silver chain was the figure of a small female with wings – a Faerie, or at least an Islander's interpretation of what one would look like as nobody had ever actually seen one or could even be sure if they existed. She had always worn this pendant, as long as Flax could remember – it had been made for Flea by her mother when she was young. Flea caught him looking at the pendant, his eyes met hers and he quickly looked away his face turning red in embarrassment.

Jumping down from her position on the wall, she walked towards him, wrapped her arms around him and gave him a gentle hug. Flax's embarrassment immediately forgotten, he hugged her back and asked.

"So what have you brought me?"

"Some fruit and some pickle."

"Well that's an odd combination."

"Not when we have it with that cheese and bread you are carrying in your bag," Flea smiled. She knew Flax and his routine well, and she would look for every opportunity to meet him on his daily work to share lunch with him.

"You mean *my* bread and cheese?" he retorted.

"Fine play it your way," she replied sitting down on the floor and taking out a pear. Bringing it to her mouth she mimed taking a bite, "Mmm delicious."

Neither of them could keep up the role play any longer. Both laughing, Flax put down his tools and sat next to her, nudging her in a playful manner as he settled down.

They ate together taking respite from the overhead sun in the shade created by the trees. As they ate their meal they chatted and laughed, relaxed and familiar in each other's company. The main topic, as with all Islanders at this time of year, was Bloom Day – *When will it arrive? Will anybody have correctly predicted the date? What colour will the flowers be? Who will be the first to see the flowers?* Many would take to waking earlier than usual in this season in the hope of being the first to witness Bloom Day. Most found this difficult to maintain and soon reverted to their usual routines.

Before they realised, the sun had moved past the high point in the sky and reluctantly Flax and Flea knew they must return to work. As always, they hugged goodbye and as Flea ran off Flax called out, "Tell your dad that I will drop the wood off later with the flonkey." Flea laughed – the joyful sound echoed through the plantation.

Flax picked up his axe smiling to himself and took to work on the nearest tree.

-6-
SHEY

The next morning Ealish woke early, lifted from her slumber by the tuneful chorus of birdsong.

She dressed herself and plaited her hair as she did every morning. She did it without any real thought as to what she was doing – her mind was elsewhere.

Slinging her bow across her back, she fastened her quiver of arrows to her belt at her left hip and placed the knife that she always carried in its horizontal sheath along the back, handle facing her left hand should she need to ever draw it quickly.

She'd spent hours practicing drawing the knife quickly with one hand, its location and the movement required to draw it in a fast smooth motion were engrained into her muscle memory. She could do it with her eyes closed, having done just that well over a thousand times in practice.

As she walked towards her door, habit prompted her to step over certain floorboards to avoid them creaking. Pausing on the threshold, she lifted her hunting bag from a hook by the door then silently continued her way through the house.

There was no sign that anybody else was up, so Ealish picked an apple from a bowl of fruit on the table and filled a small flask made from animal hide with water before heading outside.

She walked through the village, allowing the first rays of the sun to kiss her face and noticing the first few signs of morning activity. A smoking chimney from Sid Kelly the baker's house – he was always one of the earliest Islanders to wake so he could light the fires for his ovens. An empty tethering post next to the Fitchie's house – the family were responsible for tending to crops that were planted in the lower regions of the Island where they were protected from the harsh sea winds. The Fitchies were always early risers and the empty tethering post was a sure sign that they were already working the fields with their donkey.

Ealish approached The Tree. Unslinging her bow from her back she passed it into her right hand and then used her left to draw the blade from behind her back. She neared the trunk and glancing briefly in either direction over her shoulder then she drove the knife with as much force as she could muster forward and into the bark. Only, the knife did not enter the bark. It didn't even leave a scratch or any other sign that it had made contact. Ealish knew this would be the case as this had become her ritual when coming to The Tree to take shelter and observe. The first time she had tried to mark The Tree it was from sheer curiosity as she had heard the tales that it could not be felled or damaged, even with fire. She always made sure she was not being watched. She knew she could not damage The Tree. More recently she had done this daily as a way of confirming something in her mind that had been vexing her.

She lay down, placing her knife and bow next to her. She lay in this exact spot every day and observed. This morning however, she was disturbed from her peaceful state by a familiar voice.

"Room there for me?" Flax said cheerfully as he sat himself intentionally a little too close to his sister, knowing that he would get a slight rise from her.

"Haven't you got some work to be doing?" she asked, making no attempt to hide the annoyance caused by her younger brother.

"Haven't you?" he shot back nudging her again as he threw himself backwards next to her. "Anyway I wanted to come and see exactly what is so important that you need to lie here *observing*."

He looked at her expecting one of her usual witty responses. Ealish was silent. It was as if she hadn't even heard him, she appeared transfixed on a focal point above them. "I said," he began in a louder voice as he turned his head up and to the left following her gaze before continuing, "I wanted to come and see exactly what is so-"

He stopped talking immediately. His eyes were still adjusting to the shaded light under The Tree. His vision sharpened, he shook his head, sat up and refocused on the same point.

She had clearly been paying attention to her brother's reaction as Ealish too sat up, turned to him and gripped both his shoulders. He dropped his gaze and met her eyes which were a mixture of excitement, fear and confusion. He couldn't speak, he couldn't comprehend.

She spoke first.

"You see it too, don't you?"

-7-
SHIAGHT

"I see it," he replied, "I see it, I just don't…" he trailed off, his gaze returning to the focal point.

"…understand?" Ealish finished his sentence questioningly, but knew she had the right word.

"Yes I don't understand. It's, it's…. it's…" he never took his gaze from what he was entranced by.

"impossible," she finished again, no question this time.

"Yes… impossible."

Flax's body was rigid, transfixed. His mind was racing, he could feel his heartbeat, he couldn't just feel it, *he could hear it!*

He closed his eyes. *This is a dream* he told himself. *I haven't woken up yet.* He opened them, it wasn't a dream, he turned his head to his sister who was staring directly at him.

"What does it mean?" she asked – something she had been asking herself every day since making the discovery. She had come back here every morning to try and make sense of it.

Flax once more turned his gaze left and upwards. Now he had seen it he could not help but see it immediately. In any other location it would not seem out of place and would not even raise the suspicion of anybody who happened to see it. But here, here it was not something that anybody could ever expect to see. It defied everything that was known and understood about this location.

It was visible only from a certain angle and even then it was well hidden, but it was definite. There was no doubt about it. Flax could not believe that it had not been seen before.

About halfway up the trunk of The Tree a large branch reached outwards, from this branch sprouted many other sub-branches each of them sprouting further sub-branches, all of which were thick with rich green leaves.

His eyes followed along the main branch and at the point where its thickness was roughly the same as his thigh it ended, abruptly. It was clear that the wood had been broken or snapped, but in his head he knew that was just not possible. *The Tree was invincible, wasn't it?*

He took a long moment and stared more intently at the broken end of the branch. He could see when he really focused that at the point where the branch broke the wood was a different colour. It was darker, not rotten or decaying but definitely darker. *It was scorched*, Flax confirmed to himself in his head.

Yes, it was definitely scorched.

Without averting his gaze, he uttered a word in a barely audible whisper, "Dragane."

This time Ealish grabbed him more firmly by the shoulders and looked him in the eye. Gone was the excitement and confusion from her eyes, there was a look of intense determination.

"What did you say?"

They held each other's gaze for a long moment until their concentration was broken by a loud shout from the village.

"I see it! I see it! Everybody come and look!" shouted a voice, Ealish and Flax both turned and saw a figure running towards them.

-8-
HOGHT

Flax could still feel his sister's firm grip on his shoulders. He turned his face from the approaching figure and closed his eyes. His mind replayed the *ashlishyn* on a continuous sped up loop.

The lightning bolt from the mouth of the winged Dragane causing the bough from the unmistakable tree to fall. *Had that really happened?* Surely it must have because despite all known logic there was clearly a snapped branch on The Tree – and no Islander had ever been able to cause such damage. What was more was that the branch was clearly charred at the broken end.

But Draganes aren't real, Flax reasoned with himself, *and if they were, they breathe fire not lightning.*

But the evidence was there, and what he had tried, and failed, to pass off many times in his own head as a nonsense dream caused by an overactive imagination must clearly be an *ashlishyn*. A vision of incidents from the past or the future – *or both?*

The way his sister had looked at him when he had spoken the word Dragane had not been lost on him. It was as if the word had not surprised her, as if she had the same thought process. *But how could that be possible?* He had never shared the details of his vision with anybody.

Unless - he had written down his notes which he kept close to his bed. *Had she read them? Would she be able to make sense of them?* He usually wrote them in such a way that they would look like wild rambling to anybody who read them.

But now they meant something, surely. The branch was broken, severed from The Tree by a Dragane. *How long ago had that happened? What had happened to the Dragane? What had happened to the fallen branch?* So many questions raced through Flax's mind in these moments as the *ashlishyn* continued to play in his head. *Would he have to share his vision now that he knew that The Tree had been damaged?* The figure running towards them had seen it and was shouting so loudly that within moments the entire village would be aware and would want to know what force had caused the damage to their sacred tree.

He opened his eyes. His sister was staring at him with the same look of determination, as if she was trying to read his thoughts. He turned his head back towards the figure that was approaching and still yelling. He could see that it was Sid Kelly the baker. Sid was considered old for an Islander, he never let on how old he was exactly, but he must have been at least seventy blooms. He was short in stature with grey hair and a kind face, his apron and trousers always covered in dusty white flour and he always moved with short shuffling steps but could move deceptively fast for his age.

Sid stopped short of The Tree, pointing up into the mass of branches and leaves. He called out again, to nobody in particular, but everybody within earshot, "I can see it! Up there! Look at it!" His face was a mixture of excitement and disbelief.

His eyesight must be better than mine, thought Flax as he was sure he would not be able to see the snapped branch from the distance and angle that he had.

"Blue everybody, bright brilliant blue! Would you look at that."

It was at this point Flax became confused, *blue? Either Sid's eyesight is going, or he has seen something different.* He pulled away from his sister's grip and walked out to where the baker was stood. Sid, who when standing wouldn't even reach Flax's shoulder, was bent over with his hands on his knees now catching his breath – the recent overexertion now taking its toll. Flax put a hand gently on his shoulder and asked, "What is it you have seen Mr Kelly?"

"Up there," he replied taking one hand off his knee and pointing toward The Tree, "blue…". Flax pulled Sid up to a standing position and put an arm around him to support him, allowing him to calm his breathing.

"In eighty-three blooms I have never seen such a beautiful blue."

Eighty-three blooms old! Flax thought, registering that Sid had finally given away his age. *He must be one of the oldest Islanders ever.* Flax looked up towards The Tree and smiled to himself. He turned to Sid and gave him a hug, being careful not to squeeze him so hard that he may cause an injury – after all he was eighty-three blooms old today.

"Happy Bloom Day Sid."

"And happy Bloom Day to you Flax, what are you now nineteen? Twenty?"

"Only sixteen." Flax laughed, seeing the disbelief in Sid's eyes as he answered.

"But look at the size of you! Your mother must be feeding you well."

Flax was tall for his age, athletic and muscular to go with it.

"She does Mr Kelly, and I also spend my days chopping down trees and carrying wood."

"So you do, so you do. My ovens are never without firewood thanks to your hard work. My Ovens! Goodness me I need to get back to them or this batch will be burnt to a cinder. What's more, its Bloom Day, there is so much to be done!" Sid took a final look at The Tree, "Blue! Who would have guessed it? You know Flax this is the first time I have been the one to declare Bloom Day? Ovens! Must go!"

With that Sid turned and ran back to his house still yelling "Happy Bloom Day everybody!" Flax laughed to himself at the exchange he had just been involved in. It was a prestigious honour to be the one to declare Bloom Day as that person officially opened the feast that evening. Some enjoyed this more than others, personally Flax was glad that as he had approached The Tree earlier that morning he had been concentrating on his sister beneath it and not looked up to potentially be the first to see the flower.

As he looked around he could see more of the villagers coming out of their homes having been alerted by Sid's shouts. They were all looking toward The Tree, pointing and talking amongst themselves. Flax turned his attention back up to the branches and spotted the single bright blue flower that had opened from one of the many buds about halfway up. It was the colour of the ocean on a bright sunny day, it stood out clearly against the vibrant green leaves. Even as he watched he saw other buds popping open all over The Tree, their blue petals spreading out in the morning sunlight. He became aware that his sister had joined him and was also watching natures performance with a smile on her face. She put an arm around his waist and squeezed. "Happy Bloom Day sister." He said, looking down at her with a smile, putting an arm round her shoulders and squeezing back.

"Happy Bloom Day to you brother," she looked back up at him and the smile disappeared from her face, replaced by a look of deep concentration mixed with concern, "we still need to talk." She grabbed him by the arm and walked him back through the village to their house.

-9-
NUY

Ealish pushed open the door to her bedroom and walked in, Flax following closely behind.

On her walk back through the village her mind had been working overtime as her mouth and her face kept up the façade of happily greeting people they passed and wishing them a happy Bloom Day. She was now eighteen blooms old, today should be a joyous day for her, she would officially be entering adulthood. She would be able to sit in on village meetings chaired by the elders. She would be allowed to taste the fruit wines at the feast tonight for the first time – rhubarb wine, she had been longing to try that ever since seeing her mother drinking it many seasons ago.

But there was nothing joyous on her mind at the moment just a combination of confusion and determination. She walked towards her bed, instinctively stepping over the creaky floorboards without a second thought. Lifting up her mattress she pulled out a small bag in which were several papers. She started to lay them out on the floor one by one in front of Flax. She placed the last piece of paper on the floor and moved away from them as if they posed some sort of a threat. She sat on the edge of her bed and looked toward her younger brother.

She could see that he was transfixed by the papers. Only his eyes moved, darting from one to the next to the next and then back again. Even the movement of his breathing was almost imperceptible, were it not for his eyes constantly moving he could have been a statue hewn from rock.

"Flax?" she said in a voice that sounded so weak and feeble that she barely recognised it as her own.

He didn't move.

"Flax?" she said again, making a concerted effort to project her voice further and seem more confident. He turned his head and looked at his sister before turning it back toward the pieces of paper scattered on the floor. He knelt down and ran his hands across them, maybe hoping to feel something that his eyes could not see - or to check that what his eyes were seeing was actually there.

"You have seen these before, haven't you?" She said questioningly but knowing that it was more of a statement. "Well not actually these ones but you recognise them, don't you Flax?"

"I have," he replied, his voice dry and cracking as his mouth had completely dried up. He cleared his throat and then repeated, "I have, but that means…it means that you have had —"

"– the *ashlishyn*? Yes." she knelt down beside him running her own hands over the pages. Each one held an image that she had recreated from the visions that she had seen in her sleep as far back as she could remember. The images were outlined in black charcoal, but Ealish had used pigments from berries and plants to add colour to them.

She looked over them again and mentally ticked each image off in her mind as her eyes passed over it as if to confirm they were all there. She no longer needed the images as they were burned into her mind, all she had to do was close her eyes and concentrate if she wanted to recall them.

The red moon, the winged figure silhouetted against the moon, The Tree, the Dragane breathing lightning, the falling bough, the path of red light on the sea, the ship and the blood red ocean, the hill and the warrior with the spear, the spear piercing the Dragane and finally inky black darkness.

Ten images in total, snapshots that she had created of what she considered to be the key events or changing moments within the fast-moving *ashlishyn*.

"There are sounds too but I can't describe them in the images," she started to explain to her brother.

He started to speak without looking away from the images, "A baby's cry, the Dragane's roar, a war drum."

"Yes, you have heard them too?"

He turned to look at his sister, "Ealish, I see these images, I hear these sounds nearly every night in my dreams. Wait here." He got up and ran across the room, the floorboards creaking as he moved. Ealish heard him enter his own room and he returned moments later carrying his own handful of papers. She took them from him and looked down at the words that her brother had scribbled on them. They were a literary description of all the images that she had drawn, in addition there were rambling thought processes recorded by her brother on what it all meant to him. There was lots of repetition with what he had recorded and too much for her to take in quickly whilst scanning the pages. But she got the gist of his thoughts.

She too had recognised The Tree, considered sacred to all Island folk, the one that they had been laid under that very morning.

Likewise, the Dragane that breathed lightning, she had also picked up on the fact that Draganes breathed fire and not lightning – or so Island lore would have them believe.

There was not much mention of the boat in her brother's notes, he had recorded it but not in any great detail. She looked back at her own image and confirmed to herself what she had seen and recorded. The figurehead at the front of the boat was a Dragane's head, its mouth open and its multiple rows of razor-sharp teeth on display. She re-scanned her brother's notes, he had not recorded this. *Had he simply overlooked it? Or had he seen something different?*

Also, the first winged figure that crossed the face of the moon. Ealish knew what it was, or at least if her picture was anything to go by then she did. "It's a Faerie," she said out loud as her brother ran his fingers over the image of a female with wings on her back in suspended flight in front of the moon.

"How did I miss that?" he asked. "I should have known. I see one just like it every day on Flea's necklace," he added with a look of disappointment on his face that he made no attempt to hide from his sister.

"In fairness, it moves so fast in the vision," his sister reassured him. "It took me seasons and seasons to be able to slow the image in my head enough to decide that it was a Faerie, and what's more," she added, "I could still be wrong."

"No, you've got it right," replied Flax confidently as he re-ran his hands over the image. "Now that I've seen your drawing I'm certain. How long have you been having the *ashlishyn*?"

"Flax, we can't be sure that it is an *actual ashlishyn*, it could just be a random dream."

"That we both have? It's an *ashlishyn*. I've tried to convince myself it's not but there's no doubt – especially now that I know you've been having it as well."

"You're right, it isn't just a dream – I've been seeing these visions for so many seasons I can't even remember when they started. Since I found that broken branch on The Tree, I've spent every morning there trying to work it all out in my head, trying to decide what to do."

"How did you even see that branch was broken?"

Ealish looked at her brother with a smirk spreading across her face. In a hushed voice she leant towards him and explained, "The visions kept playing on my mind and The Tree was the only definite thing that I knew I could investigate from them, so –" She paused and looked around to ensure nobody else would hear what she was about to say, "– I climbed it." She sat back waiting for Flax's reaction, which was instantaneous and predictable.

"You did what?!"

"I climbed it," she said, shrugging her shoulders, as if to absolve any wrongdoing.

"But it's sacred! You can't just climb a sacred tree! Not just a sacred tree - *the* sacred tree! Have you any idea what the elders would do if they caught you?!"

"But they didn't, did they? Anyway, you know how quiet I can be. I made sure nobody would find out."

Flax turned his attention back to the images on the floor, selecting the one of the falling bough and holding it up. "Anyway we know about this part of the vision, or at least we know it has happened. Which means that a Dragane that breathed lightning must have been here on the Island at some point!" his voice grew in excitement as he finished his summary. "But where did it go?" he asked rhetorically. "Did the warrior kill it? Or is that yet to happen? Ealish this is all so confusing, we need to talk to somebody about this, we need to ask somebody who knows more about this kind of thing."

"What kind of thing is that?" came a voice from the doorway.

-10-
JEIH

Flax and Ealish turned simultaneously.

Stood in the open doorway was their father. His once golden hair showing what seemed to be more and more silver by the day. In his hands he held the top of his wooden staff that he always carried. It wasn't required for assistance with walking, yet he was never seen without it. It was the perfect height for him to rest his chin on the top of his hands. His bright blue unblinking eyes seemed to glisten like the sea under a summer sun, they stared, waiting expectantly.

There was a silence that seemed to last an eternity, Flax picked up one of the pieces of paper in his hand and looked as if he was about to start speaking.

"– About Bloom Day…and its traditions," his sister interrupted before he even opened his mouth. Taking the papers from his hands and hastily gathering up the others from the floor. Her mind raced as she tried to think of what to say next to throw her father off the scent "...And The Tree...and how long has it been here? And why is it here?" she continued, having quickly convinced herself that by asking about The Tree she wasn't technically lying to her father. And therefore, was less likely to be found out and be forced to explain the contents of the pages that she had successfully gathered and was placing back into the bag in which she kept them. This time, she kept hold of her brothers notes too.

Ealish's father said nothing, he turned his gaze to Flax, then back to Ealish. There was no anger in his eyes – she had never seen her father angry at all. There was a deep concentration and an inquisitive edge to his stare. She attempted to hold his gaze but conceded and bowed her head toward the ground knowing that her father had easily seen through her feeble attempt to throw him off.

Even with her chin on her chest she could feel her father was still staring at her, she glanced out of the corner of her eye towards her brother and could see that he too was avoiding their father's gaze.

She heard footsteps moving towards her and felt his hand under her chin as he lifted her head up to meet his eyes once more. In a calm and gentle voice, he spoke "Come with me Ealish."

She reluctantly stood and he put his arm around her shoulders walking back towards the door. The floorboard creaked as she inadvertently stood on it and she silently cursed herself. In her hand she still gripped the bag of papers. "You can leave the drawings and notes in here," her father instructed calmly, she looked at him questioningly and saw the corner of his mouth raise in a slight smile temporarily. One handed, she threw the bag behind her hitting Flax in the face with it. Such was his confusion that he didn't even react; he just stared dumbfounded as his sister and father left the room.

Ealish was led into the large open kitchen and was greeted with the familiar smell of home baked bread. Though she would never say it to Sid's face Ealish much preferred her mother's bread. It had a sweetness to it, from the honey that she added, which made it irresistibly moreish.

"Sit please," her father instructed – The sound of his voice and a chair leg scraping on the stone floor broke her temporary trance. Ealish sat feeling nervous, then ran her hands along the edge of the table away from her body and then back again until they met each other. She clasped them together tightly to prevent them from showing her nerves at having been caught lying and the anticipation of having to disclose to her father the details of the *ashlishyn*. Her head was still down, and her eyes concentrated on the rough calloused skin on the tips of the first two fingers of her left hand – caused by the constant use of the bow string.

"Dad…about just now –" she began.

"– There is time for that later," her father cut in, "Right now there is something I need to discuss with you first."

What could be more important than the fact I have proof that the indestructible tree can be damaged? And on top of that Flax and I have both been having the exact same ashlishyn of the damage happening and other events, events we can't explain but that almost definitely have an impact on what is to come! – is what Ealish wanted to say, but she remained silent, now using her right thumb to pick at the hardened skin on her left hand, this was something she did when she needed to distract herself.

"Ealish," she heard her father say in a familiar stern tone – his voice temporarily transporting her back to that plantation all those blooms ago, avoiding her father's eye due to fear of having caused disappointment.

Back in the present, she heard her father place something down on the table in front of her and looked up. On the other side of the table stood her father, both hands on the top of his staff, chin resting on his hands, his eyes still shimmering bright blue and staring straight at her. Ealish hadn't realised but her mother had joined them and was stood with her arm around his waist. Her dark hair plaited and resting over one shoulder and her large green eyes sparkling like precious stones. Her parents smiled, her father nodded his head toward the item on the table, "Happy Bloom Day sweetheart," he exclaimed.

-11-
NANE-JEIG

Ealish stood and eyed the item curiously. Whatever it was, it was wrapped in a leather sheet and its external appearance gave nothing away to indicate what it contained. She stood and lifted her gaze back to her parents asking, "This is for me?"

"Well I don't know anybody else in this house turning eighteen blooms today do you?" replied her mother as she walked around the table and wrapped her daughter in her arms, kissing her on the cheek, having to stand on her tip toes in order to do so.

Ealish hugged her mother then releasing her grip she turned her attention to the item on the table. She ran her hand over the leather wrapping, feeling the bumps and imperfections of the material with the tips of her fingers. When her fingers reached the edge of the sheet she carefully peeled it back and then gently unrolled the package across the table to reveal the contents.

She surveyed the items carefully with her eyes, then she turned first to her mother and then her father with a serious look on her face as she spoke, "Mum…Dad…"

"Yes?" replied her father eagerly – keen to know what his daughter thought of the gift. She did not reply, she held a disinterested look. A mixture of confusion and disappointment crossed her father's face as he let his gaze drop.

He could not see it as he had lowered his eyes, but Ealish was now grinning and could barely contain her laughter, her mother had caught on early as to what she was doing and was now also smiling. So many times Ealish's father had caught her out with his serious voice only to reveal he had been joking but now she had managed to turn the tables on him.

Unable to keep up the act any longer Ealish wrapped her arms warmly around her father and looking him in the eye exclaimed, "I love it!"

She let go and from the table picked up the bow. Made from a single piece of wood that curved back on itself at each end where the string was attached. Whereas her current bow had a leather-bound hand grip in the middle - this one was carved directly into the wood with an indent for each individual finger and the arrow rest was on the left-hand side of the bow just below the sight window. Ealish took the bow in her right hand at the grip and found that each finger fit perfectly in the intended grooves. She took the string in her left hand and tested the tension – immediately she knew that this bow was far more powerful than her current one, the wood felt flexible but also strong at the same time. She knew that her father was the master craftsman who had created this thing of beauty that she held in her hand. Whilst she didn't need it confirmed, it was - by the familiar signature of her father's work that she located in the recess where her thumb would rest when gripping the bow. She felt it before she saw it, when she lifted her thumb she saw the branded mark that her father used on anything he created, a blackened silhouette that was unmistakably The Tree.

Ealish kept a firm grip of the bow and assessed every inch of it with her eyes. It was simplistic in design but that made it all the more attractive to her. The wood was perfectly smooth and had been sealed with oil - it looked as if its surface was covered in a thin layer of ice. The wood that had been used to craft the bow was much darker than any that was grown in the plantations on the Island, the grain was so uniform and straight that it almost looked as if it had been drawn on with precision and care. She had seen this wood used once before, she let her eyes move from the bow to the staff that her father held in his hand to confirm her suspicion. He had not let her realisation go unnoticed and he smiled and winked at her.

Still sat on the unrolled leather on the tabletop was a quiver, not the traditional over the shoulder kind that other hunters on the Island used. This was slightly shorter, and she could tell by the way that the belt had been attached to it that it was intended to be worn on the hip. Ealish had found over the years that she could access the arrows easier when they were set in a quiver on her left hip. She had spent days and days just practicing taking an arrow from the quiver and nocking it on the string. Her current quiver was a hand me down of her fathers that she had altered to sit where she wanted it. She could tell though that this one had been created with attention to detail, still gripping her new bow in her right hand she allowed her left hand to feel the leather quiver. Unlike the leather that had been used to wrap the gift – this was smooth much like the wood of the bow. With of course the exception of the blackened brand of The Tree – she looked up at her father as she noticed this. "You did your own tannery?" she asked surprised – he nodded and smiled in reply.

Ealish joked, "I best keep this hidden from Mr Crawshaw or he will think you are after his customers." Mr Crawshaw was the Island's tanner – and a skilled one at that. That her father had dared to turn his hand to leather work impressed Ealish as much as the finished product.

Finally, Ealish turned her attention to the arrows, she counted eight of them. Putting her bow down she picked the first one up carefully in both hands. Immediately she saw they were made from the same dark wood with the straight grain as the bow. She looked down the length of the arrow shaft, as expected it was perfectly straight. She rotated it in her hands and could see the wood had been turned and then oiled expertly by her father.

Each arrow had an identical nock cut into the rear of the shaft, forward of this they were each fletched with black feathers. Just down the shaft from the fletching was the tell-tale brand of her father's handiwork.

The tip of the arrow intrigued her – she had seen and used arrows that were tipped with metals before, but she generally used ones with sharpened and hardened wood as she didn't want to destroy the meat when she was hunting. But these were tipped with what looked like some form of polished black stone – the kind she had never seen before. The arrowhead itself was triangular, widening from the sharpened tip to where it was attached to the shaft. She could see just by looking at it that the edges along each of the three lines running from the pointed tip were slightly serrated and razor sharp – they were perfectly aligned with each of the three fletches at the rear of the shaft. She eyed her father curiously, "Bit much for rabbits?" she said, raising an eyebrow.

"I think they will have their use," he said with a knowing tone in his voice.

Ealish turned her attention away from the bow and the arrows and hugged her mother and father in turn. "Thank you so much! I absolutely love it!"

"I'm glad you do," he replied, "I have waited long enough to give you it."

"What do you mean?"

"Remember the day we went to the plantation and you first shot a bow?"

"How could I forget that," Ealish said with a smile on her face – it was one of her fondest memories with her father.

"Well, that night I set to work making you this bow, with the intention that on your eighteenth bloom we could give it to you."

Ealish couldn't comprehend what her father had just told her. *How is that possible?* The size was just perfect, the finger grooves were cut exactly, the arrows the perfect length to fit a hip worn quiver – *how did he even know I would wear a quiver on my hip?*

As if hearing her thoughts her father answered unprompted, "I guess I just knew, plus your mother always wore a quiver on her hip so I figured you would too in time."

Ealish looked at her mother in disbelief, "You? Use a bow and arrow?"

"Used," corrected her mother with a smile. "But yes, I used to hunt and I wore my quiver on my hip – much like you do now – in fact that one there on the table was mine. Given to me by your father as a wedding gift, of course I wore it on the right hip, so he has adapted it, but I wanted you to have it."

"Have what?" Flax asked as he entered the room, having spent the last few minutes in his sister's room. Firstly, arranging the papers more neatly in the bag after they had been thrown at him and secondly hoping to avoid what he expected to be the inevitable conflict in the kitchen given the way his sister had been led away by their father.

Ealish was finishing fastening the belt of the quiver around her waist, she found that it seated perfectly against her hip and was not so long that it would strike her knee or interfere when she was running. "My Bloom Day gift," she replied grinning and turning to show off her new bow and quiver.

Flax carefully appraised the items, knowing instantly that his father had created them. His mind couldn't help but wonder what he would receive in two blooms when he turned eighteen – it was customary on the Island to give gifts to loved ones each Bloom day, but these were small token gifts. When an Islander turned eighteen, they would receive a gift such as the bow and quiver, traditionally the gift given would be something that would feature heavily in their adult life. Whilst he often wondered about what he might receive he knew exactly what he wanted – his own work bench and tools in his father's workshop. But he knew he would have to be patient until that time, *Traa dy liooar,* he would tell himself.

They sat down to a family breakfast cooked by their mother. The awkwardness of the earlier interruption temporarily forgotten by both Flax and Ealish. They exchanged their token Bloom Day gifts with each other and talked about the day ahead and the feast that would happen that night. Conversation turned to memories of Bloom Days gone by, some that Flax and Ealish could remember and others that they knew from stories that their parents or other Islanders had told them of. It was soon nearly noon, they all had plenty to do in preparation for the celebrations and feast that evening. Just before they parted, and out of earshot of their mother, Flax and Ealish's father shot them a quick glance and said gravely, "We will continue our earlier conversation tomorrow but for now – happy Bloom Day."

-12-
DAA-YEIG

The sun was starting to dip in the sky as the Islanders gathered around The Tree, everybody was there – nothing was more important on this day than the entire community coming together to enjoy the feast.

    Flax looked around the gathered group smiling and waving at people, wishing them a happy Bloom Day. There were one or two faces he didn't recognise but it was often the case that travellers and traders coming to the Island would attempt to coincide their visit with Bloom Day so that they could enjoy the legendary feasts. There was one figure in particular that drew Flax's attention – he was tall, thin with striking features, amber – almost golden eyes, dark hair and skin a darker tone than most of the Islanders. He wore a hooded cloak that was fastened at the neck with a silver chain, Flax could see a short sword hung in a sheath from his right hip.

"Who's that?" he asked nudging Flea next to him and gesturing with his head in the stranger's direction.

"I don't actually know his real name," replied Flea, "he is one of my father's friends from many blooms ago – I have always just known him as the Traveller."

Flax fixed his eyes on him for another few moments, analysing him, absorbing the detail. He finally let his gaze wander from the Traveller across the group again – only to see that his father was scrutinising the Traveller in the same manner that he had been.

The moment was suddenly interrupted by the ringing of a bell that brought everybody into silent anticipation.

Flea's father stood in front of the community before The Tree, its brilliant blue flowers now completely covering the outer foliage so that barely a trace of the green leaves could be seen through them. "Please everybody, take a seat."

He gestured to the large table next to him that was laden with every kind of food that Flax could imagine. Hot and cold meats, breads, cheeses, fruits, vegetables, pickles, chutneys, fish and other kinds of seafood – and that was just the first course. He knew that somewhere nearby would be tables covered in all manner of puddings and desserts, all freshly prepared today.

The noise picked up again as people moved to take a seat around the great table. Flax sat next to Flea, his legs brushing against hers momentarily as he took his seat causing his face to glow red – in all the excitement this went unnoticed. Once everyone was seated the bell rang once more, bringing back with it the silence.

Flea's father began the Bloom Day ceremony as the chosen Island elder always had and always would – solemnly announcing the names of Islanders who had died within the last year. At the conclusion of this short list those old enough to drink alcohol toasted the members of their community who were no longer with them.

After this followed the naming of those with significant Bloom Days – these tended to be eighteen, fifty and then every ten blooms thereafter. Flax looked down and across the table to see his sister reluctantly stand as her name was called, her new bow slung across her chest and the quiver of arrows on her left hip. He also saw Mr Crawshaw, who was sat opposite Ealish eyeing the leather quiver that hung from her belt. She noticed this too and quickly sat down as soon as her name had been read. A special mention was given to Beryl who today was to celebrate her one hundred and first Bloom Day. The entire table stood and applauded and then promptly sang the traditional Bloom Day celebration song.

Once the song had finished the bell rang for a third time and again a palpable silence fell, everyone knew what was imminent now – this was confirmed by the presence of a small figure carrying a lit torch approaching the head of the table where an empty chair sat. The small figure climbed onto this chair in an almost comedic fashion, Flea's father having to temporarily hold the torch to prevent any injury being caused. The figure stood upright on the chair and took the torch back from Flea's father who moved to take his seat at the table next to the Traveller.

Sid Kelly stood still on the chair for a moment looking around the table taking in the face of each Islander before he spoke, "Today I celebrate my eighty third bloom." He paused whilst everybody clapped. "And it is my great pleasure and honour to have been the first to witness the first flower of the bloom." He paused again. This time he looked up at the lower branches of The Tree which, given that he was standing on a chair, were not too far from the top of his head. "All that is left for me to say now is happy Bloom Day," and with that he thrust the flaming torch into the trunk of The Tree. Everybody clapped and gasped as the flame raced around the thick trunk, lighting small lanterns that had been placed around it as it went.

Soon the entire trunk appeared alight with a golden glow – along the length of the table further lanterns were lit by those sat nearest to them. Within a matter of moments, the entire table and its surroundings were bathed in a warm glow that counteracted the ever-encroaching darkness that was creeping in as the sun slowly set behind the western hills of the Island.

Whilst the lanterns on The Tree were nothing new – Islanders had carried on this tradition of using a fuse and multiple lanterns for years since they knew fire could not damage The Tree, Flax still enjoyed the drama of it all immensely. He sat watching the flames in The Tree flickering below the blue flowers and the green leaves, casting dancing shadows across the table and the ground beneath. He felt warmth on his hand and realised that Flea, who was also mesmerised by the lanterns, had taken his hand in hers and was gently squeezing it. She turned to look at him and leant into his ear whispering, "I made you a Bloom Day present," Flax's cheeks turned red once more but this time he was saved by the orange hue thrown on everything by the lanterns disguising his involuntary blushing – he squeezed her hand back and smiled. "But you will have to wait a bit," Flea continued, "because I am starving," with that she laughed, let go of his hand and started choosing all her favourite foods from the table to put on her plate.

The entire Island spent the evening eating, drinking, laughing, singing and dancing – nobody noticed Flea's father and the Traveller had left the party to have a much-needed conversation.

Flax was on his way back to the table, having left briefly to retrieve the present he had made for Flea, when he overheard snippets of a conversation amongst the noise of the singing and dancing. The first voice he recognised as Flea's father, the second he assumed to be the Traveller.

"…This is sooner than we had agreed…can we not have more time?"

"No it must happen now and without delay."

"But today? Surely it can wait until at least morning."

"No! It must be today…she has already set things in motion…"

"Things? What things?"

"… That does not matter…we must act…before it is too late"

"But people will notice…what will I say?"

"I do not care, we must do what needs to be done and do it now"

"– But –"

Screams cut across the village, the music and the singing stopped and were replaced by confused shouts, yells of pain and blind panic.

Flax ran towards them.

-13-
TREE-JEIG

Flax entered the clearing, his eyes struggled to take in the chaos that was unfolding in front of him. Chairs and benches were knocked over with plates of food scattered everywhere. People were running and shouting – *they were being chased!*

Small, hooded figures carrying a mixture of sticks, small daggers and other such weapons were chasing down anyone and everyone they could get close to. Flax looked towards the head of the table and could see that Sid Kelly had fallen from his chair and was laid on his back, both hands held out in front of him as he tried to wriggle backwards, away from the advancing figure that held in its hand a vicious looking curved, serrated dagger.

Instinctively Flax reached to his belt and from the pouch using one hand he drew the sling, pre-loaded with a stone. He swung the sling hard above his head twice and loosed the stone in the direction of the knife wielding figure. The stone flew true and made contact with the hooded head and the creature dropped to the floor. Sid Kelly looked in Flax's direction – his face a picture of terror and confusion. He mouthed *thank you* then rolled onto his hands and knees and scurried away.

Flax stood still for a moment to collect himself. The chaos continued around him. He had never harmed another person before and now he had most likely killed someone. He had never even been in a fight growing up – Islanders were peaceful people. They were taught to use weapons as they grew but they were taught them mainly for defence or for hunting. They were certainly not warriors. His mouth felt swollen under his tongue and all he could taste was a metallic sourness, a wave of nausea swept over him, and he started to feel dizzy.

He became aware of a blood curdling cry close by but found it difficult to focus on the source of the noise. He turned to his right to see another of the hooded figures running straight towards him. He found it strange how much detail he was able to take in in such a small amount of time. He could tell, now that he was close to one, that the figures were much smaller than the average Islander, at best the creature's head stood somewhere between his elbow and his shoulder. With a jolt he saw under one of their hoods and instinctively recoiled. The eyes were a horrible yellow colour, the nose was angular, the jaw narrow and pointed with prominent front teeth. The face was covered in wispy dark hairs and the skin beneath looked rough and leathery. In the creature's right hand was a short stick with a curved blade on the end, it looked like a scythe that Flax had seen the Fitchies use when harvesting crops in the fields.

The creature's left hand was held outward toward Flax and whilst empty of weapons it looked just as deadly, covered in more wispy dark hair through which Flax could discern five fingers with sharpened nails – and all five were aimed at his throat.

The creature was moving at speed and without breaking its stride it pushed off the ground with both feet and flew toward Flax. Shortened scythe in one hand and deadly nails on the other, its eyes were full of determination and malice. Flax had no time to reload his sling or to even draw the short hunting knife that he kept on his belt, even if he had he was not convinced that his mind would will his body to do so. He simply braced for the inevitable impact and waited to feel the sharpened blade and nails pierce his skin.

And they did. The serrated blade bit into his left forearm, instantly drawing blood. The nails of the creature's free hand dug into his right shoulder piercing through his clothing and hooking into his skin. Instinctively Flax extended his left arm, his body's way of dealing with the immediate danger and pain. Being much stronger than the creature, he was able to wrench the handle of the scythe from the creature's hand, not before the blade dug in deeper and struck the bone - giving him the leverage needed to pry it upward from the grasp of the thing trying to kill him. His right hand grabbed at the body of his attacker trying to push it away, but it clung on with its claws embedded in his shoulder. The hooded figure gave up on the blade and aimed the sharpened claws on its right hand directly at Flax's eyes.

Despite the pain, he was able to lift his injured left arm across his face to deflect what would have been a fatal attack but in doing so he stepped back. Still off balance from the creature's unexpected aerial attack he missed his footing and fell backward. As he did the orange glow that had initially served to illuminate the feast but now cast grisly shadows of violence and pain across the clearing was extinguished. Not only was he in a position of disadvantage but he was now effectively blinded too. With the savage demon on top of him Flax started to panic. The creature released its grip with its left hand and started to rain blows down with both hands aimed at his head. Flax raised both arms up defensively and as he did, his right hand felt something that it hadn't expected to. A wooden handle. The scythe that was still embedded in his forearm.

He hadn't realised that the blade was there. A mixture of fear and adrenaline from the fight had temporarily numbed the pain it had caused. Without thinking Flax gripped the handle tightly, it was wet with his blood. He wrenched it from his forearm and with one hand he swung it like an axe directly at his would-be killer's back. The creature gave a horrifying shriek of both pain and surprise before falling limp on top of Flax. He rolled to the side pushing the creature from on top of him and nausea immediately swept over him again. Revolted at his own actions he vomited onto the ground. A burning stab of pain brought his attention back to his left forearm. Whilst he could not see it clearly in the darkness, he knew it was badly injured, strangely the wound felt cold to him. Trying desperately to urge his mind to focus, Flax brought his legs into a half standing position but was swept by a further wave of nausea and dizziness which forced him back to the ground, where exhausted and injured his entire world turned to black.

-14-
KIARE-JEIG

Ealish had been sitting at the feast table when the attack began. To her right she had heard the screams and turned to see one of the Islanders slumped forward on the table, the handle of a dagger protruding from their back.

She witnessed the panic that unfolded as Islanders raced away from the table looking for the safety of cover from the attackers. In the light cast by the lanterns on The Tree and the table she saw them, small, hooded figures with cruel looking weapons attacking anybody close by.

Due to her position at the feast table, she was at the opposite end to the initial attack. Standing quickly she pushed herself back into the shadows of a nearby building whilst taking her bow from around her chest. She nocked an arrow on the string and her eyes scanned for a clear target in the chaos. Tables and their lanterns had now been knocked over and the lamps in The Tree above threw down their light on the scene casting strange shadows. In the moment Ealish found it hard to differentiate between Islander, attacker and shadows – then she saw her opportunity. Flea's father was stood between his daughter and an advancing attacker – using a stool from the feast table to keep the knife wielding assailant at bay.

Ealish identified the target. Raising and extending her right arm with the bow in it she drew back the arrow with her left hand until the string brushed against her cheek and she was able to look down the shaft of the arrow to the black tipped point. She gripped tightly with her right hand – her fingers and thumb each seating in the indented grooves that had been lovingly carved by her father. She inhaled deeply and held her breath. She exhaled and loosed the arrow.

The advancing hooded figure was completely unaware of the situation it found itself in, focused entirely on Flea's father who was still doing his best to keep distance with the chair. The creature bent low on its legs preparing to fling itself forward onto its quarry in the hope of knocking him off balance. Just as the creature began its forward momentum the arrow slammed into the right side of its chest. It fell to the ground. Dead.

Ealish had already nocked a second arrow and was scanning for the next target. She was acutely aware that she had just killed a person – *it was kill or let somebody else be killed* she told herself. She was accustomed to death and being the cause of it through her hunting and whilst she never enjoyed it or relished in it like others may have done, she was aware of the necessity of it. This was how she justified what she had just done – it was a necessity, and she would do it again.

Sweeping her eyes back and forth across what had become a battlefield, she became aware of Islander whom she couldn't identify locked in a wrestling match with one of the attackers. Held between them was a wooden stick with a spiked end – clearly a fight in which one would win and the other would die. The small, hooded figure swept at the legs of the Islander knocking them to the floor and causing them to lose their grip on the sharpened stake. Before the attacker even had a chance to raise it in readiness to strike, they were pierced through the neck by the second of Ealish's arrows.

Away to Ealish's left she heard a familiar voice calling for help, turning and taking another arrow from her hip quiver to string on the bow Ealish identified Flea surrounded by four of the attackers. One held each arm, a third stood in front with a dagger pointing directly at her whilst the fourth was placing some form of bag over Flea's head.

In quick succession Ealish eliminated the figure with the dagger and the figure who had placed the hood on Flea, striking them with arrows in their chest and throat respectively.

The figure gripping Flea's left arm turned its head in time to see Ealish select another arrow from her quiver. Ealish could see the face of the figure staring at her as she fitted her next arrow to the string. It made no attempt to move or avoid its impending death. Instead the figure just watched.

Suddenly Ealish's legs were swept from beneath her. Her bow and arrow fell from her grip and clattered to the ground far from her reach. The back of her head hit the dry earth sending a jolt of pain through her skull and white lights appeared in her vision. She shook her head but the white lights did not clear. As her vision refocussed, she realised that they were stars in the inky black sky above her. Then into her field of view came the face of one of the hooded figures – only not a human face like she expected. Whilst there were elements of a human face – a nose, a mouth and two eyes, they were all like those of an animal, a rodent to be specific.

The face was twisted in an evil grin that accentuated its yellowed protruding front teeth. The creature held in its hands a sharpened wooden staff and the sharp end was pointing directly at Ealish's chest. Extending the staff high above its head the creature prepared to drive it down hard.

Ealish desperately reached for the hunting knife that she kept always attached to her belt. With her left hand she was able to grip the handle and free it from the sheath, but it was too late.

-15-
QUEIG-JEIG

The creature brought down the sharpened stake with all its might. Unable to close her eyes and avoid seeing her own demise, Ealish met the creature's stare which had now glazed over, the eyes as lifeless as the corpse which fell across her – its weapon missing its mark and burying itself harmlessly into the ground.

A strong hand pulled her to her feet, and she found herself looking into eyes that were both familiar and foreign. Eyes that usually held so much love and compassion were still the same icy blue but now held a look of determination and fear.

"Find your brother, get to safety!" she could hear panic in her father's voice. It shocked her! She had never seen him worry, he was always a source of calm and control in a tense situation. His wooden staff was gripped tightly in his right hand, she could see the end of it was red with blood, some of which, she assumed belonged to her attacker after her father had cracked its skull.

"But...Flea?" Ealish pleaded - she too had adopted her brothers nickname for Breesha along with most of the Islanders. Ealish and her father looked up to see the two rat like figures dragging Flea away, hooded. Instinctively Ealish picked up her bow and the fallen arrow from the ground. She drew the string and let the arrow fly. It struck its target between the shoulders and one of the kidnappers fell to the ground. Her father turned to look at her but she did not return the look and was already selecting one of the three remaining arrows from her quiver. Her eyes locked on the final kidnapper, she was about to loose the arrow when the figure intentionally positioned itself fully behind Flea using her as a living shield preventing Ealish taking the shot. As the creature walked backwards it held a small dagger to Flea's throat to keep her moving.

Tracking them both down the length of the arrow strung on her bow, Ealish knew she had no clear shot. Then the creature made the critical error of leaning its head out from behind Flea's shoulder to sneer in celebration of its own cowardly cunning. Ealish's arrow struck it directly between the eyes, killing it instantly but leaving the body stood momentarily as if it was unsure what to do, a lifeless statue.

Flea pulled away from the grip of the dead attacker and fell to the floor. Ealish and her father ran towards her but found their path blocked by a dozen hooded figures carrying an array of crude looking weapons.

As they stopped and took stock of what was in front of them yet more figures appeared behind Flea and hauled her to her feet, adding rope bindings to her wrists which were pinned behind her back and a further rope around her neck on which they could apply pressure to direct her as they wished.

Ealish scanned from left to right across the scene, assessing and calculating her options. This is when she saw something that she hadn't factored in - her brother collapsed in a bloodied heap on the floor to her far right. Her father had evidently seen this too as he instructed, "Go to him." She didn't question him this time and ran to her fallen brother, not even knowing if he still lived.

As she reached him she looked back to see her father had stayed at his position. At first, she found it odd that he had not rushed to his fallen son. However, when she noticed the twelve hooded figures close in a circle around her father, she knew exactly what his intention had been. He had wanted to attract any attention away from his children in order to keep them as safe as possible.

Ealish quickly assessed her brother's condition, he was unconscious, but she could feel that he was breathing. His left forearm had an obvious wound that she wrapped with a fallen cloth from a nearby overturned table, using it as a makeshift bandage to stem the bleeding. She glanced back toward her father surrounded by the twelve hooded assailants. Not one of them had moved. She could clearly see her father as he stood a good deal higher. He stood straight and still, his staff gripped in his right hand, the base of it hovering just above the floor. He waited, turning his face to Ealish and Flax. His eyes no longer showed fear but appeared to be searching for some kind of answer to an unasked question. Ealish looked down at her brother then back at her father and nodded, giving him a thumbs up sign. That was the answer that he had been waiting for, he lifted his staff and took a double handed grip on it- one hand over, one hand under. He shifted his legs and dropped his weight slightly, taking a fighting stance, then he waited.

The first attack came, a hooded figure carrying two small sticks each with a sharpened metal blade in the end, much like two small spears, rushed at Ealish's father from directly behind him. The other eleven figures watched on, assessing, not moving.

Her father did not move, nor turn his head, Ealish worried that he had not even noticed the incoming danger and wanted to call out to warn him but then in a sudden blur her father turned to his right, sweeping the staff low. The creature was near enough to him that the staff swept its legs from beneath it. The creature let out a yell of surprise and releasing its weapons held up its hands in a defensive gesture as the end of the staff was brought down into its throat.

Two more creatures sprang forward, one carrying a curved dagger, the other a short sword. They attacked from opposite directions and Ealish watched as her father moved towards the creature approaching from his right first. This movement towards the threat was unexpected – not only by Ealish but the rat creature also as it slowed down appearing to second guess its actions. A rotating blow from the staff struck it square in the chest knocking it clean from its feet. The creature hit the ground and did not move again. Ealish's father continued to rotate his staff and turned back in the direction of the second attacker. Releasing his grip of the staff with his right hand, he allowed the momentum that the weapon had gained to continue and increased its range as his left arm extended in the direction of the oncoming rodent with the sword. The creature slashed with its weapon in vain as the longer staff connected with the side of its head.

Three more attackers moved, one of them carrying a short spear. As it ran it hurled the weapon through the air towards its target. Ealish saw her father turn his body at what seemed to be the last possible moment before the spear would hit. The weapon flew past his neck and struck one of the other attackers that had been approaching from the opposite direction with a pair of daggers held aloft. The now unarmed assailant continued directly towards Ealish's father with its sharpened claws being its only remaining means of attack. Whilst still a surprising distance away the creature leapt, arms and claws outstretched. Dropping his weight further and thrusting forward with one end of his staff her father was able to catch the creature in the stomach and using its momentum against it he flipped it over his head. The creature landed on the floor behind him. With surprising agility it changed the fall into a forward roll and sprang back on its feet, instantly turning and attacking a second time. A third creature advanced, armed with a shortened axe and got close enough to attack. Holding the axe with both hands above its head it slashed in a downward motion. Ealish's father blocked the axe attack with his staff by raising it horizontally with both hands into the path of the oncoming blade. The staff did not break under the force of the blade as Ealish had expected, instead the shaft of the axe broke under the force. The attacker was left holding the broken splintered shaft as the sharpened head fell to the floor. Still gripping the staff horizontally with both hands, Ealish's father thrust forward, smashing the staff into the forehead of the rat like figure with such force that it was thrown backwards. He then dropped to one knee, picked up the fallen axe head with his right hand and threw it spinning sideways, like Ealish had seen her father do countless times when skimming stones. The axe head struck the weapon less attacker in the chest just as it was about to leap for a second time and it crumpled to the floor, lifeless.

Six attackers remained. They had stood by and watched the demise of the first half dozen at the hands of the silver haired man and his staff. Repositioning themselves in a circle around the target they slowly began their synchronised approach. Ealish's father stood and returned to his lowered fighting stance. The attackers were approaching with more caution now, less hurried. A rodent figure to his right fell forward on the floor, the other five paused their approach to gaze at the body that lay there. An arrow was protruding from the back of its skull, black fletching feathers clearly visible. Ealish had used her second to last arrow to improve her father's odds. She was in the process of nocking her final arrow when the remaining five attackers launched at her father, limiting her chance of hitting one of them for fear of striking her own father. All she could do now was watch.

What happened next passed so quickly that Ealish could not even comprehend what had occurred. There were flurries of movement and cries of pain. Lantern light glinted from the blades of the assorted weapons as they slashed at their target. In what seemed like no time at all there was only one figure left standing.

Her father stood surrounded by the bodies of his assailants, blood discolouring his clothing and silver hair. There was no joy or excitement in his face at having overcome impossible odds, just a look of pained resignation. He looked toward his daughter and as their eyes met there was almost a look of embarrassment and shame on his face.

Observing this, Ealish was stunned at not only the speed and skill that her father had displayed but also the violence that he was capable of. She had never witnessed this side of him before but Ealish understood it was not rage or gratuitous violence that she had seen. Her father's actions had been controlled, they'd had purpose. *He is protecting us,* she told herself, *he is risking his life to do it*. He had clearly not wanted to do it. She could see that from the look that he wore.

Whilst it was always accepted that a parent would do anything for their child or children, Ealish was in the position to witness it first hand, and in that moment, her respect and love for her father deepened.

Then she saw him fall to his knees, the staff rolling from his hand.

She ran to him.

-16-
SHEY-JEIG

Flax woke up the way he was now used to. The images and sounds of the *ashlishyn* echoing in his mind until he was able to fully wake and shake them from his head.

He looked around and found that he was laid in his bed in the familiar surroundings of his room. He lifted his hands to rub his eyes in the hope of clearing away the visions of Draganes, Faeries and The Tree that felt so real yet, he knew they were not.

Feeling a sharp pain in his left arm he looked down to find it neatly bound with a white bandage. Slowly the memories of the brutal encounter at the Bloom Day feast crept into his mind, entangling with and then ultimately replacing those of the *ashlishyn*.

He remembered the details of the fatal encounter with the rodent like attacker, he remembered the dying noise of the creature as he had embedded its own blade in its back. A wave of nausea swept over him, but he was able to contain it.

He sat himself up in bed, his entire body feeling weak and tired. He waited for a long moment trying to piece together what had happened at the Bloom Day feast. *Who were those creatures? And why would they attack?*

"You're awake!" A familiar voice exclaimed with surprise. He looked around to see his mother, tears in her eyes, standing at his door. She ran to him and hugged him with a deep and obvious desperation to it that he couldn't understand.

"I will be fine in a few days mum, just a scratch that's all," he said, hugging her with his good arm and observing the bandaging on his left - downplaying the laceration that he had suffered at the hands of the creature and its scythe blade.

"I was so worried about you, we all were."

"Well, I know I'm in good hands with you and dad," he replied squeezing his mother tighter. He felt her weight collapse into him, he heard her sobs.

He thought that she was weeping due to his injury and the worry that he had put her through. But he could sense her pain, her despair - he realised that it was something more.

Releasing his grip on her so that he could look her in the eye he asked her, "What is it mum?"

"Your father, he —" she broke off and buried her head in her own hands. Flax could see the tears that had streamed from her eyes and found their way between her fingers and now ran freely down the back of her hands. He could hear the anguish in her voice.

He stood and ran from his room, past Ealish's door to his parents' room. Pausing at the door, he dared not enter for fear of what he would find inside. He knocked hesitantly, not knowing whether to expect an answer or not. When none came he pushed gently on the door and allowed it to swing inwards with its all too familiar creak, one that he knew like the back of his hand.

Flax took in the sight before him in the room and fell to his knees. Tears flowing uncontrollably down his face, for a long moment he knelt there silently sobbing, taking in what lay before him.

His father's face was pale and ashen, his eyes closed. Clutched in his hands on his chest was the staff that he carried everywhere with him. Flax couldn't move. Completely immobilised by his immediate grief, he just knelt there unsuccessfully trying to blink away the flood of tears. His father looked so peaceful. With his pallor he could have been a statue of white polished stone - if it weren't for the almost imperceptible rise and fall of his chest.

Noticing this through his tear blurred vision, he stood and ran to his father's side and took hold of one of his hands. It was icy cold to touch, not warm like he had expected. Everything that he could see and feel about his father, apart from his shallow breathing, told him that he was dead.

"Magic," came a voice from the doorway behind him, "dark magic - if there is a way to differentiate between that and good magic. Really it's all a matter of perception, I am sure any user of magic would assume that the magic they use is for their own good and therefore cannot be considered dark or evil. You see?"

"Actually it's not even really magic in this case, just a complex understanding of nature's dangerous gifts and how to weaponise them. There are few with such knowledge. I would hazard a guess that –"

"– What are you talking about?" Flax interrupted angrily without turning to face the voice.

"The arrow that your father was shot with, I examined it and found traces of what I believe to be poison. Specifically, a potent poison that can only be processed from a certain seaweed using very intricate methods and processes. *Mac Lir's Bane* - that's the name of the poison. As I was saying I could guess the source of such a poison."

Flax looked down at his father's body and only now noticed that his torso was wrapped in a bandage like that on his own arm.

"How can you be so sure what the poison is?"

"Granted, I have never seen it used before, but I am certain of it. The tell-tale sign of its use is a fogginess over the eyes that falls on its victims like the legendary cloak of Manannan Mac Lir - see for yourself."

Flax remembered stories he had been told when he was younger of the legendary sea god Manannan Mac Lir who had apparently once ruled over Mannin and the surrounding seas. In times of danger Mannin would often be shrouded in a thick sea mist making it impossible for invaders from other kingdoms to find it and land there. Over time this had come to be known as Manannan's cloak and was believed, by some, to have been sent by the god himself to protect his land.

"The curious thing about Mac Lir's Bane is that the poison actually prevents the person from dying. No matter how mortal their wound may be, the victim will not die. There are, of course, certain circumstances when that cannot be the case and the injury is so severe, beheadings and such like."

Flax leant close to his father's face and gently pulled back one of his eyelids. The bright blue that he expected to see was not there and the entire eyeball was a milky white colour, obscured by swirling clouds of grey. He checked the other and found the same lifeless fog staring back at him.

He finally turned to the uninvited guest who had unashamedly, and seemingly emotionally unmoved, observed him at his most vulnerable. Flax's watery green-brown eyes met the unblinking golden eyes of the Traveller, "How come you are such an expert on this poison?" he asked - a hint of accusation clear in his voice.

"I am no expert boy."

Flax let slip a minor involuntary reaction to being called *boy* by this stranger - Flax was taller than him and more muscular. The Traveller noticed the annoyance but did not apologise for the offence.

"I merely pick up bits of knowledge here and there on my travels - and I am acutely aware that the *Longtails* do not possess such knowledge."

This time it was Flax who noticed the involuntary change of tone in the Traveller's voice as he spoke the name Longtails.

He was aware that on Mannin Longtail was a term used to describe a rat by most - people can be superstitious and it was thought that by saying Longtail rather than rat it would keep the unwanted rodents at bay. Of course, now that he thought back to the strange features of his attacker, they greatly resembled those of a rat and so the name seemed very fitting.

"Is that who attacked us last night? The Longtails?"

"It was the Longtails who attacked your Island, but it was not last night - do you not know how long you have been sleeping?"

"What do you mean?" Flax asked with a genuine look of confusion and worry on his face.

"Summer has passed, autumn is upon us."

Flax ran to the window and looking out could see people moving around through the village. There was a cool breeze in the air but nothing to confirm what the Traveller had said. He ran to the door and out into the street in his bed clothes and bare feet. Running to the one place that he knew he would find his answer.

As he turned the corner and saw it, he stopped in his tracks.

He fell to his knees for the second time that day. Suddenly his whole body felt weak and tired. His left forearm stung where the blade had bitten into his flesh, right down to the bone. He looked up ahead of him and then back down at the bandage on his arm. His mind hurt just as much as his body, he was struggling to take in and process what his eyes were seeing.

Slowly he started to unwind the bandage, unsure of what damage he would see underneath. As he unwound the final turn his mind went into a spin. Expecting to see an ugly clotted wound from the injury sustained the night before Flax was almost disappointed to see that his arm was nearly healed. A dark pink scar ran the length of his forearm and either side were tell-tale marks where stitches had been used to sew his skin together to allow it to heal. But there is no way that the injury he sustained could have healed quickly overnight, not even in two dozen nights would it heal so well. He ran a finger across the scar- it felt both numb and tingly at the same time.

Once again, he looked up and what he saw made sense. The leaves on The Tree were a rich golden orange colour, flecked with vibrant reds and deep browns. His mind was finally catching up with his eyes. The last time he had seen The Tree in daylight had been Bloom Day with vivid green leaves, intense blue flowers and all the promise of summer. Now all that was gone. He had missed it and The Tree he saw before him now was completely different - no less beautiful - just different.

Flax slowly walked toward The Tree, stopping at the spot where he and his sister had spoken just yesterday, except it wasn't yesterday it was a full season gone by. He looked up into the foliage and through the shroud of autumnal colours it was just visible - the broken branch of the unbreakable tree.

"Keep that to yourself boy," came the voice from behind. He turned to see the Traveller staring intently at him. There was no use Flax attempting to play dumb, it was clear that both he and his seemingly newfound shadow knew what it was.

"Come," beckoned the Traveller, "we must talk."

-17-
SHIAGHT-JEIG

Flax followed the Traveller out of the village. By walking slightly behind he was able to observe him unnoticed. The Traveller still wore the same dark cloak that he had when Flax had seen him at the Bloom Day feast. The hood was worn down and only now did Flax notice that the cloak was an animal pelt of some kind. Flax felt like he recognised the patterns of the fur, but he couldn't quite place the animal.

His mind was still coming round to the idea that he had slept for a whole season. Not only that but his father was still sleeping having been poisoned with the arrow he was shot with.

Suddenly his thoughts turned to his mother, he had briefly seen her when he awoke and then had just run from the house. He felt immediate guilt and turned back to the village walking in the opposite direction to his guide.

"Where are you going boy?"

"My mother, I need to speak to her about –"

"– It is most important that we talk now. Your mother can wait," this was not a request it was clearly an order. Whilst Flax was desperate to ignore it and go to his mother there was something about the Traveller that held his attention and intrigued him. He turned to follow semi-reluctantly and continued his observations.

Every so often the cloak of the Traveller would flap back in the breeze exposing the short sword that he carried in a sheath on his right hip. The sheath was black leather which Flax could see was patterned and embedded with a shiny silver metal. He could never see it for quite long enough to discern what the pattern was. The Traveller wore black trousers of a similar design to most Islanders. His footwear was a pair of well-worn leather boots that came halfway up his lower leg. His dark hair was slicked back and tied in a short ponytail.

As they walked Flax watched the way he moved. There was no wasted energy, every movement appeared to have purpose to it. Each footstep was carefully selected, his arms and head only moved when they needed to. When Flax had first observed him at the feast he had thought him wiry and skinny. He was certainly not heavy set but now up close it was clear to see that he was not skinny, but lean. Flax could see that his bare forearms were muscle and sinew and nothing else. Flax wagered with himself that in a fight he would be able to handle himself. He kept moving onward with purpose and direction. The Traveller gave off an air of determination that Flax couldn't help but admire, begrudgingly.

"We will sit here, are you hungry?"

Flax hadn't even thought about food since he woke but now it was mentioned he realised he was ravenous. They had stopped on the top of a hill not far from one of the tree plantations that he managed. He didn't even have to look around him to know where he was and where certain features of the Island were in relation to his position. He sat on the soft grass amongst heather plants that had bloomed in their purples and whites and were now fading to brown. Looking over he saw the Traveller take off a satchel that had been belted around his shoulder, unseen beneath his cloak. He pulled from it some bread, cheese and strips of meat- along with a flask of milk.

Flax ate and drank greedily until there was nothing left. On reflection he recognised the sweet notes of honey in the bread - his mother had made it. Now that his hunger and thirst had been addressed it was time for him to talk.

"Exactly how long have I been asleep?"

"You slept for seventy-eight nights," replied the Traveller, "this summer season has been unusually short - autumn has been upon us for five days already."

"How come I slept so long? Was I poisoned too?" Flax ran his fingertips over the scar on his now exposed left forearm.

"There was no poison that I could tell of, but your wound was deep, and you became *feverish* and restless which meant your arm was not healing as it should. I used a combination of cushag and some other rare herbs that I have collected on my travels to induce a false sleep in you, to allow you to rest and heal. Your mother has fed and cleaned and cared for you and your father tirelessly since the morning after the feast. She is now in need of rest herself."

"Cushag?" Flax said almost to himself, "But that's a poison." Flax often encountered the unruly but beautiful plants with their clusters of yellow flowers on the sunnier sides of the plantations that he managed, growing at the bases of the walls or from between the blocks of stone. He was always careful not to handle them, or if he had to then to wash his hands well before eating.

"Everything can be a poison in the right amounts boy, and most things can be put to good use. I have learned and studied such techniques for more seasons than you have been alive."

"Sorry I didn't mean to offend," Flax replied before adding as a secondary thought an unconvincing, "thank you."

"When you said I was feverish," continued Flax, "there was a hesitance, a change in your voice. In what way was I feverish?"

"You did not display some of the more common symptoms of a fever such as sweating and temperature, however you were extremely restless and in your sleep you called out strange phrases that made no sense to anyone."

"What phrases?"

"You talked of a blood moon, of flying beasts and babies' cries"

Flax didn't respond. The Traveller continued, "I foolishly mistook these as signs of fever in you and treated them accordingly. However, I know now that was not the case and we have lost precious time."

"Lost time for what?"

"I started to think about some of the things you had been saying," said the Traveller, ignoring Flax's question. "And I recalled a strange conversation that I had with your father many seasons ago. He had asked me about flying beasts, specifically Draganes," – he paused – "ones that breathed not fire, but lightning."

Flax stared into the golden eyes searching for something, he could not be sure what exactly, but he kept searching regardless. His mind raced as he tried to appear calm. *His father had the ashlishyn too? He must have if he had seen a lightning breathing Dragane!* But that didn't help Flax as his father now lay in a deep sleep from which nobody knew how he could be awakened.

"Who are you?" He asked demandingly.

"I am the Traveller," came a calm, almost nonchalant reply.

"That didn't answer my question. You know things. More than you are telling me." Flax desperately wanted to grab him and shake him, to force answers from him but he knew that would not work. Instead, he decided to ask specific questions in the hope of getting answers.

By asking the right kind of questions Flax was able to learn that the Longtails were a race that lived on a small island, much smaller than Flax's Island. The Longtails island was on the eastern side of a 'T' shaped peninsula of southern Mannin, it was a four-day clear walk from The Sound marching from sunrise to sunset in summer. The island itself was named *'Guinn Y Vaaish* which when translated from the old language literally meant *pain of death* - because that is what anybody risked by going there. To most the island was simply referred to as *Vaaish* – or *of Death*.

The Longtails themselves were once people who were part of one of the ancient kings of Mannin's army. However, they revolted and tried to overthrow the great King. The King was aided by two armies from the North - mountain folk from the steep slopes of Snaefell and an army of woodland warriors from a place known as Tynwald. Flax had heard stories of the warriors of Tynwald as he grew up, a peaceful people dedicated to recording and upholding the ancient laws of Mannin. However, in times of need they would go to battle - and when they did, they were formidable fighters, especially in woodland or forest environments.

The Longtails (as they are now known) were defeated and those remaining were banished to *Guinn Y Vaaish* in exile. The rising and falling tides would completely cut off the island from Mannin at times. Even when it was accessible to cross back there was a sentry of soldiers posted on the peninsula of Mannin by the ancient King who imposed heavy taxation on anybody wanting to travel, hunt, purchase food or other goods. Over time the Longtails could not afford these taxes and they learned to be self-sufficient on *Vaaish*. They learned to live off a diet of raw fish and whatever meat they could get their hands on which more often than not was either a tough old seabird or rats that inhabited the only remaining inhabitable structure on the island. An ancient round fort with tall thick walls, this place was damp and dark but was their only option of shelter from the relentless sea storms and weather extremes that they experienced.

As the years passed the Longtails adapted to the dark damp conditions, their eyes narrowing and yellowing in the dark. Their sense of smell and hearing developed to compensate for their weakened eyesight. Their teeth sharpened to allow them to tear into the meat and fish they ate, their entire jaw structure changed giving them the appearance of having a long-pointed face leaving their top front teeth protruding. A lack of fresh fruit and vegetables stunted the growth of their bones and muscles leaving them with a short, stooped stature. Eventually they grew to resemble the very Longtails that they used for sustenance - hence they adopted the name.

They were rarely seen in daylight and were not known to have left *Vaaish* in any kind of numbers for years. Even today the current King of Mannin - a Mighty warrior named Orry (after one of the great kings of the past) kept a guard post on the peninsula of Mannin to prevent the Longtails leaving their island prison. The Traveller told of small infrequent skirmishes that occurred and usually resulted in heavy Longtail losses. Their exact number was not known as they were rarely seen but it was suspected that they now numbered well over a thousand.

They were led by a ruthless individual who was simply known as King Longtail - an almost ironic name given that all he was king of was a race of imprisoned creatures. Nevertheless, he insisted on wearing an ugly crown formed from shards of metal found washed up on the shores across his island. He was a harsh individual who ruled by fear - any subjects who refused his bidding would be taken to the dungeon of the fortress and few would be seen again. Those who were seen were only released to serve as a visible reminder to others not to cross the line, their ugly scars and physical deformities caused by the elite group of rodent warriors known as the *Roddanyn Doo*, or the *Black Rats*.

Whilst their imprisonment on *Vaaish* had caused them to physically alter and socially regress, they were not a foe to be underestimated. Flax learned that a group of at least forty Longtails had attacked his Island on the evening of the Bloom Day feast. Bodies of twenty-one of them had been found the next morning. The Traveller explained that Ealish had killed seven with her arrows, another had been found beside Flax where he lay unconscious - this being the one that Flax had slain with its own weapon. A further body had been found close by The Tree with a large welt on its head - Flax figured that this must have been the first hooded figure that he struck with the stone from his sling. Knowing that he had taken this second life gave him no pang of guilt this time, an uneasy nauseating feeling in his stomach, but no guilt - that creature would have killed Sid Kelly without a second thought.

"Ealish killed seven?!" Flax exclaimed out loud.

"Indeed, and your father twelve. Until he was struck by your sister's arrow."

-18-
HOGHT-JEIG

"My father was shot by Ealish?" Flax asked incredulously. He knew in his heart that his sister would never have shot her father, not even accidentally - he had never known her miss a shot or hit the wrong target with a bow.

"That is not what I said, I said your father was struck by her arrow."

The Traveller explained to Flax in detail the events of the night of the feast after the attack. He retold the account of the battle between his father and the twelve Longtails, the majority of which turned out to be members of the *Roddanyn Doo*. Identifiable by the blood red circle containing a black skull on the rear of their cloaks.

"So, if the *Roddanyn Doo* were there then that must mean King Longtail himself was on our Island!" Interrupted Flax.

"I was getting to that bit," the Traveller replied, clear annoyance at the interruption showing on his dark angular features.

He continued to explain that King Longtail had indeed been present during the battle. Sadly four Islanders had lost their lives fighting the raiders - Flax hung his head in genuine sadness at this news. He had known Islanders to die before but never under violent circumstances.

Many others were injured during the encounter, Flax and his father included. The Traveller explained that Flax's father had fallen at the hands of an arrow that had been shot by King Longtail himself, however this was not just any arrow - it had been one of Ealish's that the Rat King had pulled from the body of one of his nearby fallen subjects. He must have applied the poison to it before he shot it.

"The thing about those arrows of your sisters is that the black heads of them are made from a rare deposit known as *volcaan*. This is a precious mineral from the northern region of Mannin, nobody knows how it was created but it is mined from that area, and it holds certain unique properties. As you will have seen it can easily be shaped, in the case of your sister's arrows to a deadly point. If the mineral is placed in fire once shaped then it will hold its form and never break – until it is placed in fire again. When placed back into fire a second time, then an explosive element within it is activated and it creates massive destruction. In the mines of the north they will use small amounts of it to blast rock tunnels to create new mine shafts in order to extract more of the *volcaan*. Those who mine *volcaan* must be careful and there are often injuries or even loss of life in the mines.

"The final strange property of the mineral is that it has an absorbent capability – it imbibes that which is dripped or rubbed onto the surface. Mac Lir's bane in the case of the arrowhead that struck your father. That particular arrowhead has absorbed that poison and will now always contain it. Anything or anyone struck with that arrow will fall under Mannanan's cloak."

"Where would my father get hold of a rare mineral such as *volcaan*? He must have traded it with a visitor to the Island?"

"There is clearly much about your father that you do not know boy. He has travelled extensively across Mannin - and to shores beyond. Your father most likely acquired the *volcaan* during our travels around the northern mines of Mannin."

Flax could not believe what he had just heard. He had thought his father had always lived on the Island, *but he had travelled to Mannin, and to shores beyond that!?* Flax remembered tales that he would hear as he grew up of shores beyond Mannin. On clear days he could often make out dark shapes of such distant lands on the horizon, although it was sometimes difficult to differentiate the landmass from the clouds. But he had never met anybody that had visited them, well not that he knew of. Now before him stood a man who claimed to have undertaken these travels with his father.

"You and my father travelled together?"

"Yes, for a long period of time before he and your mother married, before you or your sister were born. Your father and I were – are – great friends. He is quite the fighter with that staff of his – there's not many I know who could face twelve armed opponents and walk away the victor."

"But I have never heard him mention you, I have never even met you before."

"Circumstances have been difficult and for many seasons I have been travelling, acquiring knowledge and information on behalf of your father. On your behalf too it seems. I had travelled back here on the day of the feast with the intention of sharing all I had learned with your father, but I never got the opportunity."

Flax wondered what he meant about gathering information on his behalf too, but his thoughts were interrupted as the Traveller continued.

"Now given the current circumstances it is more important than ever that I share my findings with your father. Breesha's life may depend upon it."

-19-
NUY-JEIG

Flax initially thought he had misheard, "Why would Flea's life depend upon it?"

"Flea?" The Traveller asked with a confused look on his face, although to Flax it seemed like he was trying to look confused on purpose – he could not reason why though.

"Flea...Breesha...it's a errrr... a nickname. Why would her life depend on this information?"

"She has been taken," the Traveller explained solemnly. Flax could not be certain, but he thought he saw tears form in the corners of the Traveller's golden eyes. But he blinked and they were no longer there - *if they ever had been.*

"Taken? Where?" Was all that Flax could manage to say, his voice weak and cracking with emotion. He pictured Flea in his mind, her smooth dark hair blowing gently in the wind.

The smile on her face that he liked to think she reserved only for him. He suddenly felt weak and tired all over.

"That much I do not know. The Longtails took her on the night of the feast. That must have been the whole purpose of the attack. There is no other reason they would travel with so many, and so far from *Vaaish*."

"What would the Longtails want with Flea?" Flax asked, his voice returning to him.

"They wouldn't, unless there was something in it for them, and that is worrying. *She* must have promised them something they could not obtain by their own means."

Something about the way the Traveller said she sparked a memory for Flax. He thought back to that night of the feast and suddenly remembered the conversation he had heard, or part heard, between the Traveller and Flea's father.

"I heard your conversation, the one with Flea's father." He blurted out without thinking first about how to approach the topic, he quickly refocused and fixed the Traveller with a determined stare. "You said *she* had set things in motion. You knew this was going to happen! You let this happen! Who is She? What does she want with Flea?!" As Flax spoke, he felt the anger welling up inside him, building until he could not hold it back, by the time he finished speaking he was up on his knees gripping the cloak of the Traveller and shouting in his face.

With surprising speed and strength the Traveller released himself from Flax's grip, stood, then stepped backward to create some distance between them.

"That conversation was private and not for your ears boy."

"I am no boy!" Flax yelled, lunging from his lowered position toward the Traveller in an attempt to tackle him to the ground. The Traveller deftly stepped to one side allowing Flax to grasp nothing but air, he stumbled but just managed to stay upright. Flax turned to face the Traveller and this time clenched a fist on his good hand and swung towards his head. The blow was easily blocked with a forearm by the more seasoned fighter. Flax's anger did not stop there. Thinking that the Traveller was concentrating on holding back the punch thrown with Flax's right hand he then clenched his left and threw a wide arcing punch toward the undefended back of the Traveller's head.

Just before the blow connected the Traveller rotated towards the punch and with a clenched fist of his own struck down on the exposed scar tissue on Flax's left forearm. He roared in pain and fell to the ground instinctively clutching his injured arm.

"You are weak at the moment and in no shape to fight," declared the Traveller as he tossed him a flask of water.

"Sit, drink, rest and listen," he instructed, "I will tell you all I know."

The Traveller explained how Breesha was not born on the Island nor were her parents, her actual birth parents. She had been born on Mannin at a place called *Balley Chashtal* - the place of the castle. Where the great kings of Mannin ruled. The King at the time was King Odairr - father of the incumbent, King Orry.

Her father, Murchad, had been a warrior from the western region of Mannin. Her mother, Isbal, a subject in the courts of King Odairr. They had met and quickly fallen in love at the *Boaldyn* festival, a celebration where the King would invite others from all the regions to a period of feasting and celebration in his courts to mark the impending return of the summer season

Murchad had no knowledge that Isbal had fallen pregnant and when the feasting had ended, he left to return to the western region of Mannin. He had every intention of returning the following spring and asking the King's permission to marry Isbal and take her home with him. Murchad only found out about the baby after she had been born, more than a season early, in a letter he received from Isbal. King Odairr assumed that Murchad had knowingly abandoned Isbal and the baby and so he banished him to remain in the western region for life or risk death for disobeying. Murchad wrote Isbal many letters but of course they all passed first through the court of the King who had every one of them intercepted and destroyed.

Isbal never heard from Murchad again and broken-hearted believed she had been abandoned by him. She struggled to support both herself and the child, she relied heavily upon the help of others. Unbeknown to her, Murchad had dispatched a trusted messenger to find Isbal and hand deliver a message and provide her with support in the way of coin, enough to support both her and the baby until he could figure out a way for them to reunite.

One day whilst foraging in the woods for food, or something worth trading for food, Isbal encountered a stranger. A woman approached them and showed great interest in the baby strapped to her mother's chest. The stranger could see from the physical appearance of both mother and baby that they were struggling to survive and in an unexpected gesture had offered to support them with food and coin.

When Isbal had asked what the stranger wanted in return she replied that when the child reached womanhood she must come and work for her for a period of time to pay off the debt. Seeing this as a reasonable repayment for what would ensure survival for her and her child, Isbal agreed. The stranger did indeed provide her coin and some food and as a sign of the promise that had been made, she placed a silver chain and pendant around the baby's neck.

That next morning whilst Isbal was trading some of her new coin for clothes for the baby she was approached by another stranger, the messenger from Murchad. He explained that Murchad had been banished by King Odairr and that his intention was to seek a way to find favour with the king and to marry Isbal. The messenger provided her with coin, more than she could imagine and gave her the instruction to be patient and wait for Murchad.

Isbal explained the promise she had made to the stranger in the woodland and decided she would return to find her, giving back the necklace and returning the coin she had been given.

The necklace however could not be removed from the baby's neck. No matter how hard Isbal or the messenger tried they could not remove it. Isbal travelled to the woods, leaving the messenger with the baby, to find the stranger and demand she remove the necklace and take back the coin - thus cancelling the promise of future work. Isbal never returned.

The messenger waited two days and two nights and heard nothing. He decided he must return to Murchad with the child and explain that Isbal had disappeared.

Before leaving *Balley Chashtal* the messenger heard rumour that Isbal and her child were missing and that Murchad was responsible. He also heard tell that a female had come forward claiming to be the baby's aunt, she was claiming responsibility of the child and described the child as wearing a silver necklace and pendant belonging to the aunt as proof.

The messenger stole away from the King's courts that night with the baby. Knowing that both King Odairr and the stranger were likely to seek out Murchad in the western regions in hope of finding Isbal or the baby he made the decision that the child could not go there until it was safe.

He sought temporary refuge for them at a building where holy men lived a reclusive lifestyle, a small abbey in the southern region in an area known as Rushen. He did not stay here long though. One morning one of the holy men enquired as to the origin of the necklace around the child's neck. The messenger retold the story of how it came to be there. The holy man rushed from the room and returned shortly after holding a scroll. The messenger read it quickly and soon understood the history of the necklace and the danger that the child was in. He left the abbey that day with the child and travelled west and south, his intended destination being the only place he believed the child could be safe and remain hidden until adulthood. He travelled to the Island, to Flax's Island.

Arriving by chance on the day that the Islanders referred to as Bloom Day. The messenger sought out a trusted acquaintance on the Island who knew of a couple who longed for a child but had been unable to have one of their own. An agreement was made that the couple would care for the child as their own on the condition that should the need ever arise to move her for her safety or the safety of others it would be done without question. On that day, sixteen blooms, ago Breesha was given to her parents by the messenger. When questioned by other Islanders where she had come from it was explained that she had been found in a small shipwreck by the messenger as he travelled across The Sound to the Island - there was no sign of any other persons and so knowing the child would die without immediate help he had brought her to the village to seek assistance. The villagers accepted this version of events and Breesha was welcomed as a new member of the community. Flax of course at this time had been but a baby himself and had no recollection of these events whatsoever. The only people who knew the truth of her origin were Breesha's new parents, the messenger and his acquaintance.

"And Flea has no idea of this?" Flax concluded.

"Not to my knowledge. It was always to her advantage not to know."

"The pendant?" Flax exclaimed, allowing his thoughts to vocalise.

"Go on," encouraged the Traveller.

"Flea always wears a silver necklace with a pendant of a Faerie on it." Flax pictured Flea in his mind, the sunlight glinting off the necklace that she always believed her mother had made for her as a child. *Surely she had tried to take it off herself? Although maybe not, why would she if it was so precious to her?*

"Correct, the very same pendant that was placed on her as a child, there is some strange property that causes the chain to grow as she grows."

"*She* placed it on her didn't she. The one you were talking with Flea's father about. *She* is the stranger am I right?"

"You are right again boy. The one I call *She* is actually called Meave. And *She* is a Faerie."

-20-
FEED

"A Faerie? Right."

Flax rolled his eyes and made no attempt to hide the sarcasm in his voice, temporarily forgetting that he had just been told Flea had been taken by the Longtails. Faeries, as far as Flax was concerned, were small creatures that could fly and cast magic spells, were always happy and on the side of the good in Faerie tales. He had never believed in them based on the name alone - Faerie tales. They were stories told to entertain children.

This time it was the Traveller who lost his temper, he grabbed Flax by the front of his tunic and lifted him to his feet with one hand pulling him close to his face. So close that their noses almost touched. Flax was once again startled by the strength that the man possessed.

Through clenched teeth the Traveller hissed "Listen boy, I have just told you things that I have kept secret since you were a crying babe in your mother's arms. Things that impact the safety of more than just the people on your Island. Things that others have died to keep secret - that abbey I told you about in my *story*. It was attacked just days after Breesha was moved from there, by Faeries. Yes, by Faeries! The holy men there would not give any of the information and they were tortured as a result, still they would not tell and nine of them lost their lives! The remaining men were blinded as punishment. And you have the audacity to roll your *pretty* eyes at me and make fun of what I am telling you? Well you can just carry on and I will find somebody else to help me whilst your friend is in mortal danger." The Traveller pushed Flax away forcefully to the floor.

At this last line the reality of the situation hit Flax again, *Flea was missing, his childhood friend, his best friend.*

He sat up and rubbed at his lower back where he had hit the floor.

"I'm sorry," he said with genuine sincerity to his voice, "I'm ready to listen, I'm ready to help."

The Traveller explained that the messenger had learned from the holy men in the abbey that the necklace placed around Breesha's neck was held there by a *mollaght obbee,* a dark magical curse. The records of the holy men detailed that the necklace was unique and belonged to Meave, the Faerie Queen. She had ruled the Faerie race on Mannin for over five hundred seasons. No Faerie Queen had ever lived so long, and the secret of her apparent immortality lay in the necklace and the *mollaght obbee* within.

The Traveller explained that no physical body could survive for so long without succumbing to the decay of time. Meave however, developed the curse in such a way that it enabled her to inhabit the body of the necklace wearer once they had reached adulthood. Once she had assumed the body of the wearer her old body would die and she could remove the necklace herself ready to place on her next unsuspecting victim. As such, Meave's physical appearance changed as seasons passed and there were few who outside her race who would ever be able to recognise her. Meave has to be in physical contact with the necklace wearer to enable the transition into the new body to occur. If Meave's current body died before the transformation could take place, then her Faerie spirit too would die along with all curses cast by her.

This is why the messenger had decided that Breesha should be hidden from Meave, in hope that over time her body would fail and she would be unable to transition into Breesha's body. This in turn would break the curse and allow for a new Faerie to take up the crown. In the Faerie race the females were the dominant gender, as such the successor would be another queen.

"So Faeries are actually evil?" Flax asked

The Traveller replied that this was not always the case. In ages gone by the Faerie race would interact with the other communities of Mannin and lived in peace. However under the rule of Meave the Faerie race had turned against the different races of Mannin choosing to live in isolation from others and attacking with unyielding violence any intruders who strayed into their lands. They had made their home in one of the woodlands in the eastern region of Mannin, their fortress was known as *Droghad ny Ferrishyn,* which in the old language literally meant *Faerie Bridge.* Of course this structure was much more than a bridge but it got its name as it spanned over the width of the river on which it was built.

It was not known what had happened to cause Meave to lead her race down this dark path but it was one that had brought destruction and death to any who encountered them. This meant that Breesha and any who were known to her were in grave danger.

"How do you know all this?" asked Flax. "Is this the information you have been gathering to share with my father?"

"No your father was told all this in strict confidence on the night that the messenger brought Breesha to the Island."

"If he was told it in confidence then how come you know it?" Flax asked

"Because I am the one who told him it boy," the golden eyes fixed on Flax. "My true name is Rumund - brother of Murchad the King of the western Mannin. I am known by many other names; the Messenger, the Ghost, the Keeper of Secrets but now to most I am simply known as the Traveller."

This much made sense to Flax and after what he had heard today was no great surprise. The Traveller had much darker skin than any of the Islanders, darker even than Flea. However if her father had dark skin and her mother pale then that would account for her also having a darker skin tone than that of all the Islanders. It was something he had always been aware of but had never really thought about as he saw no necessity to dwell on it, Flea was his friend - it didn't matter what she looked like.

"It was I who was trusted by my brother all those seasons ago to deliver the coin and the message to Isbal," the Traveller said softly. "I was trusted to make sure her and the child were safe and I failed my brother, I ought to have recognised that something sinister was afoot when the necklace could not be removed from the child's neck, however I allowed Isbal to go to Meave that day and that is a mistake I have regretted ever since."

"After fleeing the abbey I knew that this Island was a place I could take the child where she could be anonymous, she could be safe and hidden in the hope that Meave's body would die and the curse would be broken. I left her here and put measures in place so that I would be aware of those coming and going from the Island."

"But you were here last night, why didn't you fight? Why didn't you stop them?" Flax protested "You said it yourself - the only ones who killed any of the Longtails were my family! You could have helped with that sword you carry! Where were you?" Flax was not angry now, instead just confused and seeking answers.

"I was observing, difficult as that may be to hear that is how I serve my purpose best."

"What is your purpose if not to protect your own kin?"

"You are correct, partly. That was once my sole purpose given to me by my King. I would frequently visit the Island and Breesha whilst she was a young child and it was during one of these visits that I developed a new purpose."

"You say *my king?* I thought Mannin had one king, King Orry?"

"It is true that Orry is the king of Mannin. However the land is split into many regions. Some of these regions have their own rulers who, whilst being loyal to Orry as their King in the interests of peace, are rulers of their regions in their own right. My brother Murchad is one such King."

"And did he assign you your new purpose? The one that was more important than the safety of his daughter?"

"Let me explain without interruption and perhaps all will become clear," the Traveller said sternly before continuing, "on one of my visits to your Island I was confided in by your father. It appeared that he had been suffering terribly in his sleep. He had a recurring dream of which he could make no sense. He informed me that these dreams started the night of the Bloom Day feast that I had brought Breesha to the safety of your Island. He had spent seasons trying to make sense of them without mentioning them to another soul but he was no closer." The Traveller could see Flax had drawn closer to him and was paying clear attention to every word that he spoke, "Your father told me of a blood red moon, a baby's cry, Faeries and Draganes that breathed lightning, ships on a red sea and most worryingly The Tree with the –"

"– fallen bough," Flax could not help but cut in and finish the sentence. His mind was struggling to take in what he had just heard. *His father had the visions too? Does he know about the broken branch on The Tree?* A thousand other questions were in his head and he had the answers to none of them. He remembered the morning of Bloom Day when he and Ealish first discussed the visions with each other, how their father had interrupted them and nearly seen the drawings and writings that they had amassed - *he knew then, his father knew what they were discussing. He had even told them that they had matters to discuss.* They never got the chance to. He was brought back to attention as the Traveller continued to speak.

"It was clearly no coincidence that these visions began the night Breesha was brought to the Island, and it seemed to me that it was more than just my decision to bring her here - this event was pre-destined. The cry of the baby, this must have represented Breesha. The Faerie figure, that was Meave, or at least a representation of her. The remainder, I was unsure of and to this day I do not understand the full significance of these visions."

"How can you be sure though?" Asked Flax seeking confirmation for his own benefit.

"I couldn't be at first, but your father gave me two pieces of information that night that made me certain they were connected - even without evidence to back this up."

"What did he tell you?"

"He reminded me of something that, whilst incredible to witness, had seemed so insignificant when it happened that its potential importance was lost on me. The Bloom Day on which I brought Breesha to the Island, the flowers on The Tree were bright red that year. A fact that nobody had thought much of until the evening feast began and they looked to the sky to witness something that had not happened for generations, *Eayst Folley*."

"The blood moon," whispered Flax. He had not known that there had been a blood moon within his lifetime. In his head he ran through the sequence of the *ashlishyn* over and over. He was becoming more convinced that the Traveller was correct, *this couldn't be a coincidence.*

"The second piece of information that your father gave me was not words but something he showed me. We went to his workshop and hidden at the back beneath one of his workbenches, covered in cloth he handed me a broken limb of wood. I initially thought he was handing it to me to hold whilst he kept rummaging, but the wood was what he was searching for. This made no sense to me until he informed me that this piece of wood was hundreds of seasons old, it had been passed down from father to son in his family for generations. Despite its age there was no sign of rot or damage to the dark straight grain of the wood. This wood was the fallen bough from *The Tree*. No person outside of your father's family had ever known about it. He had been passed it by his father with the strict instructions to keep it safe as it would one day serve a purpose that was not yet known. The next morning before others awoke your father took me to The Tree and looking up from beneath it, he showed me the snapped bough that his father had pointed out to him on his eighteenth Bloom Day - proof that the events in his *ashlishyn* were real.

"That night I had visions of my own, visions that to the best of my knowledge have been revealed to me and me alone.

"I travelled the regions of Mannin and sought out information regarding these visions. Information on events that had occurred, and those that were yet to come. In order to do this I became anonymous, the Traveller, ally of all, foe of none.

"That is why I had to observe Breesha being taken without intervention, I am one of few who have travelled into *Vaaish* and lived to leave the Island again. I am seen as an individual who will offer no threat to anybody and therefore I am considered by some races to be a trusted messenger. Had I involved myself in the violence that night then my anonymity would have been lost and all communication with the Longtails with it. Difficult as my purpose is I must not enter into conflict with any of the races of Mannin for fear of upsetting the fine balance of trust and mutual information sharing that I have worked for many seasons to create.

"During my travels I was able to learn the true meaning of my own visions and of the purpose that I now serve, one that is greater than the task set by my brother all those seasons ago."

Flax cut in – "But if we had just stopped the Longtails taking Flea then Meave would not have her and the timeline of the *ashlishyn* would be broken."

"It is not as simple as that. It is incorrect to assume that the *ashlishyn* is depicted as a timeline. It is merely a collection of events that have happened or are yet to happen. It cannot be assumed that they are shown in chronological order - for example, your father described the falling bough being severed from The Tree by the Dragane toward the end of his dream, however we know that this bough fell centuries ago and is most likely the first of the events to have occurred.

"I travelled to the halls of the record keeper of Mannin in Tynwald where I have read accounts of others who had been visited with visions, some of these individuals attempted to interrupt the events of the *ashlishyn* and they, and others close to them suffered dearly."

"So what do we do? Just leave Flea to have her body stolen by the evil Faerie Queen so that we don't interrupt the visions?"

"I never said that boy, we simply need to understand what the visions mean before we act. Just because Breesha and Meave feature in your vision does not mean that they are linked. As I explained the visions are merely snapshots of events or even at times representations of events that are to happen or have already happened. Nothing can be assumed."

"So we can rescue her?"

"You make this sound a simple task like walking up a hill or chopping down a tree. But yes, we must plan to rescue her whilst gathering more information about what your visions mean. Bear in mind however, your father has been having these dreams for sixteen blooms and to my knowledge is no closer to figuring out what they mean."

"We cannot wait that long again to rescue Flea. Her body will be taken by the time she reaches adulthood, she only has two blooms until then!"

"Actually she has less time than that, on Mannin time is not measured in blooms as they do not have a Tree. Time is measured in years. A year is four seasons very much like a bloom here on the Island. However remember that Breesha was born on Mannin before your Bloom Day, over two seasons before in-fact. Breesha was born in the winter, specifically during the festival of *Oie Houney*. This is a celebration of the start of the winter season. That is when she will reach adulthood, just less than five seasons away."

"Then we must make plans straight away," Flax insisted.

"Boy, you are weak. You have been asleep for a full season and need to build your strength. More than that, you must be trained to fight, and more importantly to think. Go home and see your mother - training begins in the morning."

-21-
NANE AS FEED

Flax walked wearily back to his house, he hadn't kept track of time but it was late in the afternoon and there was an autumnal coolness in the air. His entire body ached. The Traveller was of course correct that he was in no shape to be attempting any kind of rescue of Flea.

Flea, he allowed himself a long moment to think of her, to imagine what she must be going through. Tears welled in his eyes at the thought of his friend being held against her will, far from her home and her family, far away from everything she had ever known and loved.

Flax looked around the kitchen, it was familiar but it felt different somehow, the whole house felt different and he could not put his finger on what it was.

He looked down the hallway and saw a light flickering in his parents' room, walking toward the door he stood and listened.

What he heard broke his heart.

His mother was softly singing to his father, a song that he had heard her sing a thousand times as he grew up. It was a song that until now he had always associated with happiness and good memories. However, hearing the words and the melody being sung between the sobs of his own mother he now understood the song in a completely different way. It was a song of love, and whilst most of the time love would be a happy thing it could also be the most painful thing in the world. Right now his mother was experiencing that pain, Flax thought once more of Flea and the sadness that her situation brought to him, *how much more must that be for his mother?* She had centred her whole life around his father and raising her children. Now she knelt before her husband, only it wasn't her husband it was a shell of a body, fallen, hidden under the foggy shroud of Mannanan's Cloak.

He sat outside the door and wept as he listened. The salty tears stung his eyes then raced in lines down his face. The man who had always been so strong, invincible in his eyes was now neither of those things as he lay there motionless. Held in a prison at the hands of the poison that had taken over his body, unable to either be awakened or to die of his wounds.

Flax went through so many emotions in that short space of time that he sat there. Heart ache, anger, helplessness, confusion, denial - but he settled with guilt. He could not shake the feeling of guilt that he had woken that morning after sleeping a whole season. Then, knowing that his father lay as he did now, he had chosen to spend more than half the day with a stranger rather than helping his mother and sister.

He stood and entered the room; his mother had finished singing and was quietly kneeling beside her husband. She turned and seeing Flax she managed a weak smile. Her eyes were red but were not weeping, however there were tell-tale signs of salted streaks across her face that gave away her tears.

She stood and hugged Flax tightly, he hugged her back never wanting to let go.

"Mum, I am so sorry," he sobbed.

"This is not your fault son, none of it."

"I know that but I'm sorry that I haven't been awake to help you. Then I woke this morning and I disappeared with him and left you again."

"Do not be sorry, you and Rumund had to talk, I understand that it was important." This was the first time that Flax had heard the Traveller's name spoken by anybody else, it was unexpected and it caught him off guard. He hadn't thought about the fact that his mother must have been acquainted with him due to the apparent close relationship he held with his father.

"But I should have been awake, I should have been helping you."

"We thought your wound was infected and that is why Rumund kept you asleep, however when it was clear that your words spoken in sleep had meaning we knew we must let you wake. We knew that you were having the same visions as your father."

"You know about the *ashlishyn* too?"

"Of course sweetheart, your father and I have no secrets. But just like Rumund the significance of the words were lost to me in the initial aftermath of the attack. It was only when we spoke of them again, we realised that you had not been feverish and we slowly weaned you from your induced sleep."

"Well I am here now and I will help you and Ealish to look after dad until we find a cure."

At this his mother could hold back her emotions no more and the flood of tears fell from her eyes.

"We will find a cure Mum. Every poison must have an antidote," insisted Flax.

"It's not that my dear boy, it's Ealish."

"What about her?" Flax asked, a worried look on his face

Through the sobs his mother could utter only two words

"She's gone."

-22-
JEES AS FEED

Flax woke, he blinked his eyes several times. He stared at the ceiling and realising he was in bed he sat up and rubbed his eyes.

He looked around the room, nothing was different. He sat there thinking for a moment. Trying to piece together in his head what had happened. *How did he end up in his room?* The last he remembered was talking to his mother and she told him.... *Ealish had gone*...tears welled in his eyes at the thought of his sister dead. *How had it happened? Why did he not tell me?* He asked himself angrily - referring to the time he had spent with the Traveller the previous day. *Was it the previous day?* He didn't even know what time of day it was, let alone which day.

He heard voices from down the hallway - voices, plural. He stood and ran to them. He must have dreamt all that had happened, he could clearly hear more than one voice. *If his father lay poisoned and his sister dead, then whose voices could he hear?* He ran past the closed doors of his parents' and Ealish's bedrooms. His bare feet thudding on the wooden floorboards.

He burst into the kitchen hopefully but was instantly disappointed.

Sat at the table talking to his mother was the Traveller, "Oh it's you," he muttered, his thoughts instantly returning to his sister.

"Come boy, eat. Your training starts today," he was instructed.

"Training? I'm not interested in your training. My father lies as he is and my sister is dead. I want nothing to do with you, this is your fault!"

"Ealish is not dead Flaxney," his mother interrupted, a look of pained confusion across her face, "why would you say that?"

"You said so…" he protested to his mother.

"I told you she was gone. She is not dead my sweetheart," his mother rushed to him and wrapped him in her arms. She kissed his cheek, "I'm sorry I was so upset I didn't mean to say it like I did, and then you passed out and I had assumed it was just overwhelming for you to hear that your sister had left. I see now how you my words confused you."

"I am so sorry Flaxney," she kissed him again.

"Ealish has left us? To go where?"

"She is hunting, on my behalf," answered the Traveller. "Your sister's skills are being put to use for our benefit. She blames herself for the injury that your father sustained as it was at the hands of her arrow, even though that is not the case she would not be convinced otherwise. She spent many days and nights by you and your father's side before she could be convinced to leave the house. I spent some time with her on her daily hunts and observed the way she moved quickly and silently, I also witnessed her impressive bow skill. As I said I have given her purpose and put these skills to use, sadly that required her to leave the Island. She has travelled to Mannin, I assisted her in the crossing myself."

"What purpose have you given her? What is she hunting?"

"Not what... who. I told you yesterday that the poison used to subdue your father was one that required particular skill to create, much greater skill than any of the Longtails would possess."

"I remember, so Meave must have created the poison and given it to the Longtails to help them capture Flea."

"That was my first thought and it made sense, often the simplest of explanations is the correct one. However, aspects of this explanation do not add up for me. To create Mac Lir's Bane requires a high level of skill but it also requires a very particular list of ingredients. Ingredients that are readily available on Mannin but are spread across the regions. If Meave was willing to travel across the regions of Mannin to collect the ingredients for the poison, then why would she not travel to your Island herself to take Breesha? It seems to me that somebody else made that journey and collected the ingredients then made that poison to pass to Meave, who in turn passed it to the Longtails to use."

"Maybe," agreed Flax, "but what does any of this matter, we know the Longtails took Flea and that they will give her to Meave. Why does it matter who made it?"

"Because when Mac Lir's Bane is produced the by-product of the process is the antidote to the poison."

It wasn't the Traveller who spoke this but Flax's mother. He turned to look at her questioningly.

"How do you know about Mac Lir's Bane mum?"

"Before I came to the Island to live with your father I travelled across Mannin, by myself at first and then with your father after we met. I learnt a lot in that time sweetheart, some of it I have forgotten - a lot of it I have not thought about for years. I remember spending time with a potions master in the *Slieau* region. He showed me the process for making Mac Lir's Bane. When the ingredients are mixed correctly a foam forms on top of the liquid. This foam is the antidote to the poison, not to the poison in general but specifically to that batch of poison with which it was made. To administer the antidote some of the foam must be applied to the wound. Then, the recovery is near instant. I observed the poison, then the antidote being applied on a squirrel as a test of its effects."

"Your mother is correct," continued the Traveller, "whoever made the poison and handed it to Meave will have the antidote, the cure for your fathers' condition."

"So that is what Ealish is hunting? The cure?"

"Yes, she left the Island six days ago, just as the summer season was ending. She intends to track down the source of the poison. But in addition to that I need to know where Breesha is being kept and what Meave has promised the Longtails in return for her capture."

"Do you know where she was headed? If she only left six days ago, I could catch up to her –"

"No! you are too weak boy. Your sister travels fast and light. There would be little chance of you catching up to her. In any case I need her to obtain the information that we need before we act."

"But we know where Flea is, she is at *Droghad ny Ferrishyn*, where all the Faeries are."

"We do not know that. We could assume that but we could be wrong. In my many seasons of travelling I have learnt that assuming anything can be a dangerous thing. We must gather facts and information before acting. You cannot simply walk into *Droghad ny Ferrishyn* and to do so without knowing that which you seek is within would be foolish. It could be the case that the Longtails hold Breesha with the intention of only handing her over at the time that Meave requires her, or we could be wrong altogether and the Longtails may not be working with or for Meave at all - however I find that unlikely."

"Why so?"

"You remember the conversation you overheard with Breesha's father and I?" The Traveller asked, accusation clearly present in his tone and evident by the look on his face.

Flax remembered the snippets that he had heard, "Yes, you said she had already set things in motion. What things were they?"

"I had learned that Meave had come to know the location of Breesha and that she intended to have her taken, however I did not know the exact details or timing of her plan. I travelled here immediately, arriving the day of the Bloom Day feast. I had intended to take her from here in order to protect her but as you know it was too late."

"I thought you said you had measures in place to see who was coming and going from the Island?" asked Flax.

"This is true, however sadly these measures were not designed to stop an invading army, my sentries had no time to report the arrival of the Longtails to me. Had they tried to stop them they would have surely lost their lives. They were however able to witness their escape, they fled the Island in small boats. They left one behind at the eastern dock, no longer needed due to the number of them that were killed in the attack. My sentries followed them as far as a strange rock formation known as the Sugar Loaf, where the Longtails went ashore and took shelter and rest in a cave in the rock face. My sentries waited outside for a full day but saw no movement. Tired of waiting, they entered the cave and found that it led further into the rock wall to some steps carved into the rock that led to the cliff tops. The Longtails had made good their escape on land. Unsure whether they had been spotted or not, my sentries were unable to give chase in unknown direction so they returned to me to make their report."

"Who are these sentries of yours? I need to speak to them - I need to learn what they observed." Flax protested.

"That will not be possible, their task has been reassigned."

"But –" Flax never got to finish.

The Traveller interrupted him, simply stating, "–not possible boy."

He stood from the kitchen table and walked to the corner of the room. Next to the door propped against the wall were two wooden staffs. Selecting the first one the Traveller turned and threw it one handed toward Flax. He caught it with both hands, fumbling slightly at the unexpected timing of the item being thrown to him. Once he had regained his grip, Flax held it tightly in his hands so as not to drop it. He looked at the Traveller who picked up the second staff with one hand. He spun it twice around his hand – needlessly in Flax's opinion, before gripping it firmly and heading towards the door.

"Get dressed and then meet me at the top of the hill boy. I will train you, just as I trained your father."

Then he left the house. Flax stood in the quiet kitchen. Even though his mother was there he felt lonely. He thought of his father lying motionless, unaware of all that was going on around him in the next room. Then his thoughts turned to his sister, alone somewhere on Mannin following the instructions of this stranger who had appeared in their lives shortly before all had fallen apart.

Then he looked at his mother, she seemed to have aged greatly in the time between the night of the attack and now, he stood motionless waiting for her instruction.

She looked at him with warm loving eyes. Flax could see a tear building in the corner of each of them. She softly spoke to him.

"Go."

And he did.

-23-
TREE AS FEED
- EALISH'S FIRST DAY ON MANNIN -

Ealish stood on the stone beach. Her leather boots wet with sea water clung to her feet. She watched the Traveller paddle his small boat back to the Island, back to her Island.

The crossing had been uneventful. When she had first sat down in the boat she had been full of eagerness and anticipation. But with every strong, powerful paddle stroke the Traveller had made she had become less confident, more uncertain.

The land on which she stood was unfamiliar to her, she had seen it of course across The Sound from her familiar safe Island. But now as she stood on it, she felt unsure. There was an uneasiness in every carefully selected footstep she took knowing that this now was new territory, it was the unknown.

It had been early in the day, the morning rays streaking across the sky, the sun itself hidden behind the eastern cliffs when they landed on the unfamiliar shore. Then, as Ealish had turned from the sight of her home to the unknown she watched the ball of fire begin to crest the top of the hills.

Summer seemed to be ending sooner than expected. There was a tangible coolness in the air and Ealish found the warm kiss of the sun inviting as she set off walking toward it.

Her feet stayed wet as they created fresh footprints in the dew laden grass. She scowled as she looked down at them, never liking to leave a trace of her presence. However at this time of day on this terrain it was unavoidable.

She had trained hard through the summer since learning of her task. Honing her skills of survival, learning about the many herbs and plants of Mannin. Some that would aid and sustain her, others that could harm her. She had soaked up as much knowledge as she could from the Traveller - a man to whom she formed an instant dislike. For one, he referred to her as *girl* a term that she detested. She was eighteen blooms old, she was an adult now. But it was the way he said it – like he had a bad taste in his mouth. She had, however, learned to tolerate his mannerisms to her own benefit as the more time she spent with him the more she could learn.

Her task, as he had described it had two parts to it. She must gather information to find who it was that created the poison that held her father under Mannanan's cloak, that person would also hold the antidote. She must also find out where Flea was being held and pass word to the Traveller. He had told her that when she had information to pass to him, she should light a fire by the nearest shore and into the flames cast some powdered root from the gorse plant that grew abundantly across Mannin. He had demonstrated this to her and how it turned the flames of the fire a brilliant blue. He instructed her that once she had done this his messengers would appear to her and she could trust them with the information that she had learned. Ealish was understandably very sceptical about this but had no reason to doubt what she was being told, aside from the apparent absurdness of it.

Whilst she was acutely aware of the two reasons that she had travelled to Mannin, she had a third reason - a personal reason for being here.

As she allowed her left hand to rest on top of her arrow quiver on her hip, she reminded herself of this. Looking down at the quiver her father had made for her and the arrows within she counted seven black fletched arrows, six of them recovered from dead Longtails the morning after the attack, the seventh she had not shot. Among the seven black feathered arrows was one with blue feathers, bright blue. She had chosen this colour for two reasons, firstly it reminded her of the flowers on The Tree that summer and the night that the attack happened. Secondly it reminded her of the colour of her father's eyes, that was before they turned the horrible milky grey colour that they were now.

This arrow, with the bright blue fletching, had been pulled from her father's back. It was her arrow, taken from the body of a Longtail she had killed. The poison had been applied and it had been cruelly shot into her father's back by the Rat King as he and his remaining army retreated from the battlefield with Flea as their captive. *It was a cowardly attack!* Ealish had told herself every time she thought about it. Her father was no threat to anybody at the time he was struck, he had just overcome all odds and fought twelve armed attackers single handed, with some help from Ealish who had slain one of them. This arrow, that she now stood staring at in her quiver, still held the same poison that had imprisoned her father. It had seeped into the *volcaan* tip and consumed it. This arrow would be the messenger of her third purpose in this unfamiliar land. She had vowed to herself that she would send this arrow into King Longtail's body with the full knowledge that the poison would take hold, locking him in a deathless eternity from which he would not wake.

She had to consciously shake herself from the trance in which she was trapped, staring at the arrow on which she pinned all her desire and need for revenge. She knew that her first task was to track down the Longtails in the hope of obtaining information that would lead to the source of the poison. Whilst she and the Traveller had discussed many different hypotheses, they nearly always deduced that the poison had passed from the Faerie Queen to the Longtails but this was just guesswork. Therefore, she needed to confirm this first in order to trace the movements of the poison back to its origin and hopefully the location of the antidote.

Learning of the antidote had given her purpose and focus during what had been the darkest and loneliest time of her life. She hadn't been completely alone of course, her mother had been there. However, she had rightly so been focused on nursing her father and her brother. *My brother*, she thought of Flax, who currently due to the medicine was laid peaceful and still in his bed. Before this had been administered he had tossed and turned relentlessly, unknowingly tearing at the wound on his forearm in a suspected fever. She had recognised the words that he spoke and knew it not to be feverish rambling but a vocal manifestation of the visions that he saw in his sleep - the same visions that she saw most nights. She knew that she could not share these visions with her mother, or the Traveller for that matter. She had kept them and her limited understanding of them secret, her only understanding to date being that The Tree could be damaged and she, and now her brother, had found the stump from a severed branch on The Tree. The rest of the *ashlishyn* she could only speculate at. But knowing now what she did about Meave the Faerie Queen she assumed that the Faerie in the vision was her, or a representation of her. Ealish continued to muse upon the *ashlishyn* in her mind as she walked east.

Ordinarily she would run but this was unfamiliar territory so she was cautious. She was aware that this was the direction in which the Longtails had travelled, albeit by boat, after escaping the Island with Flea. Her initial destination was the Sugar Loaf although having never seen it in her life she had no idea what it looked like. The Traveller however had assured her that she would know it when she saw it.

To get there she would have to endure a steep climb up and along the coastal cliffs and then cross a dangerous stretch known as *The Chasms*. She had been told that this was an area in which large fissures had opened up in the ground, seemingly bottomless pits that offered nothing but certain death to anyone foolish enough to fall into one.

As she climbed, she felt the cool sea breeze on her face, whipping her plaited golden hair behind her. The coolness was welcome, the steepness of the climb meant an increase in effort and despite her physical ability she felt the exertion. Ealish was travelling light to enable her to move fast and quietly. She carried her bow and quiver - of course, her hunting knife was fastened securely in its sheath on her belt and strapped to her left calf was a shorter blade. Across her body was a satchel in which she carried spare clothing, a blanket, enough food to sustain her for a couple of days - some cheese, bread and dried fish and meat. Aside from these items she carried some small animal snares, some fishing line and hooks, flint and metal for lighting a fire and a short length of rope coiled over her shoulder and around her body. Attached to one end of the rope was a three-pronged hook that Flea's father had fashioned for Ealish before she left the Island. Finally, she carried on her belt a small pouch that had been given to her by the Traveller which contained small metal discs with markings on. She had heard about these before but never seen them. In Mannin they were called coins and were used as a form of payment for things like food, clothes or even in exchange for hospitality in somebody's home. The Traveller had informed her that she may need these.

In addition to her comfortable, yet still wet, leather boots she wore a pair of grey leggings, a muted green tunic and an equally comfortable brown leather jacket. Mr Crawshaw had kindly offered to line it with fur for warmth prior to her leaving – she had taken him up on this offer and was grateful for it.

She periodically stopped and scanned the environment around her, it was important that she cover ground quickly however it was more important that she be aware of her surroundings and also of anyone or anything moving nearby. To her right was a steep drop off the cliffs into the sea, when she looked down she could see the foamy waves crashing into the wall of rock on which she stood. On the horizon to her right she found it difficult to differentiate where the sheet of hazy grey cloud met the sea, whilst she could not be sure of it she thought she could make out the faint outline of some distant land. When she looked again she could not discern the same shapes and merely dismissed them as clouds. To the north, on her left, the land rose away from her and shielded her view of anything further. This land was covered in thick spiky gorse plants. Their yellow flowers now withering and past their best, the sharp hardened spikes still a visible and physical deterrent to anybody or anything.

The path ahead of her followed close to the edge of the cliff, it was not a well-worn path but was a visible corridor of access between the gorse plants and the drop of the cliffs. As always, Ealish carefully chose where she placed her feet. As she did, she noticed evidence of animal activity on the ground, rabbit droppings and the odd track in the softer, muddier parts - she would step over these so as not to leave a footprint. These signs of animals gave her confidence as she knew that when her food ran low she would be able to hunt for meat.

She heard an unfamiliar noise to her left and stopped moving, instinctively crouching low, unslinging her bow from across her back and drawing a black feathered arrow from her quiver with her left hand. This was something she had practiced over and over in her training, knowing that being able to do it with speed and without taking her eyes off the environment could save her precious moments and potentially her life. With the arrow notched on the string she drew it back slightly, holding the bow horizontally to allow for the fact she was crouching to remain hidden below the level of the gorse. Knowing that any attack could not come from behind due to the steep cliffs, she focused on the dense gorse plants, her eyes continually scanning for any kind of threat. She saw nothing. She listened carefully. At first all she could hear was her own breathing and her heartbeat which pounded like a drum. Calming her breathing she started to pick up other sounds, the waves crashing against the rocks far below her, the odd call of a sea bird, but no rustling.

She rose slightly above the level of the gorse plants to look across the top of them, knowing this would make her an easier target she drew her bow string back a little further so that she was prepared to shoot if needed. She waited again, half crouched, watching, waiting, listening.

Nothing.

She relaxed the tension on her bow string, her fingers and forearm had been starting to ache from holding the position. She slowly turned a full circle checking for anything that could be a threat before making the decision to continue walking, this time the bow was held loosely in her hand. She continued, slightly more cautious than before.

-24-
KIARE AS FEED
- EALISH'S FIRST DAY ON MANNIN -

Ealish continued on the path along the cliff tops, still steadily climbing, the path itself was far from straight. It curled gently at times, at others it cut sharply. She had no option but to remain on it with the steep drop of the cliffs to her right and the menacingly sharp thorns of the gorse fields on her left. Whilst the climb was steep at times she did not tire, she had trained her legs hard in preparation for this journey. Often she would look over the cliff edge and see small hidden beaches and coves, accessible only from the water.

Around midday she found a good place to stop. The path at this point was heading south along the cliff top and it turned sharply left to the east. She found that by continuing south for a very short distance she could actually access the cliff edge. The edge here was a straight rock face, dropping away below her to the sea far, far below. She stopped and as she had done so many times that morning, she turned a full circle taking in her environment, scanning for any threat. There was none, or none that she could see or hear.

She noticed a strange pile of rocks, there seemed to be no reason for them to be there, maybe they were a marker of some kind. She sat at the cliff edge, her back to the pile of stones to protect her from the wind - and more importantly from view of any others on the path. Daringly she allowed her feet to hang over the cliff swinging freely. She momentarily imagined what a bird must feel like to see nothing but a long drop below them. She hadn't realised when she chose to stop but she was actually on the highest point of the cliff tops, that she could see anyway.

Away to her right and slightly behind her she could see the route that she had taken all the way from The Sound. It was only by looking back from this angle and this height that she noticed the path she had been on continued past The Sound and westward out of view around the headland. She wondered where it might lead. Looking back she also noticed that north of her position past the impenetrable wall of gorse spikes were fields that looked defined in their shape and maintained. Similar to the crop fields on the Island managed by the Fitchies. She strained her eyes and in one of the fields she could actually see animals in it, they were a whitish grey colour, she recognised them as sheep. There was a small flock on the Island whose fleeces were regularly sheared to produce fabric for making clothes and other such things.

Whilst it was no surprise to her that there was civilisation on Mannin this was the first time she had witnessed anything that resembled it. It excited and terrified her at the same time, she had heard plenty of tales of Mannin whilst she grew up on the Island but she was never sure what could be believed and what was being embellished by traders and returning travellers wishing to make their time here sound more exciting than it actually was. She silently wondered what the people were like who looked after these animals.

She looked to her left and could see that the cliffs ran in a north-easterly direction making the position where she sat the most southerly point that she could see. She knew what this meant. When she continued walking, she would soon lose sight of the Island, her Island. The place of her birth and where she had spent every day of her life since. This thought scared her. Even though she had spent the morning on Mannin she had been able to see her home. That would soon not be so. She ate some lunch slowly, subconsciously not wanting the meal to end as that meant she must continue.

As she ate her thoughts turned to her brother. She remembered a time many seasons ago when they were in their father's workshop, they had been watching him use his many tools to create something - she could not remember exactly what. Her father had been pre-occupied with his work and hadn't realised that Ealish and Flax had both selected some short wooden poles and proceeded to use them to act out a great battle with each other. They had both held the sticks two handed, one hand over and one hand under. Ealish had been a great Queen of Mannin - which to her knowledge there had never been. Flax had been the evil invader, a raider from distant lands whose intention was to steal the riches of the Queen.

They had faced each other, circling around and narrating their actions whilst creating some meaningless dialogue. With a clumsy lunge Flax had initiated the encounter, stepping forward and striking with his staff in an arcing motion. Ealish being the taller and stronger of the two at the time had easily parried the attack and as she did she had stepped to the side allowing her an advantage over her younger brother. She had capitalised on this and thrust forward with the top of her staff toward her brother's unprotected side. At the last possible moment he had been able to jump backwards so that the attack hit nothing but air. He then struck downward with his own weapon trying to knock it from his sister's hands. The two staffs connected but Ealish held tightly to hers feeling the force of the attack travel up through her staff and into her arms. Allowing the forward end of her staff to be pushed down by her brother's attack she lifted the rear end up and brought it round in a circular motion as she had stepped forward and round to face Flax. Of course, had she done this at full speed she would have struck him square in the face, so she had made sure to exaggerate her movement so that he could see her intention and he had been able to lift his staff horizontally in front of his head and block the incoming strike, pushing backwards with all his strength. The two of them had been locked in a battle of strength pushing against the other, stepping left and right conversing in character and attempting to get the upper hand. Ealish remembered feigning a step to the right hoping her brother would counter, which he did. She had then quickly changed her weight and direction and stepped to the left, catching Flax off balance and causing him to swivel backward unexpectedly. Losing his footing he had fallen backwards, striking the back of his head on a block of wood that lay on the floor. Ealish had realised almost immediately that her brother was hurt, he had made no sound at first but she could see the blood had already started to flow from his head and stain the block of wood on which it lay. His eyes had remained open but unfocused.

Unbeknown to either of them their father had stopped what he was doing to watch them play. He immediately came to the aid of his injured son. Bending down he had scooped Flax up in his arms as if he weighed nothing. Pressing a piece of cloth to his head to slow the bleeding. Flax had by now realised what had happened, and that his head hurt. He began to cry loudly, much to the relief of his father as it confirmed to him that the injury was not as serious as he had first feared. Ealish had stood, still holding her staff in one hand. Her father looked down at her and she had met his eyes, they were warm and his face smiling. He affectionately ruffled her hair saying, "Don't worry sweetheart your brother will be fine, just need to patch him up, accidents happen." At that he had left the workshop carrying her wailing brother, both of them now covered in blood.

Ealish remembered the feeling of guilt she had felt that day when Flax had injured his head - he still mentioned it now how she had *scarred him for life*, only when he wanted to tease her. His *scar* was about the width of a thumb and could only be seen if he pulled his hair to the side in just the right place. But that feeling of guilt was nothing compared to how she had felt when the Traveller induced the sleep in Flax based on the belief that he was suffering with an infection. The feeling of guilt had never actually left her, she felt it now as she ate and enjoyed the warmth of the sun on her face. Her brother was locked in an artificial prison of sleep and she could have spoken up for him. She could have explained, or tried to explain, what it was he was saying. But she hadn't and now it was too late. She made a promise to herself that when she had news to send to the Traveller, she would also send word that Flax should be woken, she just didn't know yet how she would explain it.

Reluctantly she stood, stretched out her arms and legs and picked up her bow.

She faced the Island and took a mental image of it, not knowing when she would see it again. She couldn't see her village as it was tucked away in the middle, but there was plenty for her to recognise. The southern lighthouse, The Drinking Dragane, the eastern dock, the hills that she loved to run on, the seals basking in the sun on the rocks close to The Sound. She blinked, the sun leaving bright spots across her vision, she could have sworn one of the seals was looking directly at her. She dismissed it almost as quickly as she had thought it. Had she stared at her homeland any longer then the tears that were building in the corner of her eyes, threatening to fall, would have done so. She turned to face the unknown that lay before her and started walking, blinking back the tears.

-25-
QUEIG AS FEED

Flax woke as he had every morning since he started his training – aching and hungry. His body had weakened significantly in the season that he had slept after the attack by the Longtails. He had worked hard to strengthen himself, which had been difficult due to his weak state but also the injury to his left arm which seemed to have left lasting damage. The extent of which he was not fully sure of yet. He had noticed however, that the muscles in that forearm now fatigued much quicker than the other.

He had spent the first couple of days training just walking, up and down the hills of the Island, from dusk until dawn pushing his tired legs relentlessly. On the third morning he had woken and realised that he could barely move his legs, they ached and felt like dead weight. So much so that for most of that day he was unable to do any training at all. He spent the day resting, recovering and planning how best to schedule his training. This was all he would focus on, there was no need to concentrate on work. With his father incapacitated the demand for wood on the Island had decreased. Anyway, others had been issued the job of managing the plantations due to Flax's absence of availability. Ordinarily this would have annoyed him, he had spent a lot of time and effort managing the plantations and he knew each of them like the back of his hand. To think that somebody else might have been altering his design for each of them would have ordinarily played on his mind, but his mind had an entirely new focus now.

Get fit.

Rescue Flea.

That was his all-consuming thought pattern.

Once his legs started to feel stronger, he increased the variety of his training, lifting heavy weights that he had fashioned from sections of tree trunks and climbing some of the rocky crags on the Island. He found that his fitness returned to him very quickly which encouraged him to push himself harder. He soon felt strong enough to start his proper training, combat training with the Traveller. Of course, he had learned to fight with sticks with other children on the Island as he grew but this always had an element of play to it. He would imagine that he was a knight on his mighty steed holding a lance (having to imagine what a horse looked like as he had never actually seen one - like a big donkey he had always told himself). Other days he would be an ancient warrior with a sword from a distant land, ninjas he had heard them called. He had also read stories of humans, elves and dwarves taking on mighty quests and defeating evil forces, these stories would feature heavily in his play fighting as he grew.

His training with the Traveller was like nothing he had experienced before.

"Take it easy!" Flax had said almost angrily the first time that the Traveller had struck him in the ribs with the end of a staff.

"No, if I go easy on you boy you will never learn. This is no play fight, this is real. Do you think the Longtails will take it easy on you? Did they take it easy on your father when they shot him in the back with that arrow?"

This hit a nerve with Flax. He stopped holding his freshly aching ribs and took up his staff in a two-handed grip. He lunged toward the Traveller who sidestepped just as he had on the hilltop that first day Flax had woken. This is what Flax had been counting on, as he passed by the Traveller he turned to his right sweeping the staff at the back of his legs hoping to knock him to the floor. With surprising agility his adversary jumped at just the right moment causing Flax to over rotate and leave his back exposed. The Traveller capitalised on this and struck him hard with a balled fist in the lower back.

"You are learning, but not fast enough. You have to learn how to be unpredictable with your attacks, your enemy will not just strike you in the back as I did. They will kill you given a chance. You must fight dirty if you need to in order to give yourself the upper hand."

"I managed to defeat that Longtail without fighting dirty, didn't I?"

"You did and look what price you paid for it."

Flax looked down at his scarred arm and ran his fingers across the reddened flesh.

"You can't allow each enemy you fight to take a piece of you or there will be nothing left," and with that the Traveller struck Flax hard in the leg with his stick causing him to buckle slightly, then swung the end of his staff directly at Flax's head with force.

At the last possible moment Flax was able to deflect the blow with his own stick, this stung through his weakened arm causing him to lose his grip and balance. He put his left hand on the floor to prevent himself toppling over. He looked up to see that his attacker was not relenting and was already bringing his staff around for another attack. Without thinking Flax grabbed a hand full of loose dirt and threw it in the Traveller's face.

It had the desired effect. It was an unexpected attack and it temporarily blinded the experienced fighter who instinctively halted his attack and put his hand up to his face to clear his eyes. Flax saw his opportunity and lunged forward leaving his staff on the floor. Striking the Traveller in the stomach with his shoulder Flax then wrapped his arms around his opponent's waist driving him backwards and onto the floor. Flax used his weight to pin him to the ground whilst he manoeuvred himself into a position where he could apply a choke hold. Slowly squeezing, he expected that within moments he would hear the word *yield*. It did not come. He applied more pressure. Still no sign of surrender came. Now Flax was certain that before long he would cause the Traveller to lose consciousness. He loosened his grip, concerned that he may be causing injury but this was a mistake and he knew it instantly. The Traveller had been waiting for this opportunity and he seized it, digging his fingertips into the scarred flesh of Flax's left forearm. Flax yelled out in pain and lost his grip on the Traveller who rolled free and grabbed his staff. Before Flax could even regain his focus, the Traveller was on his feet, the tip of his staff pointing directly at Flax's throat. He had no option but to speak the word he did not want to.

"Yield."

"Not a bad start boy, let's go again."

And so this is how each day went. Flax woke each morning with more bruises and cuts as a result of his training. Oddly enough though they started to not bother him, that first day of combat training he found that his bruised ribs and leg hindered his ability for the next day or two. But now his body was learning to fight through the pain. He developed ways of reducing the vulnerability that his weakened arm presented, altering his stance so that his left arm was further from his opponent. This felt unnatural at first but ultimately offered him certain advantages. Any attacker would assume the attack to be led by the rear-most arm therefore when Flax used his right arm to lead a stab or a swing with the staff it would come as a surprise, albeit with less power as he could not rotate or drive his body through the attack. Therefore Flax began to develop methods of making these weakened attacks more effective. Striking in quick repetition was one way of doing so.

In training if he was able to land three or four consecutive attacks with a right hand led strike, he could drive the Traveller back and put him off balance, allowing him to then rotate through with his left arm for a power strike. All the while reducing the likelihood of his left arm being injured as by the time he exposed it to his attacker he was already off balance. Flax found that he was holding back less in training too. If the opportunity arose for him to strike his trainer, then he would. He had felt guilty the first time that his staff had connected with the Traveller's arm, so much so that he had stopped to apologise. The result being that Flax had been struck square in the chest with a fist for his troubles. After that incident he learned not to apologise and not to hold back.

"Your enemies won't hold back boy," he heard the Traveller say in his head, and so neither did Flax.

As time went on Flax felt that more often than not he was leaving the sessions with less cuts and bruises than his trainer. This motivated him to fight harder and faster each time. It was not that he wanted to hurt the Traveller, he just wanted to prove that he was no boy, he was a man - a man who could beat others in combat. There were times when he wondered if he was being allowed to land a strike or to win a fight. He could never be sure as his newly appointed mentor never gave away more than he intended. Whenever Flax had forced him to yield, he would simply return to a fighting stance and instruct, "Again." The more he thought about it the more he was convinced that he was being coached into delivering particular strikes or attacks as the Traveller would leave intentional, though still fleeting, weaknesses in his defence.

This did not bother Flax though as such instances allowed him to become a more competent fighter, these are the kinds of weaknesses that he would have to look out for with his as yet unknown enemies whom he would encounter in his attempt to rescue Flea. *No not an attempt!* he would tell himself, *it is not something that I will try to do, it is something I have to do*! He knew that he was the only hope that his friend had of freedom and therefore he must succeed.

When not combat training with the Traveller Flax would revert back to lifting weights, running and climbing. In addition to this he practiced with his sling and knife. He would set up a variety of targets around a plantation and practice striking them at distance with both weapons. He found that throwing the blade was much more difficult than he had envisaged. Whilst the balance of the weapon between the razor-sharp blade and the handle that his father had lovingly and uniquely carved was perfect, it did not guarantee that a throw would result in the blade hitting the target rather than the handle or the back of the knife. He experimented with a number of throwing techniques, overhand, underhand, sideways. Initially he had limited success with any of the techniques as he altered the amount of power and rotation that he would put into the throw. He eventually settled on an underhand throw releasing the weapon with a relatively slow spin but high force through the back of his hand which offered him the most consistent result - even then it was not brilliant and required a lot more work.

As well as ranged attacks, he would practice at close quarters with his blade. Drawing and using it with both hands in stabbing, slashing and striking motions on targets both in front and behind him at different heights. As he practiced these techniques, he was very aware that to have to use them would most certainly result in death or serious injury to the intended target. He thought back to the way that he felt when he first struck the Longtail with the stone from his sling on the night of the attack. A watery metallic taste came into his mouth, his tongue felt as if it had swollen up. That was just from thinking about causing another injury or taking a life; he knew that he would have to find some way to manage this feeling or overcome it. He had taken two lives, the first was in order to save Sid Kelly from certain death, the second was to save his own life. After taking the second Longtail's life he had not been able to stop himself from vomiting, although that could also have been put down to the injury. But still, he couldn't be vomiting in the middle of a fight if he was to save Flea, *could he?*

He sat on a tree stump in one of the plantations pondering this one day after a hard morning training with his sling and knife. He was using his knife to slice up an apple as part of his lunch, focussing on how easily the blade sliced through the skin and the flesh of the fruit, such a simple and easy act causing such devastation and change. He hated the thought that he would have to be responsible for causing such damage to another's body. Even if his actions did not result in death, they would leave a potentially lasting impact on the other for the rest of their life. Subconsciously he ran his fingers across the scarred and tingling flesh of his own damaged forearm. That day he made a pact with himself, he would only use his blade against another or take a life if it was absolutely necessary and there was no other option available to him. Although even whilst making himself this promise he knew in his heart that he would have to hurt or kill others in order to save his best friend.

-26-
SHEY AS FEED
- EALISH'S FIRST DAY ON MANNIN -

Ealish was blinking back tears as she walked along the cliff line, the cool sea breeze whipped up spray from the foamy waves below, the saltiness causing her eyes to water further.

She could have made much faster progress but she was in unknown territory and whilst she knew she would be able to move silently she would not be able to keep herself hidden from sight. *Best to move slower and draw less attention,* she told herself. Her bow remained held loosely in her right hand and her left always hovered somewhere near to the quiver of arrows on her hip, *just in case.*

Every so often she would stop, crouch low and turn in a full circle. Looking through the watery eyes, and more importantly listening. Nothing much changed each time she looked. To her left, seemingly impenetrable gorse bushes as far as the eye could see. To her right, a steep drop to the grey blue sea below. In front and behind, the path that lay ahead and the path that she had already walked. She often scowled to herself to see footprints that she had left in the soft mud behind her. However, she had no option but to tread where she had done given the path she was on. The odd sea bird could be seen overhead from time to time, other than that there were no obvious signs of life or movement.

As she walked, she wondered to herself when the last time was that somebody else had walked this same path. There was certainly no sign on the ground of recent movement or activity, with the exception of the odd rabbit dropping. But the rabbits would be small enough to move in and under the spiky gorse bushes that acted as a natural barrier.

As far as she could see there was no evidence of any human activity on the path whatsoever. *Yet it had not become overgrown,* she thought to herself.

The cooler air reminded her of the change of the season. She knew that soon the leaves on The Tree on her Island would be turning from the vibrant greens to rich golds, browns, reds and oranges. She had been gone less than a day and already her heart yearned to be back there. *How could that be?* she thought. She had waited so many seasons to travel to Mannin and now the thing that she wanted most in the world was to be back on her Island. Running through the hills, hunting in the plantations and spending time with her family and friends.

Her train of thought was broken by an unexpected noise. She remained in her crouched position and swiftly brought an arrow to the string of her bow. Holding her breath to allow her to hear as much as possible, she strained her ears. It seemed so quiet that all she could hear for a moment was her own heartbeat which sounded like somebody marching on a rocky beach, but then she heard it again. A low rustling noise, very faint and barely audible but it was definitely there. She drew the string of her bow back slightly so that she could feel it pulling back against her grip. The same noise was getting steadily closer. She could not see what it was but it was definitely a person or creature of some sort causing the noise from within the gorse. She scanned across the top of the vegetation looking down the length of the arrow on her bow, hoping to spot a tell-tale sign of movement. There was none but she was certain something was there. Crouching back below the vegetation Ealish silently and quickly moved from her position. She knew that whoever, or whatever, was there may have seen her and could be heading towards where she was stood. Therefore, to give herself an advantage she had moved a good twenty paces - back in the direction she had travelled from. Now she waited. Her bow string now pulled halfway back ready to loose an arrow at any threat that came onto the path from the gorse.

Not far from where she had been stood, she picked up on a slight movement at the edge of the gorse, a flash of red and golden brown. She pulled the string back further, taking aim. A moment later the creature stepped onto the path from under the cover of the spiky bushes. It was a pheasant, they could sometimes be found on her Island and she had hunted them before for their meat and their feathers. They were not very clever and would often unknowingly make themselves an easy target, such as now.

She slowly eased the tension off the string of her bow and placed the arrow back in her quiver. Deciding not to kill the bird. In her head she had calculated the food that she currently had and there was sufficient for a couple of days at present. If she killed the bird she would have too much and either the meat of the bird or the food she carried would spoil before she could eat them. She therefore considered it a waste and could not justify taking the bird's life.

She stood and silently walked past the bird continuing her journey. The pheasant did not move from the path, seemingly unaware of the mortal danger that it had just narrowly avoided. She stood and watched it for a moment as it pecked at the floor then slowly strode back under the protection of the gorse bushes.

Suddenly there was more movement, deeper into the forest of prickles, in the direction from which she had come. There was definite movement toward the path. This was no pheasant. She could see entire bushes being rattled as whatever it was made its way closer and closer to the path. The movement was not slow and careful, it was rapid and determined. She could hear grunting noises too. Sounds she did not recognise or like the sound of.

Her plan of escape from this path had always been to run back the way she had come as that would be more familiar territory rather than ahead into the unknown but that was no option now. She had two choices; run or fight. Ealish quickly made up her mind, turned on her heels and ran as fast as she could in the direction she had been travelling. Deciding that whatever was coming was able to negotiate the razor-sharp spines of the gorse forest, *which means my arrows might be no good here!* She didn't want to hang around to find out if they would be or not. As she ran tears streamed from her eyes again, she had been here less than a day and was already running for her life. She was running hard, her eyes scanning ahead for potential trip hazards or other threats. Her legs and feet reacted to what her eyes saw, changing her stride or direction ever so slightly to avoid stepping on loose rocks or exposed roots. She followed the path turning left and right as it followed the cliff line, it finally dipped down into a V-shaped valley. Ahead of her a small stream ran down the gulley to the cliff edge where the water jumped from the land and fell freely through the air to the sea far below. She noticed that at the edge of the stream on her side the gorse bushes stopped and the opposite side was covered in thick heather, much like the hill sides on her Island. Smiling through her tears at the vaguely familiar site she pressed on faster to reach this boundary. Clearing the small stream in one easy jump, she then stopped, drew and nocked an arrow in her bow, as had become second nature to her whenever she stopped. She crouched and scanned the scenery behind her, observing for any pursuer. She saw nothing. She waited a long moment as she steadied her breath. Tears were still freely running from her eyes, she couldn't decide if they were from the fear, from upset or from the wind that had been whipping into her face as she ran. *A mixture of the three,* she decided.

Satisfied that she had not been followed by whatever it was, she sat by the stream and drank heavily, refilled her flask and then splashed the ice-cold, clear water onto her face.

She refocused her mind on the task she had been given. The reason she was in this strange place. She must find the source of the poison that held her father captive. *Someone in this land made it,* thought Ealish and she knew that only that person could provide the antidote to release Mannanan's Cloak. Her plan for now was simple, *Track the Longtails and find where Flea was being held.* She would figure out the next steps of the plan after this but in her mind she needed the Rat King, to make him tell her where the poison came from. Of course, the assumption was that it had been the Faerie Queen whom the Traveller had called Meave, but the Traveller also warned of the danger of making assumptions.

The need to find this antidote was more than just the personal reasons of Ealish wanting her father back, of course that was the main motivation. But second to that she needed him back because he too had been visited by the *ashlishyn*, if what the Traveller told her was to be believed – which she had no evidence to the contrary. So she needed him back at the very least so that the events of the *ashlishyn* could play out. However, she truly believed in her heart that if her and Flax could sit down with their father and discuss them, they may be able to understand at least some of what they meant.

The thought of getting her father back strengthened her resolve, she wiped her face dry on the sleeve of her top and made a vow to herself, *The next time I cry they will be tears of joy for my father's return.*

-27-
SHIAGHT AS FEED

Flax sat beneath The Tree eating his lunch, his body tired from a morning of training, he was grateful for the well-earned rest.

He glanced up whilst eating. The leaves, he noticed, had shifted their positions somehow - *most likely the wind,* he told himself. In any case the broken bough was no longer visible through the foliage. It was as if the leaves had only ever moved to allow it to be discovered by Ealish and Flax then rearranged to hide their secret once again. *That would explain why nobody else has found the broken limb!* Flax thought to himself. Since he had woken he had often wondered how nobody else had ever seen it, despite it being well hidden it was visible enough for both of them to have seen. But now it was hidden, it could not be seen from any angle or position – and he had tried them all. Whenever he was taking lunch in the village he would sit beneath The Tree, always choosing a slightly different position to allow him to look upwards without drawing attention, every day he had confirmed that the broken branch was no longer visible. He knew it was still there, it was just that The Tree did not want to reveal it to anybody. As he sat there with the low autumn sun flickering through the gaps in the leaves, he noticed a familiar figure walking toward him. The small frame and distinctive fast paced shuffle gave him away immediately.

"Good day Mr Kelly!" called Flax as the elderly baker approached, in his heavily floured apron as usual.

"How many times have I told you to just call me Sid?" Replied Sid Kelly with a wave. He shuffled towards Flax and took a seat next to him. Flax handed him some bread and cheese and he placed a small pot of rhubarb chutney between the two of them.

"Oh I don't know, at least fifty or so Mr Kelly," Flax said with a smile knowing what was coming next. He was right as he felt the playful slap at the back of his head from Sid. This had become a near daily routine and one that Flax missed if for some reason neither of them were there for lunch.

Sid bit into a slice of the bread and savoured the sweet undertones. "I really should get this recipe from your mother one day," he said through a mouthful of crumbs, "it doesn't look good when the Island baker eats someone else's bread for their lunch each day now does it?"

"Good luck, she won't give it up easily you know. But I will put in a good word for you since you are helping me."

Since Flax had started training for his mission, on the recommendation of his mother, he had asked Sid for help in learning of the folk lore of Mannin. Of course, Flax had heard lots of stories as he grew up – some he had paid attention to, some he had not. But his mother had pointed out that it would be a benefit to him to understand as much as possible about the land he was travelling to, and he didn't disagree. Ordinarily there would only be one such person that Flax would ask to teach him, but his father still lay entombed by the poison and could be of no help. Flax was reluctant at first to ask Sid Kelly, for no other reason than it reminded him that he could not ask his father. However, his mother soon pointed out that his other option would be to ask the Traveller and Flax quickly decided that to spend more time than necessary with him was not something he would intentionally do.

Sid of course had been more than willing to help. He was the self-appointed record keeper for the Island and therefore was well placed to teach Flax of such matters. He told Flax many stories of his adventures on Mannin when he was younger and Flax had sat riveted. Some of them almost sounded unbelievable but he had no reason to doubt Sid, he gained nothing from telling mistruths or exaggerating. Sid had also confided with Flax his biggest regret about his travels. He had longed to visit the great hall of records at Tynwald. Ever since he was young Sid had heard stories of this place that held thousands upon thousands of papers, scrolls and books keeping record of all manner of things from great warriors, wise leaders, cruel rulers and magical beasts to recipes for potions, ointments and medicines. There were even sections devoted to food and drink recipes, and another on how best to grow the many different crops, then another with building instructions for many ancient and modern contraptions, "Anything worth recording is recorded there," Sid would always say when he mentioned the hall, and he mentioned it often. Sadly for Sid his journeys and adventures had never led to the place he longed for the most and now in his eighty third bloom it seemed very unlikely, near impossible, that he would ever see it.

Flax told himself that if he ever got the chance then he would travel there in a heartbeat if only so that he could then tell Sid Kelly all about it.

"Today –" Sid announced as he spread some chutney on a slice of bread and topped it with a piece of cheese "– The *Moddey Doo*." He let the words hang in the air as he watched Flax's face carefully trying to gauge any reaction he might show.

Flax had heard many tales of the black ghost dog, The *Moddey Doo*, as he grew up but he was keen to see what Sid's view on it was. "Isn't that just a story told to scare children into being good?" He asked sceptically.

"It is!" Came Sid's reply.

A strange retort, thought Flax, he had expected Sid to question his doubt and set him straight with historical facts from records and first-hand accounts. Instead Sid had created even more doubt as to whether this dog ghost had ever existed.

"– but –" Sid continued, interrupting Flax just before he spoke, "–it is much more than just a story that is told to scare children, do you think tales such as this are just created from somebody's imagination? There is truth to everything young Flaxney, you just have to find it." Much as Flax reacted negatively when the Traveller referred to him as boy, he did not mind one bit when Sid called him young Flaxney - in fact he enjoyed it. He had come to see Sid as a grandparent figure, having never met his own. Also, he knew that when Sid called him 'young' that it was a term of affection. Not like when the Traveller called him 'boy', it was clearly meant to cause annoyance or raise a reaction, which it invariably did.

"So where is the truth in the tale of The *Moddey Doo*?" Asked Flax.

"Now you're asking the right kind of questions."

Sid explained that according to Mannin lore The *Moddey Doo* was a black ghost dog that was said to have guarded a castle in the western region of Mannin. The very same castle that Murchad, brother of the Traveller, called his home. However there were reported sightings across Mannin of a black dog that was as large, if not larger, than a calf. The truth, he explained, was that most of the sightings were indeed true and that people had seen large black dogs but that they were not likely to have been ghosts. Sid was aware that generations ago raiders from distant lands had travelled to Mannin seeking riches. They had brought with them large dog like creatures that Sid called wolves, the raiders had used them for hunting and to protect their camps. There were accounts, Sid claimed, that some of these wolves were large enough for grown men to ride them and they had been used in battle much like horses - only with a nastier bite. The raiders had long since left Mannin but when they did, they left many of these wolves to fend for themselves. They would roam the moors, mountains and beaches hunting for food and shelter. "These wolves are what I believe to be the cause of the many sightings of The *Moddey Doo*," claimed Sid, "there is no other reasonable explanation."

"Aside from there being an actual black ghost dog?" Offered Flax.

"Yes, aside from that of course."

"Where did the raiders come from?" Flax asked.

"From distant lands, they arrived on great wooden ships. They spoke in an unfamiliar tongue and were referred to as the *Wiggynnee* in our old tongue. They claimed to have travelled from the north so for that reason they became known more commonly as the North Men. Records point to them being savage and brutal in conflict. They fought with a variety of weapons made of iron and other metals, they carried wooden shields and were fearless warriors. They would often kill others for sport and gave no mercy to any prisoner. It was many hundreds of blooms ago that they came to Mannin, there are none alive today who encountered them so they are remembered only through the records and through stories passed down from generation to generation."

"I have never even heard of them."

"There is no record of them having ever reached our Island, that is probably why," explained Sid, "anyway enough of these North Men, learning of them will not help you on your travels. This however will do…"

Sid pulled from under his flour covered apron a folded parchment. It looked old to Flax but still appeared in good condition. As if reading his mind Sid told him, "I covered it with a fine layer of beeswax mixed with some other ingredients to give it a protection from the weather."

"I see," replied Flax, "but what is it?"

Sid didn't answer, instead he completely unfolded the parchment and laid it flat on the ground in front of them both. He spun it so that it was facing the correct way, then he sat and watched Flax's face. It didn't take long at all for the recognition to show.

"A map!" exclaimed Flax.

"A map indeed."

Flax ran his fingers across the waxy surface of the map. In the southwestern corner he could see his Island marked there, recognisable not only by its shape and location but by the stencilled outline of The Tree on it. Writing close to this described it as the *Ellan* region, Island in the old tongue. This *region* as such encompassed the Island, The Drinking Dragane, the lighthouse at the southern tip and all the small outcrops of rock that stuck out of the sea around the Island. Certain features were marked onto the map, these included the eastern dock, the northern dock, the village and some of the plantations that Flax managed - not all of them though he noted. From this he deduced that the map must be many blooms old.

North of the Island was The Sound, the deadly strait of water between the Island and Mannin, a stencil of a shipwreck served to warn travellers of the danger. Then north of The Sound lay Mannin. Flax could see that Mannin was split into seven different regions, each of the borders clearly marked and each region stained with a slightly different coloured pigment to differentiate between them. Each of them was also named, again in the old tongue - *Jiass* - south, *Hiar* - east, *Heear* - west, *Twoaie* - north, *Slieau* - mountain, *Shenn* - ancient and *Jarroodit* - forgotten.

Each region had various place names marked within them, some with words, others with stencilled diagrams - some of them Flax recognised, most he did not.

The southern region that was marked with *Balley Chashtal*, home of the great kings of Mannin. He also recognised the name of *Guinn Y Vaaish*, home of the Longtails on the eastern edge of the T shaped peninsula just as the Traveller had described. There were other places marked that he noticed and recognised such as the abbey, or at least he assumed he recognised it as the abbey from the Traveller's tale.

The mountainous *Slieau* region dominated the majority of the centre of the island of Mannin, with the eastern and western region to the right and left of it, respectively. Above the mountain region lay the vast area of the northern *Twoaie* Region, the map had very few features marked in this area and it appeared to be a large flat expanse that led away from the foothills of the northern mountain region to a very definite point which was the northern most land point of Mannin.

The western *Heear* Region hugged the west coast in a comparatively thin strip, the key feature that stood out to Flax at first glance was the castle, labelled as *Cashtal ny Raunyn*. This castle was itself a small island sitting not very far – or so it seemed on the map – off the main coast of Mannin. This must be the home of the Traveller's brother, and Flea's real father, Murchad King of *Heear*.

Within the centre of the *Slieau* region, in what Flax could see on the map to be a valley between northern and southern mountains lay the ancient *Shenn* region. On the map Flax could see that Tynwald was marked here, as was a great river named the Dhoo that appeared to run through the ancient region to the east where it disappeared beneath the mountains and then reappeared in the eastern *Hiar* region. Here it converged with another river from the northern mountains, named the Glass. This combined river then ran to the sea at a place marked as Dhoo-Glass, it wasn't difficult for Flax to figure out how the place got its name.

The *Hiar* region was much wider at its southern extreme and it then tapered into a thin sliver up the east coast of Mannin and Flax could see a few place names marked, Dhoon Glenn, Dhoo-Glass, Cornaa, Laxey and strangely the name Lady Isabella was written in this region also. On the southern border where it met the *Jiass* Region written with a large question mark next to it were words that Flax recognised, *Droghad ny Ferrishyn* - Faerie Bridge. The question mark, explained Sid, was because the exact location was not known and the fortress itself was hidden by many spells and incantations but all known information was that the fortress lay within this location straddling one of the many rivers that ran through the forests there from the mountains of the southern *Slieau*.

Finally, Flax ran his eyes up the eastern coast and at the northern most point of the *Hiar* was a small peninsula of land jutting out into the sea, on the map this area was a muted grey colour with one word written on it *Jarroodit* - "Forgotten?" Flax said out loud looking up at Sid.

"Yes, the forgotten region. As far as I am aware this area has not been inhabited since the *Wiggynnee* left Mannin many blooms before I, or anyone else who still lives, was born. Anyone who travels there simply disappears and is never seen again, they become…forgotten…" Sid trailed off, his mind focussed on something other than the conversation with Flax.

Sensing the awkwardness of the moment Flax attempted to bring Sid's concentration back to the present. "So this was your map that you travelled with?"

It took a few moments but the question registered with Sid and he snapped out of his trance. "Yes, it was, it was passed to me by my father before I travelled to Mannin. I added bits and pieces to it as I moved around and found places that hadn't already been marked on it. I have no doubt there are further places still to be mapped in the regions in which I travelled and certainly plenty to find in those I was not fortunate enough to journey to. But I am sure you will be able to add them once you find them young Flaxney," Sid smiled as he carefully folded the map and pressed it gently into Flax's hands. Even as he smiled there was a deeper sadness in his eyes.

It was clear to Flax this map meant a lot to the old baker, it was probably his most treasured possession, a record and cartographical reminder of his adventures. Even as he had the map passed to him, he could feel that Sid's fingers kept a grip on it, reluctant to let it go. It was Flax who let go first and gently pushed it back into Sid's hands, whilst patting the old man on the shoulder and letting his hand rest there. With a caring smile and a compassion in his voice that belied his young age he broke the silence, "I can't take this from you. Thank you, but this clearly holds many important memories for you. I appreciate the overwhelming generosity but really, I can't take those memories from you."

A tear formed in the corner of one of Sid's eyes and despite him blinking repeatedly, he could not stop it swelling and finally falling down his face. Unashamedly he tried no more to suppress his tears and they fell freely across his cheeks. They struck the waxed parchment of the map and beaded away leaving no trace that they had ever been there. Neither of them spoke for a long moment, Flax kept his comforting hand on Sid's shoulder and Sid kept his head bowed and shed tears of sadness over things that were far beyond Flax's knowledge and understanding.

Sid spoke first raising his head and putting his hand upon Flax's as it rested on his shoulder. Shaking away the tears he said, "You're right Flax there are many memories in this map for me, some sad but most of them exciting and happy. But this map is far from finished and let's be honest..." Sid smiled, "I'm a bit past my prime so it won't be me who finishes it," With that he pressed the parchment back into Flax's hand before he finally let go.

"I'll be sure to bring it back with many new places to tell you about Mr Kelly."

Sid Kelly leant forward and embraced Flax with surprising strength.

"I know you will young Flaxney, I know you will. If I'm honest I would have given it to your sister before you, had I known she would be travelling to Mannin. But I did not learn of her departure until after it had occurred. Perhaps you will be able to catch up with her on your travels and then you can both benefit from it."

Flax hadn't thought of Ealish yet that day, but now his mind turned to thoughts of her. *Alone on Mannin, a strange and unfamiliar land, without so much as a map to aid her on her quest.*

-28-
HOGHT AS FEED
- EALISH'S FIRST DAY ON MANNIN -

Ealish finished filling her flask with the clear stream water, then stood up and did a quick mental kit check to ensure she still had everything. She was satisfied she had not dropped anything when fleeing from the unknown creature in the gorse or that she had left anything whilst she rested. Turning her back on the stream and the spiky forest which had dictated the direction of her journey for most of the day, she looked ahead of her as the path rose once again up along the cliff line. The footpath was visibly worn, presumably by the many people who had trodden it before her, but this time it was bordered by low level heather bushes as opposed to the ferocious razor-sharp spikes of the gorse on the previous section. She realised that should she wish to, or need to, she could move further inland than she had yet been able to. The bushes themselves were no higher than her waist and due to the manner in which they had grown there were zig-zag routes between them leading across the open moorland that lay to the left of the path. She stood for a moment weighing up her options, the path was easier to navigate as it was visible but it had the downside that others may be along it too and whether they were friend or foe she wasn't ready, or wishing, for any company on her journey.

If she walked through the heather meadows, that were now past their best pinks, purples and whites and turning rusty brown, she knew she could avoid unwanted company. But it would make it harder to find her way to the Sugar Loaf.

"And the easiest way to get to the Sugar Loaf is to follow the cliff path," Ealish surmised to herself out loud. Her mind made up she strode out along the worn cliff path, still wary of her surroundings but she now had the option of fleeing into the heather meadows and taking cover if needed.

As she walked, she gently hummed a song to herself. She had never been particularly musically gifted growing up but she could just about hold a tune. The tune that had subconsciously entered her head was one that her mother had sung to her and Flax when they were younger. There were words to go with the tune but at this moment Ealish was more than content with the warming feeling that the familiar notes brought to her. Which was just as well because as she looked ahead of her, she saw a blanket of dense sea fog being slowly blown in by the breeze.

She stopped in her tracks and observed the natural phenomenon she has witnessed many times back on her Island. But there she had known where she was and how to get home safely. Here there was nowhere that she could call home and feel safe. The fog advanced on the land swallowing it up in front of her as the tide does the beach. The steadily advancing wave of swirling grey gloom finally reached her and slowly enveloped her. She instantly felt the change in temperature and pulled her jacket close around her body, fastening it up to her chin. She looked to where the sun had been hanging in the sky and found that it was no longer visible, its rays unable to penetrate the thick soupy haze in which she now found herself.

As she looked ahead at where the path had been visible just moments before she could now only see a short distance ahead of her. Without warning or intention an image of her father appeared in her mind. He was laid in his bed with his eyes closed, the image magnified in her mind so that all she could see was his face. Suddenly his eyes opened, but they did not look at her. They were unable to as they were the cloudy grey-white colour they had been when she last looked upon them. *This must be what his eyes see all the time,* Ealish thought to herself as she shook her head to take the upsetting image from her mind.

Aware that she could not dwell on the upsetting thought, she slowly turned in a full circle on the spot where she stood, looking and listening.

She was once again faced with two options, continue in the fog or return to the stream and wait it out. In reality she had no idea how long it would persist. On her Island she had known sea fog to last for days at a time. Therefore, waiting it out was simply not an option. She pressed on in the hope of finding some form of shelter where she could eat and possibly rest through the night.

Her progress was much slower given the conditions, she could not see all that far in front of her, which also meant she could not see all that far to the side of her – this was a much bigger problem. The ground just ended at the cliff top and dropped away to the sea below, any fall from such a height would mean certain serious injury and most likely death.

Ealish planned to keep as far to the left-hand side of the path as she could, following the line of the heather meadow and hoping that if the path suddenly changed direction or if there was any threat that she would be able to see it in time through the murky greyness.

She slowly walked forward sticking to her plan, conscious of the fact that a trip or fall could result in her own demise. She used the heather on her left as a guide, walking so close to it that she could feel it brushing reassuringly against her leg. If for some reason she could not feel it, such as a small gap between plants, she would stop and check that she was still on the right course. On one such occasion she looked down to find that she was periodically leaving footprints in the softer mud of the path that ordinarily she would purposefully step over. She silently scolded herself but quickly self-reasoned that this was preferable to falling off the edge of the cliff. If anybody was out there and tracking her in these conditions, *then fair play to them,* she thought.

She progressed slowly, stopping every hundred paces or so to look and listen for anything different, she didn't want to stumble into anything that she was unaware of. Looking was still fairly pointless given the weather conditions, so she listened all the more intently for any sounds of danger.

She had been travelling for some time when on one such occasion of stopping she thought she heard something unfamiliar. She held her breath and opened her mouth slightly so that her jaw put less pressure on her ears - she had found this helpful when tracking animals on her Island. She strained to hear the sound again, and she did.

A faint but definite scratching sound was being carried on the breeze. She struggled to determine exactly which direction it was coming from as the fog swirled around her.

Ealish crouched low and listened again, *had the sound stopped?* She strained her ears, *no,* it was definitely there still. *Was it moving closer or further away?* Difficult to tell.

Ealish waited a long moment, whether it was because she had been concentrating so hard on the sound, she wasn't sure but now it was the dominant sound that she was registering. Her ears had focused in on the specific vibrations and her mind seemed to be amplifying them above those of the waves hitting the cliff below or the odd sea bird calling through the impenetrable fog.

It's getting closer, Ealish told herself realising later than she would have liked, *this was why the sound seemed to be taking over.* She could tell now that the sound wasn't a scratching but more of a brushing sound. A sound that she was familiar with, she searched her mind to place it. She put her bow over one shoulder and around her body, she couldn't see much further than a couple of bow lengths in front of her. *A ranged weapon is no good here,* she decided, it would mean that any attacker would almost be upon her before she could register the threat and shoot. Likewise, if there was no threat she may shoot before registering who or what the sound was and injure or kill someone or something completely innocent.

She drew the hunting knife from her belt as well as the shorter blade from her calf sheath, holding the larger of the knives in her left hand with the blade up and the smaller in her right in the reversed grip with the blade pointing down.

She had experimented with different variations of grip with the two blades before leaving the Island and had found this one to offer her the best combination of defensive and offensive options in close combat. She had practiced by moving through the thicker areas of the plantations treating each low branch she encountered as a threat, striking, stabbing, parrying and slashing her way through the maze of outstretched limbs. As with anything that Ealish took to, she took to it obsessively. If she mistimed a strike or a block she would start the entire section again, and again, and again if needed until she had a perfect run at it. She was by no means a master of close combat but she had become the best she could in the short space of time that she had available to her.

Now she would have to potentially use these skills in anger for the first time, and no amount of training in the plantations could prepare her for the reality of a close and violent encounter using blades – for a start the trees never attacked back and they certainly didn't carry weapons of their own.

Ealish could feel her heart rate increasing as the brushing sound grew closer, *could she actually hear it beating in her chest?* She had turned her back to the cliff face reasoning that whatever was approaching could not be coming from that direction, this allowed her to scan a wide arc of vision which captured what she could see of the path and the start of the heather meadow through the grey blanket of fog.

Suddenly her mind registered where she had heard the noise before, it was the sound of something moving through the heather. She had heard it because she had been making the very same sound since the fog had closed in on her as she had brushed her leg against the plants as a guide.

The movement through the heather was determined and it was heading directly towards her.

She stayed crouched, her head just above the level of the plants. Straining her eyes to search into the misty gloom that lay before her, she could still see nothing.

She shuffled back, the knuckles on her hands turning white as they gripped the knives tightly.

She looked again, still nothing. She could hear steady breaths, but they were not her own.

She started to panic, fear was taking hold of her. *I'm not prepared for this*, she told herself. She shuffled back again but was less steady on her feet this time. Moving her left foot back again she found nothing solid for it to plant in and to her horror she realised her back was at the cliff top, her left leg hanging over the grey nothingness. She quickly glanced over her shoulder as she fought to regain her balance. She could see nothing below but she knew that the ground fell away to either the sea or the rocks - neither of which did she fancy her chances with.

She had trapped herself between her unknown attacker and the drop to certain death. She considered her options quickly in her head. *I could lower myself over the edge and hang out of sight hoping I don't get seen,* was one of her first thoughts. But there wasn't all that much to cling to, she didn't know how long she would have to, or be able to, hang there and if she was spotted then she would be completely trapped without any possibility of fighting back.

I could run along the path in either direction, was another thought. Running to her right into the unknown would not be a sensible option, she did not know what lay ahead. Running left would take her back in the direction of the stream and where she had come from. Neither of them were desirable options in the fog, a misplaced step or not seeing a turn in the path in time would cost her dearly.

Standing her ground and fighting was an option but she was at a great disadvantage with her back at the very edge of the cliff. If her attacker had any size advantage over her then a simple push could easily end the fight on unfavourable terms for Ealish.

She decided the best option was to move forward into the heather meadow. Preferably she would look to hide amongst the plants and wait for the danger to pass. However if it came to combat, she would rather be in a larger arena than the limited space she currently held. At least in the meadow she knew she could move around with comparative safety.

Taking a deep breath she moved onto her hands and knees, still gripping a knife in each hand, and she prepared to move forward into the unknown.

But when she looked forward, she realised she had left it too late pondering her options. There, directly in front of her, barely visible was a pair of pale blue eyes staring ahead at her through the greyness.

She froze, hoping that somehow she had not been seen, this hope was lost from the outset. The eyes were staring directly at her.

These eyes were not human.

For what seemed like the longest moment of her life the eyes stared intently, she dared not move.

She heard a low guttural growl. Her grip tightened around the knife handles and she came up on her haunches preparing herself to leap forward and attack if it came to it.

The creature stepped forward. Ealish stayed her ground. The greyness swirled like smoke as the beast stepped forward again, displacing the fog between the two of them.

For the first time Ealish saw the creature's dark spectral form, her face turned pale as her voice croaked and she whispered two words to herself, "*Moddey Doo.*"

-29-
NUY AS FEED

Flax breathed hard, pushing himself as fast as he could up the hill through the plantation. Low hanging branches whipped at his face. These annoyed him. Not because of the pain they caused him but because whoever had been managing this plantation in his absence had neglected to trim them from the trunks. Putting his annoyance to one side he continued to run, the bag weighted with rocks pulling down on his shoulders making each step feel as if he was running in deep mud.

His arms pumped forward and back, propelling him up the steep hill. His head was down concentrating on his feet so as not to trip on any exposed roots. It almost came as a shock to him when he broke through from the gloomy shade of the trees into the bright autumnal sunlight. His eyes were unadjusted and the sunlight stung them as he glanced ahead of him to the end of his training run, the summit of the hill.

Looking back down he willed his legs to move faster as he drove his body up using his last reserves of energy to crest the peak without stopping.

He collapsed in an exhausted heap as he reached the top. Sweat dropped down his face stinging as it ran into the small cuts left by the branches. He sat for a long moment and then drank deeply from a flask on his belt, the cold fresh water cooling him. He brought himself up to a seated position and worked on controlling his breath, he took long deep regulated breaths and before long he felt refreshed enough to stand.

He stood in the cool breeze as it danced around him. From his vantage point he looked north across the water to Mannin. It was his seventh day since he woke, that meant his sister had thirteen days head start on him. He couldn't envisage how he might make up the distance of such a head start to be able to meet up with her. But somehow he would have to, she had been sent ahead of him to obtain information vital to the success of his mission. He needed to know where Flea was being held in order to rescue her and he needed to know who had made the poison so that they could track the antidote. *What if it comes to a decision between rescuing Flea or getting the antidote?* Flax asked himself. It was not a choice he wanted to even think about having to make, yet for some reason it was a recurring thought that kept coming back to him.

He traced his eyes along the shoreline of Mannin and watched as it rose into steep climbing cliffs running away to the east. One thing he was certain of was that this would be his initial direction of travel towards the rock formation the Traveller had referred to as the Sugar Loaf. He knew that Ealish had travelled this way too in hope of picking up the trail from the Longtails.

The wind had finally cooled the sweat from his brow completely, and standing on the exposed hilltop he felt a slight chill as the cold wind pressed against his sweat soaked top. He retraced his gaze back down the cliff line to the shore north of The Sound, then back across the water to the northern dock of the Island.

He blinked, then blinked again hoping that his eyes were not playing tricks on him.

They were not.

At the northern dock an unmistakeable figure was steadily dragging a small boat from within a low walled area down the rocky beach and into the water.

Flax did not waste a moment. Ditching his weighted bag at the top of the hill he began to run. Purposefully bypassing the plantation on the way down as he knew that the branches and trees would only slow his descent. He ran faster than he had ever run, determined and angry. He cursed under his breath as he pushed himself to run faster, nearly stumbling as he misplaced a foot on top of a mossy rock causing it to slip but regaining his balance at the last moment.

He entered the village and almost ran head long into Mr Crawshaw as he went about his business. Neatly sidestepping him, Flax continued on through the village. He could hear that something was shouted after him but he was already too far gone to register what was actually being said.

At the north end of the village Flax continued on the track up the much lower hill than the one he had run up this morning. His legs weren't ready for another fast incline run, they burned in pain and his mouth felt the watery taste that preceded nausea. He took in huge gulps of air as he ran hoping that would help him. As he crested the hill he didn't even take the time to look up, he pressed on down the hard path, his boots pounding on the solid ground. He was running so fast he felt that his body might overtake the speed of his legs causing him to fall forward, to counter this he pulled his head and shoulders up. As he did, he looked, and he realised he was too late.

About halfway across The Sound, passing close to the eastern edge of the Kitterland was a single boat with a single passenger, a dark cloak pulled up over their head as they used a single bladed paddle to propel the vessel smoothly across the water.

Flax reached the walled dock which stood four or five boat lengths from the gently lapping waves. With all the energy he could manage he screamed at the top of his voice, "Get back here now!" His voice was a painful mixture of anger, upset, confusion and disappointment.

"I know you hear me. Get back here now you coward!" He had hoped this insult would cause the head to at least turn but it did not. The small boat was now in the dangerous rip tide that cut through The Sound, its sole occupant was putting more effort into their strokes with the paddle as they fought through the cross current, but they still made it look easy.

He had no more energy to shout. Sinking to his knees and then onto his backside he leant back against the low wall and just watched the figure in the boat paddle farther and farther from him. The boat finally beached at the other side of the strait. The figure climbed out into the shallows and pulled the craft onto the shore and up away from the water line, leaving it in an identical walled dry dock on the other side.

Flax watched in disbelief as the hooded figure walked along the shoreline up onto the cliff path and slowly out of his view.

With a final burst of energy summoned from deep within Flax let out an animalistic cry, hoping somehow that it would invoke a response from the figure, to cause them to turn back. It didn't.

Flax couldn't move, paralysed by a combination of exhaustion, betrayal and disbelief. He sat there late into the afternoon staring across the water, trying to contemplate what had happened and what it meant for him. He finally decided to stand as the sun dropped low to the west, scattering a carpet of golden light across the smooth surface of the sea.

As he turned to head back toward the village something caught his eye, a piece of parchment was fastened with a nail to a wooden post that stood in one of the corners of the walled dock. Flax could have sworn it was not there when he ran down but his attention had been focussed on the boat and its occupant.

He looked around slowly to see if anybody nearby could have placed it there whilst he had sat. In the late afternoon sun he noticed a couple of young rabbits that had ventured from their burrow, they paid no attention to Flax as they nibbled at the grass. Nor did the sea birds gliding low across the water, their wing tips tracing across the surface as they searched for fish.

He took the paper from the post and as he did so he felt a pair of eyes watching him, he turned towards them and sighed to himself as he saw a seal laid near the water line watching him with curiosity.

As he opened the folded parchment he could see that it was a handwritten note, not a very long or informative one though.

It read:

Boy,

I must leave earlier than I had planned.

You know what you must do.

Find your sister.

Find Breesha.

Do not fail.

"He didn't even bother to sign it?" Flax exclaimed to the seal who was still eyeing him. Regardless, Flax had no doubt as to who had left it, The Traveller must have known that Flax would see him leaving from the hilltop. That must be why he had instructed him to run up earlier that day as part of his training. "Why would he not just explain himself in person?" Flax questioned the now disinterested looking creature.

He carefully read the note again and tuned it over in his hands checking that he hadn't missed anything on it, he hadn't.

He looked up from the paper. The sun was now half sunk behind the watery horizon, it was throwing splashes of pink, red and orange across the thin wispy clouds. Flax realised he had wasted a half day by the water's edge. He turned his eyes toward Mannin and came to a decision, he had wasted enough time, tomorrow he would make the crossing.

-30-
JEIH AS FEED
- EALISH'S FIRST DAY ON MANNIN -

Neither Ealish nor the creature moved, they were in standoff. Their blue eyes locked intently on each other. Ealish tried to figure out what the animal was thinking whilst also working on a plan of action.

The sight of the black dog surrounded by the ever-moving fog had initially frozen Ealish with fear. Now that she had taken a moment to think, she started to take in what was in front of her. She was still crouched low and the beast's head was higher than hers. She reckoned that if she were stood then the pointed black ears of the dog would be somewhere around her midriff. It's mouth was slightly open revealing sharp white fangs, one of them was snapped but looked no less dangerous. The beast was not completely black, its chest and nose held patches of a lighter grey and white fur, as did its lower front legs, one of which was completely white from the knee down giving the appearance that it was wearing a sock.

Ealish gripped the knives in her hands and assessing the threat she came to a realisation – the dog wasn't growling, nor had it tried to attack her. It wasn't crouched down on its haunches preparing to attack, it just stood, staring at her. Seeing no threat she hoped that she had judged correctly as she slowly stood tall. Once stood, Ealish could see the dog's entire body, it looked thinner than it should, not unhealthy but definitely under fed. She took instant pity on the animal, which for her was uncharacteristic. She had always been fascinated by animals and their behaviour but she had seen them as either sources of food when hunting or as tools to be used, such as the donkeys on the Island. But something about the dog had resonated with her and she saw no threat, just a vulnerable animal. She slowly slid the smaller of her knives into her belt, being sure to keep the larger one gripped in her more competent left hand in case she had completely misread the situation and underestimated the threat. With her right hand she opened her satchel bag and fished around for a moment. She pulled out a small piece of dried meat it and held it out in front of her to show the animal, then gently threw the snack toward the still slightly open mouth of the creature. The meat hit the dog on the end of the nose and bounced on to the small stretch of ground between them. The dog cocked its head and eyed the piece of meat quizzically but made no move toward it.

The standoff resumed. Ealish was very aware that she was still backed against the cliff top and any sudden movement could startle the creature. Even in its apparent underweight condition it would be heavy and powerful enough to knock her off balance, causing her to fall to her death. Keeping her eyes fixed on the dog's and her left hand gripping the knife she used her right hand to search for another piece of dried meat. She found one and held it in her outstretched hand towards the dog's mouth, this time rather than throwing it at the dog's mouth she dropped it just in front of it on the floor. Ealish did not want to rush the dog and this would allow it time to smell the snack she had thrown it before deciding whether to eat it or not. Another reason, and one Ealish hoped would not be necessary, was that the dog would have to lower its head to the food to eat it which would offer her a slight combat advantage if needed.

Ealish held her breath and waited, the dog didn't move, she waited some more. Still there was no movement. With an audible gasp she breathed heavily not realising that she had been on the verge of going dizzy from lack of air.

At this gasp the dog twitched, moving backward slightly. Ealish realised she had scared it; *the poor creature was frightened, it was no threat to her.* She slid the knife from her left hand into its sheath along the back of her belt then knelt down and reached forward for the piece of meat on the floor. She still eyed the dog carefully but it didn't move. She picked up the food and placing it in the palm of her hand she held it out in front of her, just below the dog's nose. The animal still did nothing.

"Hmm," Ealish said aloud, as she did so the dog's ears twitched, registering the sound of her voice. Accepting that she may be in for a long wait she readjusted her position and sat cross legged with the piece of dried meat in her hand, the other piece was still on the floor to her right where it had bounced off the dog's nose.

Ealish didn't want to risk moving away from the dog in case she startled it and it either attacked her or accidentally knocked her from the cliff top. Also, this was the first company of any kind she'd had since arriving on Mannin and once she realised that the dog offered no threat, she began to enjoy the encounter.

After what seemed like an age the dog finally made a movement. It cautiously licked the dried brown meat, testing it. It licked again, this time its rough tongue tickling across Ealish's palm causing her to laugh aloud and move her hand.

The dog stopped, so did Ealish.

She straightened out her hand again, this time the dog gently took the food from her. It held it in its mouth and stared into Ealish's eyes, she tried to read its emotions but to no avail. Slowly it lowered its head and started to chew the food. Cautiously Ealish reached out, her hand visibly shaking, the dog kept its head low but looked up at her and let out a low growl from its throat. Ealish's mouth felt dry, she didn't move her hand away but instead reached out further and felt her fingers connect with the dark fur on the animal's head. The dog never stopped chewing and the growl quickly subsided. Ealish allowed her fingers to ruffle the surprisingly soft, warm fur on the dog's head, she maintained eye contact and started to speak in a low soothing voice, "Good dog, there you go, you were hungry, weren't you?" Her voice cracked at first given how dry her mouth and throat were. She gently cleared her throat then spoke more soothing words to the dog. Now she was able to concentrate, she assessed the dog's condition. It was definitely underweight as thought and it had visible scratches and scars on its body and face. The most noticeable running from above its left eye, down across the eyelid onto its cheek and to the left corner of its mouth. This was an old wound and had healed into a greyish pink scar and no fur grew on it. "How did you get this?" She asked aloud as her fingers brushed gently across the top of it. The dog finished eating the snack, Ealish kept one hand on the animal and reached with her other to take up the meat that had fallen to the floor when she had thrown it. No sooner had she held it out that the dog greedily and eagerly took it from her hand, its broken fang unintentionally grazing her palm. She didn't mind or show any reaction. She just kept scratching behind the beast's ears, as she did it would cock its head to that side pushing its head up into her hand as if silently encouraging her to continue.

The dog finished its second bit of meat quicker than the first and then it crept forward and nudged at Ealish with its head. She laughed and scratched at its chest. It nudged her again forcing its head under her right arm. "Oh you're not dumb, are you?" She exclaimed, realising the dog was trying to get to her bag for more food.

"Okay, okay," she conceded, reaching into the bag she produced a piece of smoked fish. The dog clumsily rushed to her and almost knocked her off balance. Using her free hand to steady herself and quickly appreciating how close she still was to the perilous drop behind her she held out her hand and firmly said "Ey!". Unsure of what reaction she expected from the dog she was pleasantly surprised to see it step back a few paces. "Well that seemed to work," she quietly told herself. She now felt confident enough to stand, still holding a hand in front and towards the dog to show that she meant business. Once stood, she eyed the dog and showed it the dried fish, it shuffled back ever so slightly and to her amazement and amusement it sat and cocked its head, never taking its eyes off the food. In an exaggerated movement she threw the snack in a low arc towards the dog's mouth. This time it knew exactly what to do, it lifted up on its back paws, caught the fish in its mouth and softly landed back down. It then sank onto its belly with its front paws stretched in front concentrating on its latest snack. Ealish took this opportunity to step away from the dangerous cliff edge and to the dog's side. She knelt down next to it and rubbed her hand up and down along its back, she could feel each of its ribs beneath its thick, soft fur.

"Where did you come from?" She asked, expecting no reply. "You gave me quite the fright at first, I thought you were The *Moddey Doo*. But you aren't scary at all are you?" On cue the dog rolled on its side and lay at what appeared an award angle but was clearly comfortable given that it stayed there. It raised its front right paw used it to nudge her, she took the hint and rubbed at its warm belly fur.

Ealish lost track of how much time she had spent with the animal. As she rubbed the dogs belly it lifted its front paw and scratched at its nose. Then, with what Ealish could have sworn was a sneeze, it rolled all the way over away from her and onto its belly. From there it stood, shook its head and sneezed again then without even looking at her it turned and stalked back into the heather meadow, stopping only to cock its leg against one of the low plants before striding away into the mist and out of sight.

Ealish stood, confused and saddened at the loss an unexpected yet most welcome companion on her journey. She didn't know how long she stood there but as she did the fog around her slowly thinned and then cleared. She could tell from the sun's position that it was now late in the afternoon, she scanned across the meadow hoping to see the shadowy figure of the beast. "Dog?" She called out as loud as she dared for fear of alerting any other animal or person to her presence. She waited, nothing.

"Dog?" She called once more, her voice quieter this time, with a hint of desperation to it. Still nothing.

"Goodbye boy," she whispered sadly as she turned and continued on her path.

-31-
NANE-JEIG AS FEED
- EALISH'S FIRST DAY ON MANNIN -

Ealish's progress was much slower than it had been during the morning. When she set foot on Mannin she had been unsure yet determined, and that determination had spurred her. Her encounter with the dog had put her through so many emotions in a short space of time but had ultimately ended up in a deep feeling of loss. This instilled in her a sense of loneliness that she couldn't shake. Now emotionally exhausted her progress was affected, her strides were shorter and lethargic, she paid less attention to her surroundings and her foot placement, which meant she was leaving footprints and other evidence of her journey along the path.

There was a heaviness in her chest and gut that she could not help but dwell on, it made her head hurt. She sipped on water to try and alleviate the feeling of pressure at the back of her head, it helped a little. She snacked on a piece of smoked fish, but that brought flashes into her mind of the dog chewing on the same snack.

"Oh for goodness sake, snap out of it!" she cursed herself out loud. She had spent an insignificant amount of time with a wild animal that at first she had feared would attack and possibly kill her. And now she felt such a disproportionate sense of sadness and loss and she was letting her emotions take control of her actions. She could not understand why this encounter had affected her in such a way.

As she walked, she tried to figure out the reasoning behind it. She concluded that since the night of the attack on the Island she had only known loss: her father, her brother and, by virtue of her leaving her homeland - her mother. The brief moment she spent bonding with the dog, was a positive connective experience but again this had ended in loss.

The day was growing old and as she walked east along the cliff tops she could see fingers of pink and purple light reaching across the sky from the slowly sinking sun behind her. She stopped and turned to look at the fiery orb, it seemed to grow in size as it sank closer and closer to the horizon. She needed to find somewhere to rest, she could not risk travelling this path in the dark, one wrong step and she could fall to her death. As she turned to walk along the path something across the meadow caught her eye for a fleeting moment, she shook her head and then continued on the path.

Now as she walked, she systematically gazed to her left every fifteen paces or so, her eyes had not deceived her as she first thought.

A smile crept across her face but other than that she did not react. Instantly the aching in her head subsided and there was a fresh bounce in her step. She checked again, yes, it was still there, he was still there.

Stalking her from the heather meadow she had seen the dark shadowy figure of the dog, matching her pace and direction but remaining at a distance from her. She stopped, so did the dog - her smile widened. It was not trying to hide from her, yet at the same time it was sinking its body low on its legs to prevent it standing out fully above the heather plants. Ealish continued walking and so did her canine shadow. After some distance she stopped and beckoned the dog, she called out to it and waved her arms invitingly, hoping to convince it to come to her once more. The dog didn't move closer, cocking its head to one side as if questioning her actions. This did not dissuade Ealish, who continued walking in the hope of finding shelter, now confident that the dog would follow her if only from a distance.

She decided to strike camp for the night, then work on encouraging the dog to come to her. She had been so captivated by its return that she hadn't realised ahead of her was a structure that she had not yet encountered on Mannin. One that made her stop and pay attention to her wider surroundings for a long moment before she would move forward again.

Ahead of her she could see that the path was dissected by a stone wall that ran through the heather meadow, across the path and ended abruptly – as you would imagine, at the edge of the cliff. The wall stood as high as her chest but because of the way the land fell away on the far side she could see nothing beyond it. In the fading light she noticed a wooden ladder attached to the wall.

Her eyes keenly scanned around her in systematic sweeping arcs. There was no sign of any other person or creature nearby, except for the dog which stood still as a statue watching her every move away to her left. She followed the line of the wall up through the heather meadow, its dark form snaked along the ground rising and falling in line with the undulations. At its farthest visible point it crested a hill and presumably flowed down the other side out of her view.

Just prior to the wall she noticed the path split and offered a left-hand fork. She stepped forward cautiously to this fork, the dog matching her steps. She looked to the left and could see that this path didn't go far at all, she followed it into the heather for around twenty paces and it opened into a large circular clearing of short grass. Around the perimeter of the clearing large stones had been set at regular intervals. These stones were partially buried in the ground, quite clearly intentionally placed there for some purpose, what that purpose was she could not even begin to guess. She tried to beckon the dog again but it did not react to her attempts.

The light was fading even more now, she decided to look over the wall purely as a means of establishing what lay ahead of her. If there was no immediate threat or more suitable option for her camp then she would return to the strange stone circle and use the shelter that it offered as her camp for the night.

Stepping cautiously on the bottom step of the ladder allowed Ealish to see to the ground on the other side and she quickly satisfied herself that there was nothing that would alter her plan. On the other side of the wall the terrain looked similar to the side she was on. The path was visible and still followed roughly along the cliff top line as far as she could see in the limited light. There was also, she noticed, a second path that ran to the left along the wall line and up to the crest of the hill she assumed, although she could now not see that far in the ever-increasing darkness. There wasn't much more that she could see and she stepped back down off the ladder as her mind briefly pondered the second path - *that is a decision for morning,* she told herself as she returned to the circular clearing in the heather. She looked up to check on the dog, she could no longer discern its shape but she could see the last rays of the sun's light reflecting from its eyes, making them appear like two yellow-green hovering spheres in the gloomy darkness. Had she not known what they were they would have surely been a frightening thing to encounter. She sat with her back against one of the embedded stones so that the entrance to the opening was to her right and the dog away to her left.

The temperature was dropping now that the sun had set below the horizon. She pulled her fur lined jacket tight around her body and fastened it. Opening her satchel bag she pulled out the thin, but very warm, blanket that she had packed. She wrapped it around herself and then put her hand back into the bag. Bringing out some bread and cheese she looked up to see the dog now sat in front of her. She could hear him panting in anticipation of a potential meal. She thought back to her encounter with the pheasant and wished she had shot the bird as the food rations she carried did not factor in a second, and very hungry, mouth to feed. However, she would not deny the undernourished dog a meal. She placed a chunk of the bread and cheese on the floor between them and stroked the animal's head with one hand as she ate with the other. When she had eaten, she pulled the blanket close around her body and sat back, resting her head against one of the hard, upright stones. The dog had finished well before her and was laid looking at her, his front paws out in front of his chin, which rested on the ground.

She thought about lighting a fire, but not knowing who or what may be alerted by the light and the smoke she dared not. She shivered and pulled up the fur lined hood on her jacket for extra warmth. Now that the sun had sunk fully her eyes had adjusted to the low levels of light and she could make out clear shapes within a reasonable distance of where she sat. She was aided by the brilliant blue-white light that the half-moon cast down. She looked up and as her eyes adjusted thousands of tiny stars came into focus, studded into the dark velvety blanket of the sky.

She smiled to herself, she recognised these stars, they were the same ones she had gazed at hundreds of times on her Island. In that moment she felt closer to home than she had all day, despite the fact she had never been farther from it. She felt a warmth across her legs and looked down to find the dog had moved up close to her and laid his head across her thighs. She stroked his head affectionately and in return he ran his rough tongue along her arm. Ealish wrapped her arms around the dog and pulled him close to her. There in the strange stone circle, with her unexpected companion she fell into a deep sleep beneath the twinkling stars.

-32-
DAA-YEIG AS FEED

Flax looked across the stretch of water that he had wasted the previous day gazing at – angry, confused, abandoned but eventually – determined. Today, there was no question about what he must do. Today, he would leave his Island and cross The Sound to Mannin. Taking the same journey that the Traveller had the previous day, and his sister fourteen days before.

He stood alone. Having said his tearful goodbyes in the village the previous evening, knowing that he would rise and leave at first light. He had requested that his mother, or anyone else for that matter, did not come to the beach with him.

He said goodbye to his mother and his permanently sleeping father but he had also visited Flea's parents before he left. They had hugged him for so long he thought they would never let go. There was such a deep desperation in their eyes.

He knew their only hope of seeing their daughter again lay in him, and he knew they knew it too. Before he had left their home Flea's mother had given him something. It now hung round his neck on a silver chain. It was a Faerie, an exact replica of the one that Flea wore, the one she could never remove. "Let it be a reminder of your true purpose," she had said to him as she gently kissed his cheek and then turned away, unable to hold back the flow of tears from her eyes. Flax thought them to be strange words.

Of course Flea is my purpose for travelling but so is rescuing my father from his poisoned state.

Surely she knows that? Flax pondered these words as his hand instinctively felt the pendant.

He eyed the small wooden boat that he had pulled from the dry dock. He had packed and repacked his bag a number of times. Second guessing what he should and shouldn't take. Much like his sister he had chosen a bag that could be worn over the shoulder and close to his body. It contained food, additional clothing, a blanket, a flask of water, a small pouch of coins and snares for hunting. On his belt he carried his hunting knife, identical to Ealish's, the blade flat across the small of his back with the handle toward his right hand. Placed into a specifically drilled cavity in the bottom of the handle was a small fire striking stick. He also had his pouch containing his pebbles and sling. Around his body he carried a length of rope with a three-pronged hook that was again identical to Ealish's, having also been forged by Flea's father. He had offered him the finest sword he could make but Flax had declined, stating that he been afforded little time to practice with a sword and so opted to take his fighting staff.

The true reason he had declined is that the sword offered no option but death or serious injury to any would be attacker and that was still something that did not sit easy with him. The staff gave him the option to deal with attackers in a less brutal and final method. However if it came to it then he was well practiced with his hunting knife and knew he could be deadly at close quarters or at range with it if he absolutely had to be.

His staff lay attached to his bag, wrapped in cloth having been oiled the previous evening. His coat had been lined with warm fur by Mr Crawshaw and safe in an interior pocket he had placed Mr Kelly's map and a writing stick.

Reluctantly he pushed the boat into the shallows and stepped into it. He knelt for a long moment pondering his thoughts, mapping out in his head what he must do. Taking up the paddle in his hands he propelled the boat forward into The Sound with strong steady strokes.

The small vessel was designed to carry more weight than one passenger and a bag so it rode high in the water but felt stable enough. The bow sliced through the calm rolling waves of the northern shoreline, making for hasty progress into the channel of The Sound. He pointed the bow to the eastern edge of the Kitterland, hoping to follow the same line that he had seen the Traveller take the previous day.

He hadn't appreciated quite how far the stretch of water was until he was on it. He normally looked down upon it from the hills, from where it seemed much narrower than it actually was. Ahead he could see where the two currents met and the deadly rip currents were formed. The water here did the opposite of what would be expected. There were patches that looked so smooth they could be a sheet of ice and then next to them the water frothed and bubbled as if it were a boiling pot on a stove. He brought the boat to a stop, accepting that whilst he was a competent paddler he had never encountered waters such as this and he had no idea how he would navigate his way across the deadly strait. He looked around considering his options, his eyes were drawn to something in the water to his right. He leaned over the edge of the boat and stared down into the water, what he saw made him recoil back in shock. A ghostly pair of dark eyes were staring back at him from beneath the surface. He steadied himself and looked again, this time knowing what to expect. Still the black unblinking eyes stared at him. He was able to make out, now that he stared for longer, the outline of a head to which the eyes belonged. Slowly the entire body of the creature came into view, and with relief Flax saw that it was a seal laid on its back just below the surface. Its powerful tail swaying hypnotically allowed it to stay in position next to the boat despite the movement of the waves. Its eyes locked with Flax's and he could not place it but he saw familiarity within them. He studied the animal. It's coat was dark grey and was mottled with splashes of white and lighter shades of grey and brown. He watched as the seal rose in the water, its face breaching the surface. Its nostrils, which had been tightly shut, opened and took in deep breaths of air. Its wet whiskers glistened in the mid-morning sun. The seal had been injured at some point, the injuries looked old but its right flipper was definitely damaged. It looked as if it had been torn or ripped and was about half the length of the left one. The fur around the right flipper also looked damaged, as it if had been burned with fire. Flax brought his gaze back to the eyes of the animal, desperately trying to place where he recognised them from. He couldn't and told himself that most seals eyes looked alike – and he had seen hundreds of them on the Island. Being so close in the water was something else though, he was amazed at how such a large animal, that moved so awkwardly on the ground, could be so graceful and sleek in its aquatic environment.

Suddenly aware that his boat was beginning to drift closer to the opposing currents, Flax grabbed the paddle and dug it hard into the water to halt his progress. When he looked back down into the water, he was just in time to see the seal turn onto its front and dive deep into the gloomy depths of the blue-green water, its tail the last thing to disappear from view.

He turned his attention back to the pressing issue of navigating The Sound, deciding that the best course of action was to use his strength to put in long powerful strokes in the hope of punching the craft across the ever-nearing contradicting currents. After all, he had seen the Traveller cross the same strait the previous day, and Flax reckoned himself to be stronger than him.

He regretted this decision as soon as he had committed to it. The nose of the boat entered the current at a right angle and was immediately caught by the surface current that ran from his right to his left. The front of the boat began to turn, pushing the nose in a westerly direction to the open ocean. He reacted quickly, altering his grip on the paddle and putting in wide arcing strokes on the left-hand side of the boat in an attempt to turn the nose back toward Mannin. But the current was far too strong and all his efforts achieved was to temporarily hold the boat at such an angle in the current that the frothing waves spilled over the sides and into it.

The cold water was a shock. It brought him quickly to his senses, "I can't fight this current," he said angrily to himself. He lifted the paddle from the water allowing his craft to be turned fully west, letting the current carry him. He passed the rocky Kitterland to his right and briefly cast his eye across the small island. He saw multiple pairs of eyes watching him as he skimmed by, the seals were oblivious to the situation he had gotten himself into. But he was not overly concerned, he scanned ahead looking for something in particular, he saw it.

About ten boat lengths ahead of him, past the far western edge of the Kitterland, the choppy water ceased and there was a smooth patch of water that he took to be a pool or an eddy, *perhaps created by some rocks beneath the surface*. He planned to navigate into this eddy then re-assess where to enter the next current to allow him the safest passage to the shore of Mannin.

Flax thought again about the Traveller simply gliding across the water yesterday, never having to alter his stroke. Then a realisation hit him, *he was on the water much earlier in the morning than the Traveller had been*. Flax had neglected to think about the tides and how they affected the currents! He cursed himself aloud. He had been so intent on leaving the village at first light to avoid meeting anybody and having to say more farewells. He cursed himself again. He knew that the tides made such a difference to The Sound, he had been taught it by his father for as long as he could remember. He bet his sister hadn't made such a stupid mistake.

It was too late to turn back now, he was so far across the first current that he would be unable to paddle back across it and to the safety of the Island. That's what he told himself at least, whether it was true or not would not change his mind, he was stubbornly continuing with his initial plan in the face of his blatant and potentially deadly error.

He drove the paddle into the water at the stern like a knife allowing it to act as a rudder, applying pressure, fighting against the current to push the boat across at an angle. He was now about two boat lengths from his entry point into the eddy and was on course to enter its safety. He was straining to hold the boat on course, the strong current relentlessly biting against the flat blade of the paddle.

The moment that the bow crossed from the choppy waters into the smooth Flax realised he had made another misjudgement. *It was not an eddy at all!* The smooth water was a current flowing strongly in the opposite direction. The boat was quickly turned about on itself before he had chance to stop it. He was now facing East, Mannin to his left and the Kitterland and his Island to his right.

He quickly lifted the paddle from where it trailed at the stern and thrust it deep into the water on the front left side of the boat hoping the force of the current would pivot the craft around the paddle and into the next opposing current. In this fashion he planned to force his way from one current to the next until he reached the safety of the shore-bound rolling waves on the Mannin side of the channel.

The moment the paddle entered the water it was violently snatched away from him by the ferocious undercurrent flowing in the opposite direction.

It was pulled backwards and out of his grip. In an ill-judged desperate attempt to keep hold of it he leant over the side of the boat toward the water. He immediately realised the danger he was in when cold seawater sloshed over the side and into the bottom of the boat. This made the craft more unstable in the water and as Flax threw his weight back into the centre of the boat the seawater within moved from one side to the other. The momentum of both Flax and the seawater moving caused the opposite side to dip below the smooth surface of the fast-running tidal current. Before he had a chance to react the entire boat was swamped with water. It listed heavily onto its side causing Flax and his belongings to slide into the biting cold sea. His whole body froze in shock, his lungs wouldn't work and he gasped in vain for air. He was pulled under the surface by the snarling current. He opened his mouth to breath but all he got was a mouthful of water. He kicked his legs as hard as he could and pulled with his arms, fighting to reach the surface. His hand breached the surface first but he had to keep fighting to get his entire body into the top layer of water to have any chance of surviving and prevent himself from being dragged along under the water, and even then, the chances were slim.

His lungs screamed for air and his legs and arms burned with exhaustion. It took everything he had not to open his mouth and inhale. He felt his head break the surface of the water. He inhaled deeply, just in time as he was dragged back under, his legs still caught in the lower currents. Now that he had air in his lungs, he was able to think more clearly. He stopped fighting against the current and instead he straightened his body and put his arms together above his head making himself more streamlined. This allowed more of the fast-flowing current to move past him and it slowed his progress in the wrong direction. Next, he began to kick both of his legs together like the tail of a fish, he pointed his arms at an upward angle and used the powerful kicks and the momentum of the current to drive him along and up. This worked, as when he broke into the upper current near the surface his entire body entered it at nearly the same moment which prevented him from being dragged back under. This time he was ready for the change of direction in the top current and once he felt that he was fully in it he tucked his legs into his stomach and rolled onto his back. He straightened out again and continued with the powerful kicks as he now felt himself being propelled in the other direction. He was concentrating so hard on keeping horizontal and straight in this top current that he was unaware his face had broken through into the cold autumnal air. Only when the urge to breath overcame his ability to suppress it did he open his mouth and breathe in deeply. He opened his eyes and squinted as the low sunlight bounced along the shimmering water. It felt as if he had been under the surface in the murky gloom for an age but it had only been a matter of moments. He was completely disorientated as to where he was, he looked to his left and recognised his Island. He figured out that his feet were pointing west, his head east and he was also travelling east, floating at an almost leisurely pace in the current. He lifted his head looking down toward his feet hoping to see some sign of his boat, there was none.

Then he remembered he had been pulled under and in the opposite direction of the more buoyant boat – which would have stayed in the top current. That mean that his boat was somewhere ahead of him to the east. He rolled laterally onto his front so that he could see in the direction he was travelling. He could see his satchel bag, with the staff attached, being pulled along the surface. There was no sign of the boat. He aligned himself with the bag and put his face in the water to streamline himself. He began to propel his body forward with determined powerful strokes of his arms, coupled with kicks, raising his head every fourth or sixth stroke to breathe and check he was still on track. He was gaining steadily on the bag but due to his position in the water Flax had failed to notice something. Between him and the bag, sat just below the surface and moving more slowly, due to being full of water, was his boat.

He was mid-stroke when he caught up with the slow-moving boat, his forehead collided hard with the stern of the craft. He had no idea what had just happened as he still couldn't see the submerged boat beneath the smooth flowing surface. His left arm hit next, his scarred forearm coming down heavily on the top edge of the wood. With pain in both his head and his arm he instinctively stopped swimming and brought his other hand to his head, he rubbed it and on examination could see that there was blood on it. It was a washed-out pale pink as it mixed with seawater. But it was definitely blood. He suddenly felt dizzy and in this temporary confusion he allowed his legs to drop and his body went vertical in the water.

In an instant he was pulled under the surface once more by the much stronger undercurrent. He hadn't time to take in breath before being pulled below, he tried to straighten his body as before but the current felt much stronger here. Either that or he was weaker in his exhausted and now injured state. He couldn't align his body properly in the current and this resulted in him being rolled and tumbled along in the water, he lost his sense of direction and couldn't be sure which way was up or down. He opened his eyes searching for a sign of the daylight above but the low rays of the sun didn't penetrate deep enough into the water.

His whole body screamed for air, he was panicking, his head felt like it was being slowly crushed. Darkness began to creep into the edges of his vision and he realised he was losing consciousness.

He tried to kick his legs but there was no energy there, no fight.

He couldn't keep his mouth closed any longer, as he opened it water flooded in. His vision faded as his limp body tumbled away into the darkness.

-33-
TREE-JEIG AS FEED
- EALISH'S SECOND DAY ON MANNIN -

As she ate a breakfast of bread and cheese with the dog, Ealish realised that the previous night's sleep was the first time since the *ashlishyn* had started that she hadn't had the visions. She couldn't understand why even though she had run through several different scenarios and possibilities in her head. But none of them made sense, *then again neither did having the same dream every night for seasons at a time.*

She was pulled back to the present by an affectionate nudge from the dog. She stared into his eyes, "You need a name. I can't very well keep calling you dog, can I? I'm guessing you will be around for a while since you follow me like my shadow."

A smile crossed her face as she thought of the word for shadow in the old tongue, "*Scaa*," she said aloud patting him on the head. She found this name fitting since he had followed her like a shadow since they met. There was also double meaning since the dominant feature of the dog's face was the ugly scar that ran almost the length of the left side and the old tongue word sounded similar to the new tongue word - *scar*.

The sun had not long risen and its rays were creeping across the top of the heather plants that surrounded the strange stone circle in which they had spent the night. The morning dew was not heavy enough to hold off the gentle heat of the sun and a light steam rose from the ground and the plants. Curling fingers of vapour reached upwards, twisting and rolling like seaweed on the seabed, it made the whole environment appear alive.

Now it was daylight Ealish could see that on each of the stones forming the circle there were strange markings. Markings that she did not recognise nor could she make sense of. She traced her fingers across them, each stone held three marks in a vertical line. She noticed that the bottom marking on each stone was the same. Slowly she made her way around the circle, Scaa at her side stopping and sitting next to her as she crouched at each one. When she reached the short entrance path that led into the circle, she saw two larger stones stood either side. She hadn't seen these the previous night due to them being partially obscured by the heather plants. On each of these pillars was one large symbol, the same as had appeared on the bottom of each of the other stones.

This played on Ealish's mind as she packed her blanket into her bag. She knew that it would likely have no impact on her quest and therefore was insignificant, but she liked to understand things and it frustrated her when she didn't.

She cursed herself for not bringing any parchment or a drawing stick with her, she would have liked to have copied down the symbols to study.

She sighed, resigned to the fact that she wouldn't be able to decipher the meaning of these strange markings.

"Come on then Scaa, time to move," she called. The dog looked at her, cocking his head to one side quizzically. He had clearly heard her voice but didn't understand either the words or the intonation of it.

"Hmm might take some time for you to learn your new name." Again the dog tilted his head at the sound of her voice but didn't respond.

Ealish tried a different tack and leant forward on her knees excitedly patting them and calling out to him repeatedly, hoping that her body language and tone of voice would encourage the dog to come to her. They didn't, Scaa didn't budge from his position in the circle. She considered using some more food to get him to come but her rations were already running lower than she would have liked given that she had been feeding him too.

Instead she opted to trust that he would follow her as he had done the previous day, he was after all her shadow. She threw her bag across her shoulder and then carefully placed her bow over her other one. She had done it in this order intentionally, so that if needed she could quickly arm herself with her bow without the need to mess around with her bag strap. She attached her quiver to her belt and fitted it against her left hip, she counted the seven black fletched arrows and the one blue. She checked that both blades were in position on her belt and her left calf. She scanned around what had been her makeshift campsite for the night to check that she had left nothing she needed, and more importantly to check she had left no trace of her presence. Satisfied that she had not, she walked back to the main path and climbed onto the wooden ladder by the wall, as she had the previous night she stopped and scanned the environment ahead of her.

As far as she could tell nothing had changed in the immediate vicinity. But what she had taken to be another heather meadow the night before she could now see was more gorse plants. This meant that once she continued, she would be stuck on the path she was on with no reasonable hope of escape inland as she had been offered the previous afternoon. She looked at the path to the left snaking up to the crest of the hill, she longed to know where it led. However she knew that she must stick to the cliff path to reach the Sugar Loaf. She followed the line of this cliff path and saw that it stopped at another wall, funnelled to this location by the gorse on one side and the cliffs on the other.

In the wall there was a wooden gate that offered access to whatever lay the other side, she didn't like being forced to move in such a restricted direction. She was used to running free across the moorland of her Island, choosing her own path. Reluctantly she would go the way she must. She climbed higher up the ladder and stopped to look around once more. The dog was stood off to her left, nothing else moved. She brought her legs over the wall, sat on the top of it and looked down.

She studied the ground on the other side of the wall and saw no footprints or sign of other recent activity, she could see that a few of the rungs of the ladder on the opposite side had rotted away probably destroyed over time by the prevailing wind driving rain and sea water into it.

Looking once more to her left she was not surprised to see Scaa jump on to the top of the wall in an effortless movement. He stood on the top, his eyes fixed on Ealish, waiting for her next move before he made his.

Ealish pushed herself forward from the wall with her hands so that she moved out past the broken ladder, she landed on the soft floor with a quiet thud, bending her knees to soften the landing. She remained in this crouched position and scanned around. No movement from anywhere with the exception of Scaa gently landing on the ground further up the path to the left.

She stood and proceeded down the cliff path. She had not travelled far into it when she felt something brush against her left leg. There was no need to look down to know that it was Scaa now trotting alongside her, almost pushing himself into her leg to keep away from the sharp barbs of the gorse plants. Ealish had suspected that he would come close to her down this path rather than attempting to navigate through the treacherous plants as he had through the much softer and sparsely grown heather yesterday. Whilst it was comforting to have Scaa close to her it also concerned her. His reluctance to travel in the gorse confirmed to her that whatever had come at her through the gorse forest the previous morning was not Scaa. Therefore she had yet to encounter whatever it was, and whatever it was she did not want to encounter since it was clearly impervious to the razor-sharp spikes of the gorse plants. It made her wary of the area to her left and so she kept scanning it for any sign of movement.

Before long she reached the gate in the wall, a sign attached to it confirmed what she had thought would be on the other side.

The sign read:

BEWARE!

Chasms - Danger of Death!

-34-
KIARE-JEIG AS FEED
- EALISH'S SECOND DAY ON MANNIN -

There were two things that tempted Ealish to turn back and take the inland path rather than enter into the area known as The Chasms. The first, and most obvious, was the clear danger they presented. The *'danger of death'*, as the sign so succinctly highlighted.

The second, and less obvious reason, was that the writing on the sign was not weathered. The ladder she had crossed had been rotted away by the elements, this sign however - and the gate on which it hung - had not. That told Ealish that there were other people in the area, and that made her feel uneasy.

She had only been on Mannin a day, until now she had encountered a small bird and Scaa. That was not strictly true as there was the unknown *thing* in the gorse forest too. But she liked the semi-solitude of just herself and her canine companion and didn't wish to meet anybody else anytime soon. The truth was that Ealish had always been slightly awkward around others, until she really got to know them anyway. But that was the problem, she didn't like to put in the effort of getting to know new people. She knew what she liked and that was running and hunting and spending time with her family. But she was in a strange land now so she had to accept that she would meet new people eventually and there was no real way of avoiding them, especially if she were to be successful in locating Flea and finding the antidote to her father's poison.

Her father, the thought of him gripped her for an instant as she realised that she hadn't thought of him yet that morning. A deep pang of guilt sat heavy in her chest, he was the main reason she was here and she had been busy looking at weird markings on stones and playing with the dog. "Stop it," she scorned herself aloud, "you can't be so hard on yourself!"

She shook her head and cleared the negative thoughts from her mind. Then she eased open the gate and stood at the entrance to The Chasms taking in what was before her. What she saw was rather unremarkable, at least compared to what she had envisaged.

The area was, as outside the wall, bordered on the left by the gorse forest and the right by the cliff tops. But unlike outside the wall there was no clear worn path along the middle. The area between the gorse and the cliffs was much wider than the path she had been walking and was scattered with an assortment of gorse and heather plants, as well as long grasses and other low-lying shrubs that she didn't recognise. These plants had grown in such a way that there were many thin paths that weaved and interlaced their way through to a wall at the other end with a gate much like the one she was stood at. At first she saw nothing that posed a danger of death. But when she looked to her left, she saw the first chasm and it made her appreciate just how real the danger was.

Partially covered by a shrub was a fissure that had opened up in the ground. She cautiously walked towards it, the ground felt firm around it. She got on her hands and knees and crawled slowly to the edge so that she could peer down to the bottom, only she couldn't. She couldn't see the bottom at all. The light wasn't strong enough to penetrate to the depths of the dark abyss. She picked a loose rock from the ground next to her and dropped it in, then listened. She could hear it bouncing off the walls of the chasm on the way down but never heard a definite noise of it hitting the ground. Scaa had edged up to her and he inched his face over the side, seeking the stone that had been dropped. He whimpered and cowered backwards away from the edge. Ealish crawled away from the edge just as Scaa had done before she dared to stand. Heights had never bothered her, she would climb trees all day long but something about not being able to see the ground below gave her an itchy feeling across her body that she didn't like.

She took in her surroundings again, this time paying no attention to the bushes and shrubs. She started to notice more and more chasms in the ground. How she hadn't seen them before she didn't know, but now she had seen them they were all she could focus on. She walked back to the gate and stood in the gap in the wall looking across to the gate at the far side. In her mind she worked backwards from there to her position mapping out what seemed to be the clearest way through the maze of spiked bushes and bottomless pits. Several times she hit what looked like a dead end and started the whole process again. She finally completed a route that seemed to work and took in the least dangerous looking paths, even then it would still mean she would have to jump across some of the cracks – not something she was looking forward to. She visually remapped the route twice. Knowing that once she was within the naturally created maze she wouldn't have the benefit of seeing the path ahead, or even the gate at the far end given that the land dipped away slightly from where she currently stood.

She noticed the sun was nearing midpoint in the sky to the south. She decided it would be best to eat now then start what she expected to be a slow journey through The Chasms once she was refreshed.

She backed out from the gap in the wall to the safe side and sat on the soft grass, Scaa copied, sitting down next to her and nuzzling his head against her arm.

As they ate she mentally travelled the route over and over in her mind, satisfying herself that she knew it. Once they had finished she stood and stretched, then walked to the gate and paused for a long moment, turning her head back the way she had come and seriously considering the path that led inland. *No,* it would lead her away from her intended destination she knew she could not take it.

She walked slowly from the gate into the enclosed maze, turning left and right along the pre-determined path she held in her mind. Scaa walked tightly at her left-hand side, so close that at times it felt like he was leaning into her. She kept reaching down to ruffle the fur between his ears with her fingers, he would respond by lifting his head and rubbing it against her hip. She was grateful for his company.

They were soon into the middle of the maze, surrounded by gorse and heather in every direction. She looked toward where she knew their exit lay but due to the way the ground dropped away above the bushes all she could see was blue sea, blending seamlessly into the blue sky. She looked down at Scaa and then to her right. She suddenly felt dizzy and stumbled back half a step, not realising how close she was to the edge of one of The Chasms. She had looked down expecting to see the path only she saw nothing but blackness falling away into the ground. She took a moment to steady herself then continued on.

Ealish stopped. Something wasn't right. She was stood at a dead end! Surrounded by gorse bushes on three sides, their menacing barbs taunting her, daring her to try squeeze past. She replayed her steps in her mind, she was sure she had made the correct moves. But if she had then she wouldn't have ended up where she was. She scolded herself and tried to work out where she had gone wrong. She surmised that it must have been when she had looked into the chasm and thrown herself off balance, she must have turned herself round whilst steadying herself and then moved in the wrong direction from there. She sat for a long moment and scrunched her eyes tight, conscious of Scaa's presence close to her she could feel his breath on her face. She tried as hard as she could to block it out whilst working out a reverse path back to where she had gone wrong. Confident that she had worked it out she began to retrace her steps, she quickly became frustrated at herself for being so conscious about leaving no trail. Had she left footprints in the soft grass and mud like most people then this would have been so much easier.

They eventually found their way back to the point where she suspected they had gone wrong. She replayed the path in her mind and confirmed that she had indeed set off the wrong way after her dizzy spell. She turned to face the way they needed to go and set off walking, this time intentionally pressing her feet into the ground to leave footprints should she go wrong again. It felt like they had been in there most of the day, but when she looked up at the sun's position she realised it had not been all that long. She was conscious however that she wanted to be through The Chasms and safe on the other side of the wall before the sun began to set.

She knew they were about halfway through the maze, and she knew what was coming next. Beside her Scaa had stopped and stood still, looking ahead. The path ahead was dissected by a chasm, she cautiously walked toward it, Scaa didn't move. As she neared the edge she got on her hands and knees and as before and crawled to the lip. Looking down, it was no different to the previous chasm she had peered into - darkness. Using her hands she tested all the ground along the edge of the drop, making sure it was sturdy enough to take her weight. She judged the distance of the crossing and figured she could make the jump without a run up. It was not much wider than a long stride so she reckoned that a static jump should do it.

She walked back to Scaa and knelt down beside him. Ruffling his ears and then putting an arm around him, she whispered in a calm voice, "It's okay boy, it's just a little jump, I'll show you how to do it then you follow. Okay?"

She checked her boot laces were fastened securely, then physically checked herself from her feet up to her head to make sure nothing was hanging loose that could catch her arms or legs and trip her up or disturb her concentration. Satisfied that she was ready, she walked to the edge.

"Okay," she said aloud, she breathed deeply, psyching herself up, "on three."

"One,"

Deep breath in.

"Two,"

Deep breath out.

"Three!"

Nothing happened. She hadn't moved from the spot where she stood, she couldn't physically bring herself to take the leap across the black void.

"Come on you can do this!" she slapped her hands against the side of her thighs a number of times. She looked at Scaa who still hadn't moved. "Come on do it, do it!" She turned back to the chasm. She crouched low preparing to push herself forward.

"One, two –"

She jumped on two, knowing that if she allowed herself to count to three her body would stop itself again. She pushed off on her left leg, driving the right leg forward and easily cleared the gap, landing softly on the other side. An instant rush of euphoria flowed through her body at her achievement. "Yes!" She congratulated herself, turning to look back at the gap she had crossed, "your turn now boy," she called to the dog. She bent forward and enthusiastically patted her legs calling him, "Come on boy, come on Scaa, you can do it boy!"

Scaa came running and in what seemed an effortless leap he cleared the divide and continued running towards Ealish without breaking his stride. She rubbed his head then lead the way on through the maze.

They crossed three more chasms, on the third Scaa took the initiative and crossed first without the need to be cheered on by Ealish. The fifth chasm they came to was no wider than any of the others, Ealish sized it up and checked the ground as she had with the previous four. As before it felt firm and sturdy, she readied herself for the jump and took a deep breath. She sprang forward off her left leg, leading with her right, out across the chasm. Her right foot touched down on the ground on the opposite side. Instantly she knew something was wrong.

The ground beneath her foot wasn't firm, the grass had grown there but it was covering loose slate shale below it. The shale started to shift as soon as her weight pressed down on it. She quickly tried to bring her left leg forward to find some grounding and to regain her balance but she was too late. Her right foot had started shifting sideways and her attempt to keep herself upright had served only to exaggerate this movement. She felt a sharp snap in her right ankle as it over extended and she let out a yell of pain as she fell sideways and backwards. Her left leg now on the ground on the other side of the chasm acted as a lever causing her body to rotate backwards faster than it should have done. The back of her head connected hard with the rock wall of the chasm and darkness threatened at the edges of her vision. She threw her hands up and desperately clawed for a hand hold as her left leg slipped into the chasm. She turned vertically and began to fall feet first. Owing to the way that she had fallen she was having to reach backwards over her head. Her right hand grabbed onto something that felt firm. Her fall was arrested and she hung there, her back scraping against the wall of rock, her feet dangling above the dark abyss scrabbling hopefully against the wall, seeking some kind of purchase.

She rotated around so that she was facing the wall, her right forearm was now starting to burn from holding her weight, she wasn't sure how long her fingers could keep a grip in this position. She searched with her left hand for something to hold onto, to take some of the pressure from her other arm. The rock face was craggy with plenty of natural handholds but whenever she tried putting any weight on them the flaky slate broke away sending shards of sharp rock and dry soil raining down onto her face and into the chasm below. Sweat and dirt mixed and ran into her eyes stinging them and blurring her vision, she could feel warm blood trickling down her neck from the open wound on the back of her head. She gripped her right wrist with her left hand and kicked her feet against the wall with all her might pulling herself upwards on her right arm. She was about an arm's length below the surface and now she looked up she could see through the dirt in her eyes that she had managed to take hold of a large gorse root that had grown through some of the smaller fissures in the rock and hung exposed over the chasm. She managed to pull herself up so that her face was almost at the level of her right hand, her knuckles had turned white and her fingers were beginning to feel numb from gripping so tight. Her eyes darted left and right seeking the next handhold. There was nothing, no more roots, no natural hollows in the rock, nothing at all. Panic was setting in. Her breathing was no longer controlled and her heart was beating so hard and fast she was sure that she could hear it.

Finding nothing to hold on to she gripped the root with her left hand too, this allowed her to relax her right and let some blood start flowing back into the fingers. She tried to control her breathing to help her think clearly. Her eyes still searching without result.

"Think! Think! There must be something!?" She shouted desperately at herself. Her feet still scraped unsuccessfully against the wall, her stomach being pushed away from and then back into it by the movement. Only it wasn't her stomach hitting the wall she realised, she suddenly had an idea. She stopped kicking her legs and she hung still and vertical for a long moment as she worked to steady her breathing. Now slightly calmer, she started preparations to implement her plan. She released her left hand from around the root, taking a tighter grip once more with her right. With her left hand she lifted the bow, that was strung about her body, over her head and let it hang on her left shoulder. Next, she lifted the coiled rope over her head and let it hang on her other shoulder. The first part done, she gripped the root again with her left hand and relaxed her right temporarily to allow it to recover. Once the tingling feeling in her right hand had subsided she let go with it completely, dropping it low she allowed the rope that was hung around her right shoulder to slide down her arm. She stopped it from falling by bending her wrist to make a natural hook that caught it. She gripped the coiled rope with her right hand and lifted it up to hang around her neck. She knew she would have to use her more capable left hand to carry out her plan so she took hold of the root again with her right. Her left hand had begun to burn with the effort of holding all her weight in the lifted position. She spent a long moment holding the root with alternating hands whilst she clenched and unclenched the other hand, preparing for the next stage of her self-rescue. Once she felt ready enough she took a firm hold with her right hand, using her left and her teeth she untied the simple knot on the rope that hung coiled around her neck. She then slowly allowed her right arm to extend, lowering her back down into the chasm - she could not hold herself up in the higher position with just one hand long enough to complete her plan.

She wiped the sweat and dirt from her eyes with the back of her left hand and then wiped it dry on her jacket. Then taking the coiled rope from around her neck she allowed the weight of the three-pronged metal hook to pull some of the rope though the loose grip of her hand, naturally uncoiling as it did so. Once enough rope had fed through her hand – what she judged to be roughly double the distance to the top of the chasm – she gripped the rope tight to prevent any more feeding through. She prepared to swing the rope and hook to the top but realised a flaw in her plan. There was no way she could generate enough swing with the hook extended below her feet, a simple error that she had made in her panicked situation. Painstakingly she had to single-handed feed the rope back through her hand, she used her left leg to trap the rope against the wall to allow her to grip the rope lower and pull it up then repeat. This wasn't easy given that the three-pronged hook constantly worked against her wanting to pull the rope into the chasm below.

Eventually she felt metal with her left hand and knew that she had fed all the rope back through, she gripped the hook in her hand and extended her arm out to her left. With as much energy as she could muster, she threw the hook upwards in a wide arcing throw. She looked up and saw it disappear from view over the top of the pit, her left hand snatched at the rope as soon as it stopped feeding upwards, knowing that the hook had ended its journey. She pulled hard on the rope, hoping that it wouldn't budge, telling her that the hook was lodged securely. That didn't happen, the rope pulled toward her, she gripped higher up and pulled again, still the rope moved, she repeated the action, the rope moved again then started to move faster. She looked up and saw the hook fall over the edge back into the chasm and toward her head.

She raised her left hand to protect her head and by nothing more than luck the hook hit her arm and fell toward her body leaving the rope trailed over her arm. She trapped the rope against her body, stopping the hook from falling into the darkness below.

She changed her grip and was able to grab the hook again and repeat the throw. Taking hold of the rope once more she pulled, her heart sank as the rope moved toward her again. Sweat beaded from her forehead mixing with the dirt, it ran down her face and into her mouth. She spat it out defiantly as she pulled the rope again, it went taut, she tested again, *definitely taut*. The prongs of the hook had done their job and snagged on something strong enough to hold fast. She let out a cry of relief. She allowed about half of her weight to be supported on the rope as a test, it held. She let go of the tree root with her right hand, thankful for the temporary reprieve. She hugged her right arm across the rope, trapping it to her body whilst she stretched out her fingers. Then she took hold of the rope with both hands, wrapping her legs around it she slowly began to climb. Every fibre in her arms ached for a rest, she knew that she wasn't far from being able to give them a well-deserved one. She was within reaching distance of the lip of the rock wall and the air smelt fresher and sweeter with every breath.

Unexpectedly the rope moved, she dropped back down into the darkness. As quickly as she began to fall, she stopped. The rope went taut and her fall was arrested with a sharp jolt. Her hands burned as they struggled to hold onto the rope. Her right arm became entangled in it, she couldn't free it and the rope tightened around her forearm, biting down onto it through her jacket. Her left hand held onto the rope. Blood seeped from between her fingers where the rough fibres had shredded her skin. She had no idea what had happened but assumed that whatever the hook had initially snagged on had moved somehow. She had to let go of the rope with her left hand to reach higher so she could try free her trapped arm. As she let go the rope tightened harder than she could have imagined, the thick leather of her jacket was all that stopped the rope biting through her skin to the bone. She let out an animalistic scream as she reached up with her free hand and gripped the rope again, taking her weight on her left arm she struggled to unravel the rope from around her right. Whilst trying to do this she failed to realise that the rope was slowly being pulled back into the chasm.

She quickly found out when she was hit in the face by an avalanche of dirt and broken rock. Above her laboured and increasingly panicked breaths she heard a noise. As she looked up through another shower of dust and shards that stung and slashed her face, she realised what had happened.

She could see Scaa's front paws silhouetted against the blue sky, scrabbling over the edge of the chasm. Before long, his head came into view. The rope held tightly in his jaw. His head being pulled low by Ealish's greater weight. She could hear Scaa whimpering as he desperately tried to pull the rope backwards and bring her to safety. His head disappeared from view again as she felt herself move upwards slightly, the hope that this gave her was short lived as he was dragged back to the edge and into her view once more, sending another load of stones and dust into her face. She looked around hoping to find something to hold on to that would let her take some of the weight off the rope. There was nothing, above her she could see the root she had originally held onto. It was well out of reach.

"Scaa, let go boy! Let go!" she screamed.

She came to a realisation that he wouldn't be able to pull her out and if he didn't let go – she would pull him into the chasm on top of her. It was no use, he held as tight as before and continued to fight against her weight. His front legs were all but over the edge now, sharp rocks rained down constantly onto Ealish's face like hundreds of tiny insect stings. She couldn't let go of the rope as her right arm was still trapped in its bindings. "Scaa? Please!", she begged, "let go, get away! Leave!"

Nothing worked.

Ealish let go with her left hand causing her weight to drop further, a larger cloud of dust fell from above as it pulled Scaa further over the edge. With her left hand now free she reached to her back, with practised movement that had been ingrained into her finger muscles she slipped the sharp hunting knife from its sheath. She reached up and ran the blade across the rope around her arm, the blade was sharp enough to slice through the taut fibres of the rope, once it was halfway through them her body weight did the rest. The rope was no longer strong enough to hold her weight and it snapped.

Scaa was thrown backward to safety by the sudden release of the weight. The hook and short length of rope still attached to it fell to the ground beside him.

Ealish and the remainder of the severed rope fell into the endless darkness.

-35-
QUEIG-JEIG AS FEED
- FLAX'S FIRST DAY ON MANNIN -

Coughing up a mouthful of tepid seawater Flax awoke, gasping for breath, he turned onto his side and coughed out more. His throat felt raw and dry from the salty water. He reached instinctively to his belt for his flask, it wasn't there. He remembered that for his travels he had chosen a larger flask and packed it in his bag, his bag that he had last seen floating away from him in the currents of The Sound.

He tried hard to remember what had happened. *How did I even come to be washed up on the beach?* The last he remembered he had been swimming and then…then he couldn't be sure. He rubbed his eyes hard trying to clear away the salt that stung them. His hands brushed over his forehead and he felt a stab of pain. He touched it again, more cautiously this time. It felt sore to the touch and swollen. He remembered now. He had hit his head on the sunken boat and then been sucked under by the current and pulled out to sea. *So where am I now?*

His head throbbed and the low autumn sun bouncing off the water shone directly into his eyes as he sat up. He blinked hard, then rubbed them again, then blinked hard once more – trying to make sense of what he could see.

He was looking at his Island! He could see the low stone walled boat dock that he had sat beside just the day before.

"But how did I get here?" He asked himself. His voice came out weak, his throat sore from the salt water he had swallowed. He sat looking back across The Sound trying to make sense of the situation, as he did so he checked himself over. Other than the bump on his head and the dull pain pulsing in his scarred arm he was fine. He didn't seem to have lost anything from his person either, the silver Faerie necklace, the waterproof waxy map, his sling and his knife were all still in their respective locations.

He put his hands either side of himself, intending to push up to a standing position, his right hand pressed onto something that wasn't stone. He looked down to see his satchel bag laid next to him, next to that laid out with a large rock on each corner to weight it down was his blanket, next to his blanket were his spare clothes, also weighted down. He looked inside the bag and his water flask was there, without question how the items got there he opened it and drank greedily. The ice-cold water soothed the heat that the salt had created in his throat. When he had drunk his fill, he turned his attention back to the bag, the snares were there as was the food he had packed. Whilst the snares could be used again most of the food was spoiled. Only the cheese, due to the way it had been wrapped, and the apples had survived. He took out the soggy dried meat, fish and bread, he nibbled at each and that was all the confirmation that he needed, he cast them into the water.

He double checked the snares and was thankful to find they were not damaged – he would be able to catch more food when needed.

He looked at the sun's position and judged it to be after lunch. Whilst he didn't feel all that hungry he knew that he had to eat. He had used a lot of energy swimming and was losing more as he sat shivering on the beach. He ate one of the apples and some of the cheese, soon realising just how hungry he was.

As he ate he tried to work out how not just he, but his items too, had come to be on the beach. It was clear that somebody had rescued him, nothing else could explain it. His clothes and blanket had been taken from the wet bag and placed out to dry. But his bag had been floating ahead of him on the current, whoever had saved him had also rescued his belongings. He looked left and right along The Sound, there was no sign of any other boat nearby save for the one The Traveller had left in the dry dock.

He pushed himself to his feet, his legs felt heavy and weak from the swim that nearly cost him his life. He turned in a full circle trying to make sense of how he came to be on the beach. There was nothing near him with the exception of his belongings, now he was stood he also noticed that his staff - still wrapped, lay on the floor close by to him. He looked to the Island hoping to see some movement or sign of life that might indicate it was one of his fellow Islanders who had come to his rescue. There was nothing, *Anyway they would have stayed until I was awake and checked I was okay*, he told himself. It was on the second, slower turn that he turned that he noticed it.

High on the cliff top away to the east there was a silhouette, no real detail was visible due to the distance and the angle of the sun in his eyes but it was definitely the figure of a person. Something suddenly triggered in Flax's mind and the image of the warrior with the spear from his *ashlishyn* flashed across his vision.

Had this person helped me?

Why didn't they stay to speak to me? Flax questioned. The figure did not move, Flax could tell that it was facing towards him and it was clear that the person could see him but they made no attempt to move toward him or to communicate in any way.

Cautiously, Flax raised an arm and gave an uncertain wave to the shadowy figure. Inadvertently his arm blocked the sun from his view and his eyes quickly adjusted, sharpening his vision. He saw that the figure wore a dark, hooded cloak, he also thought the figure to have a darker skin tone than his own. He could tell that it was a male and for a moment he could have sworn it to be The Traveller.

Why would he leave only to wait about for me?. Only the figure did not wait about, as soon as Flax had begun to wave the figure turned from him and walked out of sight along the cliff line to the east. As the figure turned Flax noticed a detail on the stranger he hadn't seen until now, his right arm was significantly shorter than the left, as if part of it were missing.

-36-
SHEY-JEIG AS FEED

The stranger turned his back on the golden-haired Islander on the beach below.

He had not wished to intervene, *it was not yet time.* But he had been given no choice. The boy would have surely drowned without his assistance.

In his mind he questioned if the boy was up to the task before him, given that he had nearly failed at the very first step.

Only time will tell.

As the stranger walked away he stopped to pick up his possessions, that had been placed neatly on the ground.

A spear, the wooden shaft curiously joined in three distinct sections, the sharpened head a smooth black stone with a deadly point and serrated edges.

The other item – a shield made from the pelt of a creature, soft to the eye and the touch but as hard as precious stones to any weapon that tried to cleave it.

The stranger fitted the shield to his right arm – or what remained of it – it fitted more like a gauntlet than a shield. Once in place his right arm looked no shorter than his left.

He stopped and for a long moment gazed at the sea far below. His mind lost in the continuous motion of the waves.

He snapped back to his senses and strode out along the cliff path to his next destination.

-37-
SHIAGHT-JEIG AS FEED
- FLAX'S FIRST DAY ON MANNIN -

Flax slowly trudged along the beach, cold seawater squelched from his wet boots with each step. He had gathered up the clothes and blanket, they weren't yet dry but he couldn't afford to wait all day whilst they did. When he set up camp later on he would light a fire to help them dry quicker. He had slung his bag about his shoulder with the wrapped staff attached to it, then set off in the same direction as the stranger he had seen on the cliff top. The stranger who – he could only assume – had earlier that day, and for some unknown reason, saved his life.

Whilst he had trained hard since waking up from his long-imposed sleep he still tired quickly and his progress was slower than he would have liked. He didn't want to admit it, but the swim had been tough on his body, as had the near drowning. His legs ached and he could have quite happily set up camp for the remainder of the day on the edge of the beach above the tide line. How he would have loved to sit and watch his Island from a different perspective. Seeing aspects of it from new angles for the first time in his life.

The cold metal of the Faerie hung around his neck reminded him that he could not do that. He had a mission, a purpose that he must fulfil. The words of Flea's mother repeated again in his mind, '*Let it be a reminder of your true purpose.*' He was still not sure he fully understood the weight and the meaning of her words.

As he walked he gripped the pendant between his thumb and forefinger pondering the words. He noticed that no matter how much he held it, the metal never warmed to the touch. It remained ice cold.

He assessed the steadily rising path before him, it meandered through a couple of low-lying meadows before climbing steeply in a direct line up onto the cliffs. He knew that his sister had walked this very path not so long ago. He walked along it looking at the ground, searching for signs that she had been there. Of course he knew that his sister was too careful to leave footprints. In any case it was many nights since she had passed through and the weather would have washed away any such prints.

He slowly continued, not willing to lift his gaze from his feet in case the seeming impossibility of the climb overcame him. He had to make progress, no matter how small, before he would allow himself to rest. With every energy sapping step his legs felt increasingly heavier, his mind could focus on nothing other than the staff that was strapped across his bag knocking against his back every time he moved. It frustrated him to the point of anger in his exhausted state. Reluctantly, he stopped to take it from his back, deciding he would use it as a walking stick. The cloth it was wrapped in was still cold and damp from the sea water, he worked the knots in the twine that held it and they steadily loosened to the point where he could start to unwrap the cloth from the top of the staff to bottom. He realised instantly that something wasn't right, this wasn't his staff! He unwrapped it fully and held it. He sat back on the hillside and turned the wooden staff over and over in his hands.

Not his staff, his father's staff.

The one he rarely saw him without.

He had studied it before, he knew every detail of it. Made from the same strange dark wood as Ealish's bow and arrows. A number of grooves were cut around the circumference near to the top, perfect grips for fingers when using it as a walking pole. In a small recess where the thumb sat was his father's brand, the blackened silhouette of The Tree. The staff itself was carved with intricate swirls and patterns and down the centre at the front of it three words were etched. They brought tears to his eyes as he heard his father saying them in his head *Traa Dy Liooar*. Two sections of the shaft were undecorated and the wood was polished to a smooth finish, these allowed the staff to be held two handed as a weapon. He had never seen his father use the weapon in anger but had heard from The Traveller the account of his father killing twelve Longtails on the night of the attack.

Flax was numbed as he sat there appraising the staff over and over. The fact that he was sat holding it brought back to him the realisation that it was only possible because his father lay poisoned.

It was clear that his mother had switched it with his own staff at some point after he had said goodbye to his sleeping father. Because when he had last visited him, the staff had still been clutched to his chest. At first seeing it saddened him. But the more he thought about it, the more positive he became. He was alone in this strange land but he no longer felt it. He had something of his fathers, something so familiar to him that it felt like a piece of his father was with him. He smiled and pushed himself to his feet with a newfound energy, his legs were still tired but he no longer felt the sapping exhaustion that he had before.

He was unaware of how long he had been sat but he noticed the sun was on its downward journey toward the horizon. He turned and pushed on up the hill, the staff now gripped firmly in his right hand, aiding him with every step, his fingers tightly curled around the lovingly carved wood. His thumb pressed purposefully onto the brand of The Tree.

As he climbed he noticed that he was now pinned onto this route, trapped between the gorse plants on his left and the cliffs to his right. This didn't bother him, he walked steadily and cast his gaze around taking in the environment, out of pure interest at the new land in which he found himself. He was unknowingly a lot less cautious than his sister had been when she trod this very same path, he did not envisage himself encountering any kind of threat and his thoughts were on progression along the route and nothing more.

He followed the twists and turns for some time, the light continued to fade as the sun sank lower and lower toward the sea. He was aware of this and pushed himself to move faster. His legs burned with the exertion but he continued on, keen to find a suitable place to spend the night.

He was no stranger to spending the night outside under the stars. He fondly remembered nights spent out on the hills of the Island with his family. His mother and father would point out patterns in the stars to him and his sister. On occasions they would see streaks of light moving quickly through the night sky, '*shooting stars!*' his mother called them, they fascinated him. Even now he would often spend nights outside hoping to glimpse the shooting stars.

He remembered one such night when Flea had joined him. They had hiked up one of the hills with a picnic and shared a meal together before lying down and star gazing. He had pointed out the same patterns in the stars that his parents had taught him. They had given them all their own names to remember them by. He remembered how after pointing them all she had just laid there in silent awe and wonder, her eyes sparkling with the reflection of a million tiny lights in the sky. Flax had turned on his side and whilst Flea had watched the stars, he had watched her. He hadn't thought of that night for so long but now it warmed him to remember it. He had never talked honestly with Flea about the way he felt for her. He had always just hoped, and assumed, that she knew and that she felt the same. Little did he know that most of the Islanders also knew how he felt about Flea, they had been almost inseparable for most of their lives. He felt the ice-cold pendant against his chest and instinctively his hand raised to grasp it between his fingers, "Next time I get chance I will tell her," her told himself out loud.

His progress in the later part of the afternoon had been much faster than the earlier part and before long he found himself at a high point close to a strange pile of rocks. The path here was slightly wider and it turned sharply left at the cliff edge. He quickly appraised the site and decided it would be suitable for him to spend the night, he didn't think much to the prospect of walking any further in his tired condition in failing light next to a perilous drop.

He unpacked the damp clothes, blanket and the cloth that had been wrapped around his father's staff and he laid them out, placing small rocks on them to hold them down. Next, he got on his hands and knees and rummaged around the edge of the gorse forest, careful not to catch his arms or face on the barbed plants. He found what he had hoped for, plenty of dead fallen branches from the plants. They felt dry enough, they were protected from moisture by the plants above and the ground was fairly dry as any rainfall quickly drained away and what remained was sucked from the ground by the gorse plants. He took off his leather jacket and used it to protect his hands as he lifted the spiked dead wood and carried it to his makeshift camp site. He piled them up leaving a small hollow beneath, in here he placed a small strip of the cloth that had been wrapped around the staff. The cloth had soaked up some of the oil from Flax's staff before his mother made the switch. So even in its slightly damp state it didn't take long for it to catch a spark as he struck the blade of his hunting knife against the fire striker from the base of the handle. He coaxed the spark by gently blowing it, a small flame flickered and took hold. Before long the wood was ablaze and Flax was bathed in the warm glow of the dancing orange flames, a black finger of smoke curled up into the sky.

He had noticed some animal droppings beneath the gorse plants so he returned and set a couple of snares in what he thought to be the most likely places for him to catch some food, hoping to bolster his decimated supply.

He returned to the warmth of the fire, and as he sat he gazed west and silently watched the half-sunken sun throw rays of orange, pink, purple and strangely some green across the thin feathery clouds. They created a blanket of colour in the sky over his Island. Sunset was one of his favourite times of day for this very reason, each and every one was unique. The perfect sunset needed just the right amount of clouds, at just the right height and just the right density. This evening he was lucky enough to have just the right conditions. As he sat and ate some fruit from his remaining rations he thought of nothing more than the moment he was in. He laid back against the pile of stones and before long was struggling to keep his eyes open, the events of the day getting the better of him.

Flax fell into a deep dreamless sleep, oblivious to the pair of yellow eyes that watched him from within the gorse forest.

-38-
HOGHT-JEIG AS FEED

The eyes did not belong to an animal, nor did they belong to a human. The creature whom they belonged to watched the figure that lay asleep against the pile of stones.

The watcher had been observing the golden-haired male for most of the afternoon. Ever since he saw him approaching the gorse forest up the hill.

There were not many who travelled this path but the watcher saw all who did. There had been a few in recent days, including a golden-haired female who carried a formidable looking bow and arrows.

This male was less aware of his surroundings than the female had been, he carried a stick and the watcher had also noticed a knife on his belt.

The watcher waited for quite some time and saw that the male did not stir, he dared to move forward onto the path. He paused and waited, then waited some more. Still the male did not move.

The watcher crept forward. His yellow eyes keenly fixed on the sleeping form.

The watcher stopped as the male turned his head to look directly at him.

The glowing embers cast orange light across the face of the male, his eyes still closed tight in slumber.

The watcher continued his cautious progress toward the male. He observed the objects laid on the floor around the fire. Items of clothing, the stick, a bag, a blanket that was half pulled over the male's legs.

The watcher took hold of the stick and lifted it from the ground, finding it too cumbersome and long for him he placed it back down then turned his attention to the bag.

Quietly rummaging through the bag he found some food items. He took a piece of the fruit and placed it inside his pocket. He turned his head back toward the male and eyed him suspiciously, checking that he was not being observed, the watcher did not like to be seen.

He turned his attention back to the bag, seeing what else he could find. He took out a block of something wrapped in wax paper, he lifted it to his nose and sniffed, *cheese*, he placed that inside his pocket too.

The male stirred slightly. Not wanting to outstay his welcome the watcher retreated slowly backwards to the gorse forest, never taking his yellow eyes off the golden-haired male.

-39-
NUY-JEIG AS FEED
- FLAX'S SECOND DAY ON MANNIN -

Flax's eyes snapped open. He didn't know how long he had been asleep but daylight was breaking across the sky from the east.

The fire in front of him had all but died, a few of the coals held small flecks of orange on them and he could see the last of the heat rising from it into the cold autumn air.

He was unsure as to why he had woken so abruptly, then he remembered he had heard something, *but what was it?*

He sat forward from the pile of stones and stretched his arms out. He heard a scuffling sound away to his right - *the snares.*

He stood – his legs no longer aching from the exertion of the previous day – and turned toward the gorse forest and the snares he had set the previous evening.

He scanned from left to right, noticing that the first snare was empty and still set. The second however had caught something, and *something* was entirely the right word to use.

Flax had been hoping to catch a rabbit or a hare, what he had caught was neither.

Staring at Flax with a pair of eyes that were bright yellow, was a peculiar creature that stood roughly just more than half Flax's height and was squat and muscular in build – caught by its left ankle in the self-tightening snare. It wore a pair of brown trousers that looked to be made from a thick heavy fabric, the kind of which Flax had never seen before. Its feet, upper body and arms were bare – well not exactly, they were covered in a coarse spiky brown hair, not uniform enough in its coverage to be classed as a fur. Around the waist of its trousers was a leather belt and attached to that belt was a menacing looking club, tapered to a handle at one end, the other end was much wider and with a multitude of spikes protruding from it at varying angles. Flax recognised the spikes instantly, they were from the gorse plant, now he looked more closely the entire club was fashioned from a branch of a gorse bush.

The creature's head was covered in a similar hair but was groomed into a plaited ponytail, as was its beard. The skin that was visible on the face looked tough, like old leather that had been left to the elements.

"Well," came a gruff and completely unexpected voice, "let us out then!" demanded the creature.

"You can talk?" Flax replied in surprise.

"Course I talk. Idiot! Thinks I can't talk, does he?"

"Who are you talking to?" Flax asked, still in wonderment at the sight of the trapped creature before him.

"You! Course! Thinks I'm talking to someone else? Nobody else here! Let us out!"

"I'm sorry," Flax stuttered, "I just didn't expect you to talk that's all."

"Course I talk! Idiot!"

"So you said already," Flax couldn't help but laugh.

"Not funny. Let us out!"

The accent and the style of speech was so strange to Flax that he struggled to contain any further laughter, however the anger shown by the creature and the fact he had the spiked club attached to his belt helped him decide that unduly annoying him further would not be the best idea, even if he was currently caught in Flax's snare.

Flax carefully stepped toward the creature and knelt down to release the snare, being sure to keep one eye on the weapon that hung menacingly close to his face.

The metal wire of the snare was strong and would bite hard into the skin and flesh of any animal caught in it. As he released it from around the creature's ankle Flax could see that it had barely left a mark on the thick hair covered skin of the creature.

After releasing the snare, which required fingers nimbler than those of the creature to work the mechanism, Flax allowed his eyes to meet the creature's. Neither of them spoke, neither of them blinked, rich green-brown bore into dazzling yellow. Flax spoke first "You're welcome."

"Welcome is it!" shouted the creature, "welcome? Could have killed us, idiot! Been trapped here most of the night!" The creature looked down at his ankle and rubbed it.

"I apologised already, and I am not an idiot," Flax replied defensively. "An idiot would be someone who, having stupidly gotten themselves caught in a snare, then finding themselves unable to get out, simply sat all night instead of doing the obvious thing – asking for help. Then, upon receiving said help not even uttering a word of thanks. That would be the behaviour of an idiot." With that Flax turned his back on the creature, inwardly smiling at his well worded response, oblivious to the club being unclipped from the creature's belt.

Flax walked back to his makeshift campsite and started to collect his things together. He gathered up the clothes and blanket, which due to the light morning dew were still not completely dried yet and folded them into his bag.

The creature had taken a step closer, the club held menacingly in his right hand. The anger at having been called an idiot clear on his face.

Suddenly Flax reached for his staff, taking it in one hand, as he came standing to full height he wheeled on the creature and held the staff at arm's length toward it.

"My food!" he said, the accusation clear in his voice, "you stole my food!"

The creature still held the club in his right hand but let it hang loosely at his side, there was no way he could outmatch Flax given the reach advantage that the staff held over the club.

"Didn't steal. Borrowed. Needed it."

"And so did I!" protested Flax, "Give it back!"

"Can't," came the simple reply.

"Why not?"

"Eaten it," the creature said, shrugging his shoulders. "Told you, been stuck all night," and with that he turned toward the gorse forest, ducked low on his hands and knees and started to crawl under the bushes muttering inaudibly to himself.

Flax watched dumbfounded for a moment, frozen in disbelief at the brazen honesty of the creature, *no honesty was not the right word,* thought Flax. *It was blatant thievery!* and he decided to do something about it. Even though he was only a short distance from him, the creature was beginning to disappear from sight, its coarse brown hair almost indistinguishable from the mess of branches and grass beneath the canopy of the gorse forest.

Flax dashed forward onto his hands and knees, he had to reach into the branches but managed to take the creature by one of its feet. He gave a hard yank backwards.

"Oi! Let us go!" The creature protested, trying to pull its leg free. This only encouraged Flax to try harder, he reached forward with his other arm too and taking hold of the same leg gave an almighty heave. The creature yowled, Flax was unsure if this was in pain or in remonstration, most likely both given that he had taken hold of a handful of the hair around the creature's leg. It almost felt sharp to the touch but this didn't dissuade him from hauling the creature back into the morning sunlight from its shady hideout.

The creature was strong, but Flax was stronger and had a clear weight advantage. It came out from beneath the gorse feet first and face down. Flax instantly capitalised on this and laid himself across the creature, effectively pinning him to the ground. Beneath him he could feel the creature fighting to get from beneath his weight, however Flax was able to quickly counter every move he made by shifting his weight slightly or using an arm or a leg to pin whichever limb the creature was trying to wiggle free. Eventually he felt the creature give up, whether through exhaustion or resignation to the loss, it didn't matter to Flax. He sat atop the creature as he took off the length of rope, that in his tiredness the previous night he had neglected to remove from around his body. He bound the creature's hands tightly behind its back and then when he was satisfied that he had secured the thief he finally relaxed his weight and sat to the side, keeping a tight hold of the rope with one hand.

"Firstly," Flax breathed heavily due to the exertion it took to subdue the thief, "you owe me an apology for calling me an idiot." He gave a sharp tug on the ropes to emphasise this point and then he waited. No apology came, he gave another sharp tug, "I can wait all day."

The creature muttered something inaudible.

"I can't hear you," Flax replied, turning the creature onto its side and then pulling him up into a sitting position so that he could face his captive. He sat and stared into the yellow eyes, waiting expectantly. He was unsure how long he had sat there but he clearly made his point as the creature was first to break the silence.

"Sorry…"

"Sorry for what?"

"Calling you idiot," the creature said with a look that made it seem like each word tasted awful.

"That's a start," Flax declared pushing himself to stand, still breathing heavily, sweat starting to bead along his forehead beneath his golden hair. He looked at his arms and noticed that they were streaked with blood. He hadn't realised at the time but when he had reached in to grab the creature the spiky gorse bushes had cut into his forearms, the cuts were not deep and the blood had already started to dry. "And Secondly –" he continued, "– you owe me some food to replace what you stole, what is there around here that I can eat?" He cast his eye across the gorse forest seeing nothing that looked remotely edible, let alone appetising.

"Worms is good," offered the creature.

Now it was Flax's turn to look like he had a bad taste in his mouth. "You eat worms?"

"Sometimes," the creature shrugged, "easier to catch than hoppers."

"Hoppers?"

"Yep hoppers. Big ears, fluffy tail, pointy –"

"– Oh you mean rabbits?" Flax interrupted.

"Yep, hoppers. Not easy to catch, fast they is."

Flax was slowly getting used to the strange manner in which the creature spoke, he wondered to himself where he lived and more than that, *what was he?* He looked down at him sat on the floor, his hands tied behind his back, defenceless. He couldn't help but feel sorry for the creature, despite the fact he had stolen food from him.

He must have been hungry to resort to stealing, thought Flax. He had never been truly hungry in his life, he had never had to go without food for more than half a day so he had no idea what it would feel like to be truly in need of food, and in turn he no idea what measures he would resort to in order to get food in such a situation. The anger that he had previously felt toward the creature had subsided completely, it was not in his nature to be an angry person or to hold a grudge.

He knelt down behind the creature and worked his fingers at the knot he had hastily tied during the struggle.

"What you doing?" Called the creature, unable to turn his head to see - panic and uncertainty were heavy in his voice.

"Just hold still a moment."

Flax managed to loosen the bonds enough to pull them over the stubby hands of the creature. As he did, he said, "I am sorry if I hurt you, I didn't mean to."

"Hrmphh!" exhaled the creature as he brought his arms round to a more natural position by his side. By this Flax could tell that the only thing that was hurt was the creature's pride.

He had expected to see him scuttle away under the gorse but instead he sat there, not moving. Flax stood and walked over to his bag. He took out the two remaining apples, leaving just one piece of cheese remaining in the bag. He eyed the apples in his hand, then without hesitation threw one to the creature, who had been watching him carefully. Flax was surprised at the speed with which the creature reacted and caught the apple cleanly with one hand. He quickly bit into the flesh of it, juice running from his mouth and down his beard into the hair on his bare chest.

The creature stopped, aware that Flax had not started eating and was watching with curiosity.

"Thanks," the creature said through a second mouthful of fruit, and with that Flax sat and in silence ate his own apple, still watching the strange creature.

-40-
DAEED
- FLAX'S SECOND DAY ON MANNIN -

"Flax."

"What's a Flax?"

"I'm a Flax. I mean my name is Flax, that's who I am," Flax explained when they had both finished eating.

"From that Island," this wasn't a question. It was a statement.

"Yes I am, have you ever been there?" Flax asked, eager to talk of his home.

"No, can't swim," the creature replied bluntly, "don't like water."

"Oh right," Flax replied, "there are boats that can get you there you know? In fact - I would definitely not recommend trying to swim there." Flax said with a knowing smile on his face as he recalled his near deadly swim the previous morning.

"Don't like water," the creature replied gruffly, giving nothing more away.

"What do you like?"

"Grub," the creature said eyeing Flax's bag greedily.

"Well I know that, and there's not much left so that apple will have to do for now until we can catch something."

"Hopper?" The creature asked, with a genuine look of excitement on his face.

"Yes a hopper, come on you can help."

Flax walked over and offered a hand to the creature to help him to his feet, he didn't take the offer but stood and picked up his spiked club.

"We won't need that," Flax explained holding up the snare that he had released the creature from that morning. He walked to where he had set the other snare the previous night, hoping to find it had worked but it was empty. He picked it up and walked along the cliff path until a bend took them from out of view of his camp site, he then got on his hands and knees and crawled along the edge of the gorse forest staring intently at the ground. All the while the creature stood back at a slight distance watching him with interest.

"Droppings?" He asked in his minimalist conversational manner.

"Exactly," Flax replied.

Flax found what looked to be a recent trail with droppings along it so he stopped and carefully set one of the snares. He stood and looked around, he noticed some small plants that he recognised as dandelions. They had managed to grow on the side of the path, just outside the shade cast by the gorse plants. He picked some of the leaves and pulled up their roots, laying them as bait at the mouth of the snare.

"Here," called the creature. Flax turned to see that the creature had imitated Flax in looking for a possible place to put the other snare. Flax walked over and assessed the ground that the creature was pointing at, it looked promising. He set the second snare and laid some more dandelions as bait.

With the snares set Flax had no option now but to return to the campsite and wait, he was desperate to make progress along the coast but with only one small block of cheese he wouldn't get too far before having to stop to find food. He hoped that the snares were far enough away that his, and the creature's presence, would not dissuade rabbits from venturing out to eat in the early morning light before the sun rose too high.

Back at the campsite he stoked at the embers of his fire from the night before. They had all but died but when he held his hand over them there was definite heat there. He rummaged around for some dried gorse branches and found more than enough. Placing them on the warm ashes he was able to coax the fire back to life again without need of his knife and fire striker. He wanted the coals to be nice and hot as he was hopeful that before long his snares would catch something.

"Kibbin," he heard the creature say behind him.

"Pardon."

"Kibbin, I'm Kibbin, means –"

"– Spike," interrupted Flax, "Kibbin means spike in the old tongue, right?"

"Yup," nodded Kibbin the creature.

"Where do you come from Kibbin?" asked Flax.

"Here, course." It became apparent to Flax that he would have to ask questions a certain way to get the answers he desired. Kibbin was clearly not one for giving too much information away and would answer in as few words as possible. Not, Flax suspected, through any distrust – it simply appeared to be his way.

"Sorry I mean, where specifically? Where do you live?"

Kibbin didn't answer, he just pointed to the dense spiky gorse forest that lined the path.

"You live in there?" Flax asked

Kibbin nodded.

"But do you have a house or a home in there?"

Kibbin didn't answer but instead asked Flax a question of his own, "Where you going to?"

Flax thought about his answer before he gave it, he knew his sister would be curious before telling anything to a stranger. He wondered if he should tell him anything at all. After all, he had no idea who Kibbin was or who he was loyal to in this land. *He could be allies with the Longtails or the Faeries.* He was about to answer when he was interrupted by a sound that he recognised.

He stood, and as he did he heard the sound once more. He couldn't believe his luck as he walked toward the snares and found that a rabbit had been caught in eachone. It temporarily saddened him to see the defenceless creatures lying dead in the traps he had set, but he knew that he needed the food to survive. The traps had killed the animals near instantly so he knew that they hadn't suffered long. Kibbin shuffled up to one of the snares, having earlier seen Flax release it from his ankle, he was able to quickly release the carcass.

"Yummy Hopper," he said to himself as he lifted the rabbit and walked back toward the campsite, leaving the snare on the floor. Flax too released his rabbit and reset both of the snares before walking back to the fire.

At the camp he expertly skinned and butchered the rabbits then set them to cook on the coals of the fire. All the while Kibbin watched him closely, taking in the movements of the knife and the way the meat was prepared. Flax was sure he could see him salivating as the food cooked.

As Kibbin watched the food, Flax watched Kibbin. He was fascinated by the creature and was desperate to ask him more questions, the main one being – *'What are you?'* But he resisted the temptation for now, he didn't want to offend or anger him.

Before long the rabbit was cooked. Flax set half of the meat to one side and then divided the remaining meat into two portions. He placed half of the meat on a flat stone in front of Kibbin and encouraged him to eat. He didn't need much encouragement, nor did Flax. They both ate greedily in silence. Sea birds overhead showed interest, this didn't go unnoticed by Kibbin who kept his spiked club close to hand. Flax had no doubt that anyone or anything that tried to take food from him would have a bloody fight on their hands.

Once they had eaten Flax started to pack away the camp site. He wrapped the remaining cooked meat in the wrapper from the cheese that Kibbin had eaten the night before. He placed it carefully inside his bag with the remaining block of cheese and his spare clothes and blanket. He recoiled the rope he had used to bind Kibbin and placed it over one shoulder. He spread out the embers of the fire and placed some large flat stones on top to cover them over. Scanning around he checked that he had not left anything, his staff was leant against the pile of stones, he walked over to collect it.

"Got to add a stone," Kibbin called to him.

Flax turned to look at him, unsure what he meant.

"To the pile," Kibbin insisted pointing one of his stubby fingers in the direction of the heaped stones. "Called a cairn, everyone adds a stone," as he said this, he picked up a small stone from the floor and walked over to hand it to Flax.

Kibbin was too short to reach the top of the cairn so Flax took it from him and placed it on top of the pile. It seemed a strange ritual but he didn't wish to offend Kibbin. As he stood back and observed the cairn something occurred to Flax, *there were hundreds of stones in this pile.* That meant hundreds of people must have used this path over time, how had he never seen anybody walking this cliff line when he was on the Island?

"Kibbin, have you seen people put stones on here before?"

"Course. See everyone who comes by."

Flax thought of his sister.

"Kibbin did you see a girl? A woman? With golden hair like mine?"

"A female? Course."

"When Kibbin? When did you see her?"

"Hmm, 'bout two weeks ago."

"Weeks?" Flax hadn't heard this term before.

"Week, week is seven days," Kibbin explained as if Flax was stupid.

"So fourteen days?" Flax said as he subconsciously submitted the meaning of the term week into his mind.

"Course," replied Kibbin, "tried to talk to her. Silly female ran off. Only wanted grub."

It was not like his sister to run from anything thought Flax, she was a hunter, and a very skilled one at that. He thought it more likely that Kibbin would have ended up with an arrow embedded in himself for his troubles. *Would an arrow pierce that thick skin?* Flax wondered as he eyed Kibbin's hair covered hide. When he had been wrestling him from the gorse bush it felt thick, like the bark of a tree. *It would have to be for him to move through the gorse forest without causing himself serious injury.*

"Where did she go? Did she say anything?" Flax questioned

Kibbin pointed a hand in the direction of the path to the east and said, "Ran off."

"Thanks," Flax said as he set off walking in that direction, bag and staff in hand.

"Hang on!" Called Kibbin, breaking into a trot to keep up with Flax on account of his much shorter legs. "Who's the female?"

Flax didn't answer immediately, he questioned as to whether he should share anything about himself, his family or his mission with Kibbin. Instead he replied with a question, just as Kibbin had earlier.

"Why should I tell you? What is it to you?"

"Just wonderin'. Not seen anybody for over a season, very quiet. Now four folk in two weeks!"

"Four?" Flax replied without even thinking of who the other two could be.

"Yup, gold-haired female, dark-skinned male with hood, dark-skinned male with one arm, then you." Once again Kibbin was blunt with his answer.

Of course, thought Flax, *the Traveller and the Stranger had both walked this way in the last two days.* Kibbin truly did see all who passed. Flax reached the snares that he had reset and was disappointed to find them both empty. He gathered them into his bag and slung it over his shoulder, ready now to continue on his journey.

"Well it was nice to have met you Kibbin, I am sorry that I had to tie you up but hopefully you understand."

"Wait, the female? Tell us who she is."

"Why are you so interested?" challenged Flax. He wondered again about who Kibbin might be allied to. But he could see instantly that there was no malice or ill meaning in Kibbin's line of questioning when he shrank back at Flax's challenge.

"Just wondered. Like knowin' stuff, you asked 'bout her first, see?"

He made a valid point, it was Flax who had first mentioned her, he could see no harm in disclosing who she was.

"She is my sister, Ealish."

"Ay-lish!" Replied Kibbin as if the word had surprised him. "Where's she goin'?"

"Honestly," Flax paused "I can't be sure, but I need to find her."

"Why?"

"Because…because both she and I need to save some people very dear to us," Flax thought of Flea and his Father, he had not thought of them since waking that morning and he instantly felt guilty because of it.

"Save from where?"

"Not from where, well not exactly, more of from who," Flax said.

"Bet them rats did it!" Kibbin replied angrily, Flax noticed a change in his body language and his voice.

"You've seen the Longtails?" he asked – urgency and desperation heavy in his voice.

"Course." replied Kibbin.

-41-
NANE AS DAEED
- FLAX'S SECOND DAY ON MANNIN -

Flax walked steadily, accounting for the slower, more relaxed pace of Kibbin. He listened intently as the creature talked in his strange fashion. His conversation had initially been minimal, but at the mention of the Longtails it was as if he could hold his tongue no more and he opened up, telling Flax the history of his kind.

Kibbin explained that his ancestors had lived in the forest in the *Shenn* region and that they had fought in the great battle in support of the King of Mannin against those who had revolted to try and seize power, those who ultimately became the Longtails. His ancestors were part of a small group who had been sent forward as scouts to infiltrate the enemy camp and learn of their battle plans. But one of the group, having spent time amongst the enemy, altered his allegiances and defected. In doing so he disclosed the identity of the other spies. Many of the scouts were captured, tortured and killed – their broken bodies left on view in the camp as warning.

Those that weren't caught fled and were pursued relentlessly, most were quickly captured and taken back to the battle camp to face the same fate as the others. One group had been hunted for days by their enemy, in desperation they had crawled into one of the many gorse forests found across Mannin seeking refuge beneath the spiky branches. The pursuers had kept watch on the edges of the forest for days, indiscriminately shooting arrows and launching spears into the forest in the hope of hitting their quarry. They lit fires along the edge of the forest to prevent escape, this forced the group deeper into the forest. There they remained for seasons, hiding in fear. They were unaware of the outcome of the war or even that the revolting army had been banished to *Guinn Y Vaaish*. They remained in hiding – fearful of what may happen if they were caught, having witnessed first-hand the horrors that were inflicted upon their captured comrades. They lived off small animals such as mice and rabbits along with whatever edible plants they could find growing amongst the dense vegetation. When food supplies were low, they resorted to digging in the soil for worms or other bugs to eat just to stay alive.

Seasons became years and over time the group hiding in the gorse physically changed, adapting to their environment. They left the forest infrequently, choosing to remain hidden and safe. Over generations they became shorter in stature so that they could move below the canopy with ease, their skin grew thick and tough to prevent the sharp spikes causing them injury. Thick coarse hair grew all over their bodies, this helped to camouflage them amongst the brown lower branches when they came close to the edges of the forest. Their eyes had all changed from the greens, browns and blues that they once were to the bright yellow that they were now. This yellow was the same colour as the flowers that grew on the gorse bushes, again this helped them to blend into their environment. The group used this camouflage to their advantage and relying on their skills in espionage and scouting they became gatherers of information – listening to conversations, observing movements, stealing useful items when possible. Some of the information they learned they would trade but Kibbin offered no further comment on this as to who with or for what.

Kibbin told tales of how he had stood within touching distance of people who had no idea that he was there. Flax was fascinated and saddened to hear the story. He saw similarities between the story told by Kibbin and that of the Longtails told to him by The Traveller - but the Longtails' misery was of their own doing. Kibbin's ancestors' was not, they were working to prevent the war that came. Of course they eventually learned of the outcome of the war and those surviving that had been part of the uprising had been banished to *Vaaish* where they too had physically altered and become the race known as the Longtails. By the time this information was learned, and confirmed through eavesdropping on multiple accounts, the group had already begun to transform and they decided not to return to their former home. Only the Longtails that had chased the group into the forest knew of their existence, they had long since passed and over the generations they were simply forgotten about.

The group referred to themselves as the *Moanee*, which simply means moor in the old language - this chosen as they lived in the gorse forests found on the moors across Mannin. In the common language they referred to themselves as Moor-men - there were of course females within their population but the umbrella term of men was still applied.

The Moor-men had grown slowly in number over the years but were far fewer than the Longtails. As each generation was raised, they were taught to both fear and hate the Longtails from an early age. The entire history of their race stemmed from the pain caused at the hand of them. The main population of Moor-men was in the mountain region, on the slopes of a great mountain named South Barrule, here they had excavated a series of underground chambers and tunnels beneath the gorse forest. However Moor-men were posted across Mannin to listen and gather information on the comings and goings. Kibbin, along with two others, was posted to the southern region of Mannin. He would not say where the other two currently were but he did say that he was the only one of his kind in the immediate area. His task had been to watch the southern coastal path and the water crossing to the Island.

"You watch The Sound? The water? Did you see who rescued me?"

"Rescued you? Didn't see you cross. Lookin' for grub." Kibbin went on to describe how he had been in the area since the start of the summer season but it had been difficult to find food since arriving. The *'hoppers'* were too wary of him and too fast whenever he got near, so he had been surviving on plants and worms. There was little opportunity for him to steal food given the remoteness of the location - until he had seen Flax sleeping that was.

"You said you have seen the Longtails?"

"Course," replied Kibbin in his usual way. Flax smiled inwardly, he had quickly become used to this reply - so much so he could predict when he received the one-word response.

Flax waited for him to explain more but he didn't, he hadn't given anything away unprompted – Flax had asked countless questions as they walked to get the information from Kibbin. In that time they had followed the cliff path as it wound its way east, dropping down and over a small stream at one point before climbing once more, this time with less densely growing heather bushes along the side of the path. The scenery was stunning, Flax had taken little of his surroundings in but every now and again he would avert his gaze from either Kibbin or the path ahead to appreciate the landscape around him.

He had lost track of the time and how late in the day it had become, the sun was now behind them and low in the sky. Ahead of them he could see a wall, the first sign of any civilisation he had seen on Mannin, with the exception of Kibbin - *if he could pass for civilised*, Flax thought as he eyed him.

As they neared the wall Kibbin took a left turn through a narrow pathway and into a clearing, "Stay here tonight," he announced.

Flax hadn't given any thought as to where he might stay but now he was in the rounded clearing it seemed as good a place as any. As he looked around he noticed strange stones surrounding the circle but thought nothing more of them.

"You're staying too?" he questioned Kibbin, "not that you're not welcome," he added, not wanting to cause any offence. "It's just, well if you don't mind me asking … why are you still here?"

"Grub," replied Kibbin pointing to Flax's bag.

Flax laughed as he sat down against one of the stones that surrounded the clearing, he placed his bag on the floor beside him. Before he had time to stop him, Kibbin was in the bag rummaging around.

"Hey, a little patience would be nice," he called out.

To his surprise though when Kibbin removed what he had been looking for it was not the wrapped-up rabbit meat that he had cooked earlier, but the snares.

Kibbin scurried off into the shrubbery behind Flax and returned a few moments later, having set the snares. "Hoppers, yummy," he declared with a grin.

They sat around a small fire and ate the remaining rabbit caught earlier that day. Flax asked again about the Longtails Kibbin had seen, and this time through asking specific questions he got the information from him.

Kibbin had seen the Longtails retreating after the attack on the Island, marching along the coast further east of the Sugar Loaf, he had also seen a female with them.

"That's Flea, she's my… she's my friend," explained Flax, becoming unintentionally emotional at the mention of her name.

Kibbin described how he had been desperate to set about the Longtails with his spiked club, but he was outnumbered and it would have done him no good and certainly led to his death. So instead he had done what he always did, what he was meant to do, he watched and he listened. He trailed the group for around half a day moving unseen amongst the gorse that lined the cliff path, matching their pace - which given the reluctance of Flea to travel at any speed was not difficult.

They had spoken little and when they did it was in hushed whispers, likely to avoid Flea hearing what they said.

Kibbin had been forced to leave the group as they started to descend the cliffs to the beach far below, unable to follow unseen he had sat up on the cliff edge, curled tightly, his head tucked down just tight enough so that his eyes could see above his arm. To anyone or anything looking at him they would have seen a dried-up gnarled bush - anybody close enough to see otherwise would have had Kibbin's club to contend with.

He had watched the Longtails escort their prisoner onto the beach then along and into the mouth of a cave and out of sight.

He pondered what he had seen for some time before slowly returning to the cover of the gorse and making his way steadily back west to see what else or who else he could observe.

"So you saw where they took her? Can you lead me there?" Flax asked impatiently.

"Course, cost you though,"

"Well I don't really have much –"

"– grub!" Kibbin interrupted, "Give us grub and I'll show you."

"Grub it is then," Flax smiled and nodded in agreement. Flax had so many questions he wished to ask Kibbin but his mind and body were still tired from the ordeal of crossing The Sound. His eyelids grew heavy as he sat back against one of the stones and pulled his blanket up around his body. He gazed up at the multitude of diamond white stars studded in the consuming dark blanket of the sky and let the questions race through his mind along with thoughts of his home, of Flea, of the strange land he found himself in, of the night of the attack - he traced his fingertips across the scarred flesh of his left forearm. The motion felt hypnotic and allowed his body to surrender to much needed sleep.

-42-
JEES AS DAEED
- FLAX'S THIRD DAY ON MANNIN -

Flax woke to the smell of meat cooking. He blinked in the early morning sunlight, his face wet with the fine morning dew that had settled.

Kibbin sat in the middle of the stone circle, close to the fire, he was using a knife to prepare a rabbit – a second one was already prepared and cooking on the fire.

Flax watched as he worked the knife along the carcass – removing the skin with expert ease. He woke fully when he realised that the knife Kibbin was using was actually his.

"Hey," he called as he sat himself up, "how did you get that knife?" he felt the empty sheath attached to the back of his belt.

"You was sleeping, easy," came the reply, Kibbin didn't take his eyes from the rabbit and continued to move the blade with skill.

"Where did you learn to use a knife like that?" Flax asked, standing and walking towards the fire.

"From you," Kibbin replied, "watched you and learned."

Flax was fascinated, "But I only used it once," he thought aloud, and the way that he now moved the blade would make anybody think he had been doing so for many seasons.

"Fast learner," Kibbin shrugged.

"I see the snares worked?"

"Course!"

Kibbin clearly had his mind on food over conversation this morning. Flax was impressed at the speed with which he had learned to prepare a rabbit – it had taken him many, many attempts under the watchful eye of his father to get anywhere near an acceptable standard. Now that he thought of it – Flax remembered how quickly Kibbin had learnt to set the snares having only seen it done once. He truly was a master of observation, but not only that he was able to apply learning from what he saw, and quickly it seemed.

Flax walked the perimeter of the stone circle, casually casting his eyes across the strange marks on them, "I wonder what these mean," he said aloud.

"Graves," Kibbin called, not taking his eyes from the rabbit cooking on the fire, "*Wiggynnee* graves."

Flax waited for him to explain further, but he didn't so Flax pressed for more information.

"How do you know that?"

"Everyone knows." Flax felt foolish at this answer even though it would not have been Kibbin's intention. "They are all over Mannin," explained Kibbin.

"Oh right, we don't have them on my Island," Flax replied as he studied the markings on the North Men's gravestones. Again his head was filled with questions but given the limited flow of conversation he decided not to ask them. Instead he quietly packed up all of his belongings into the bag, he found the snares next to Kibbin, both of them having been successful through the night. Kibbin handed Flax the knife, still wet from the butchery, Flax wiped it down on some grass before sheathing it on his belt.

Whilst the second rabbit cooked on the coals they ate the first. Flax watched his newfound companion with intrigue as he ate. He was still fascinated by the story of how over just a generation or two his kin had adapted so quickly to live in such an inhospitable environment as the gorse forests. *Surely there had to be some kind of magic involved?* thought Flax.

Kibbin's yellow eyes rose to meet Flax's and he quickly averted his gaze, worried that Kibbin had somehow read his mind. In that moment Flax understood why his eyes were such a vibrant yellow, they had taken on the colour of the gorse flower. Such a bright and inviting yellow flower that disguised the pointed barbs amongst which it sat, *was there a deeper meaning to be learned there? Was Kibbin dangerous behind those yellow eyes?* Flax had certainly struggled to control him during their physical encounter the previous morning, he had a strength that was certainly unexpected.

That aside he could see no threat from Kibbin. Whilst he did not yet trust him, he had no reason to be overly suspicious or worried of him, as long as he kept him fed anyway.

They finished eating and Flax carefully wrapped the meat from the second rabbit and placed it into his bag. He scattered the coals and covered them with some wet grass, steam rose from them so he piled on some more until he was satisfied they were extinguished.

He followed Kibbin out of the circular graveyard, as he left a thought crossed his mind. He shuddered at the realisation that he had spent the night sleeping within an ancient burial site. Had he known that the night before he would have opted to stay elsewhere, but the *Wiggynnee* graves had offered the perfect opportunity for shelter and protection.

As they climbed the ladder over the wall Flax saw he had a choice of two paths before him. "Which way?" He asked Kibbin.

"That one," he pointed a short hairy finger toward the path ahead, "they went in there, to The Chasms."

"Flea went in there? I thought you said you saw them to the east of here? Near the Sugar Loaf?"

"Not Flea!" Kibbin replied impatiently, "Ealish!"

"Ealish? You saw Ealish go down there?" Flax asked excitedly, immediately lifted by the idea he was still travelling toward his sister.

"Course."

"Well why didn't you say?"

"Never asked," shrugged Kibbin.

Flax couldn't argue with that logic, "Hang on, you said *they*...was Ealish with someone else?" his mind instantly thought of the Traveller, but there was no way he could have caught up with Ealish. He was only one day ahead of Flax.

Probably slightly more given the time he lost crossing The Sound and recovering after.

"That flippin' mutt," scowled Kibbin, "always scaring away them hoppers."

"A dog? Ealish was with a dog?"

"Good riddance to it I says," Kibbin continued, "saw 'em go in but not seen 'em since, been busy looking for grub."

"But that's the same way we're going right?" Flax asked eagerly.

"Course," and with that Kibbin set off along the path toward the stone wall. He could move surprisingly fast when he wanted to, he wasn't running but his short legs powered him forward at a pace that meant Flax had to break into a jog to catch up with him. Once he was alongside it was no trouble for him to match pace. They spoke little as they walked down the path. Flax wanted to talk but it was clear Kibbin was not in the mood to converse. Whenever Flax asked something he got a grunt or a one-word answer in reply so eventually he gave up and spent the time taking in his surroundings. To his left was another patch of the gorse forest, he could see across the top, it stretched up the hillside as far as he could see, the green and brown spiky branches still dotted with the remaining yellow flowers from summer, staring back at him like a thousand of Kibbin's eyes. It unnerved him to think a Moanee could be watching them and he would have no clue, *would Kibbin even know?* he wondered.

Ahead of him, growing ever closer was the wall that hid The Chasms from view. *Who built these walls up here?* he wondered. They had walls on the Island around their fields and plantations that were built with purpose but Flax had seen no other sign of human life up here, *so who had built them? And why?*

Before long they reached the wall, Flax read the sign attached to the gate and chuckled aloud – again, he was unknowingly a lot less cautious than his sister had been.

"Any grub before we go in?" Kibbin asked hopefully as he greedily eyed the bag slung around Flax's shoulder.

"We haven't been moving long, and the sun is nowhere near its peak," Flax replied pointing up to the sky. "We need to get through The Chasms, rather than stopping now." In truth he was conscious that he now only had the one rabbit and a small piece of cheese left, he needed Kibbin to show him through The Chasms safely and if he had no food left as incentive then he had doubts as to how helpful Kibbin would actually be to him.

Kibbin made no effort to hide the disappointment on his face, "This way then," he huffed as he slowly shuffled through the gate in the wall before grumbling, "who lets the sun tell 'em when to eat grub?" Flax followed feeling slightly guilty but knowing he had made the right choice.

Kibbin clearly knew his way through The Chasms, he moved steadily through the maze taking turns left and right. Flax had stopped to gaze into the first chasm, straining his eyes to peer into the light absorbing depth. He couldn't see much detail at all past the first few arm lengths into the darkness, this didn't concern him at all as he stepped across it. Before long the distance between the safety of hard ground either side was increasing and Flax became concerned that Kibbin would struggle to clear the gap safely, he needn't have though. He stood dumbfounded as he watched the short creature clear what was the widest one yet with ease from a standing jump, what's more his landing was near silent and not at all clumsy or loud as Flax would have expected.

"That was impressive," Flax couldn't help but exclaim.

Kibbin looked back at him from the safety of the other side and shrugged his shoulders.

"Tis easy, just jumping," he turned and continued along his predetermined path, not even stopping to check if Flax had made it safely across - which of course he did.

They had been moving most of the morning without stopping, Kibbin turned to Flax and asked hopefully, "Time for grub?"

Flax tried hard to avoid his yellow eyes as he replied with a question of his own "How far are we from the end of The Chasms Kibbin?"

"Hmmm, not too far."

"Well I would feel much safer eating on solid ground rather than next to one of these bottomless pits," Flax said pointing into the chasm next to him, "could we please just get out of here and then stop?" Flax felt bad for lying to Kibbin but still the thought that he may become useless to the creature once his food had run out niggled in the back of his mind. He couldn't be sure where this thought had come from, *probably ever since noticing the yellow of the gorse flowers matched Kibbin's eyes.* He hoped that he was wrong but did not want to take that chance, especially in the middle of the maze of drops that almost certainly meant death for anyone who fell.

"Course," said Kibbin shrugging his shoulders and making it clear that he was not at all disappointed by Flax's response, this made Flax feel even worse. He chose not to dwell on it though and followed on after his guide.

Kibbin took a couple of steps run up at the next chasm they encountered, this allowed him to clear it and the broken ground on the far edge with ease. Flax chose to do the same, he waited until Kibbin had cleared the landing area then he stopped a few steps short of the edge and prepared to propel himself forward to jump when something on the ground caught his attention. He stopped dead in his tracks and stared, his eyes not registering at first exactly what it was but they knew it was definitely foreign to the environment.

As he got closer to it his mind caught up with what his eyes were seeing, he dropped to his knees and lifted the item up in his hands. The three-pronged hook in his hands was identical to the one that he had attached to the rope coiled around his chest. Only this one had just a short length of rope attached to it, the rope had been severed, not only that but it had bite marks in it too. Flax's mind caught up once more and he scrambled to the edge of the chasm, he desperately looked into the blackness, he couldn't see anything.

"Ealish? Ealish!" He called into the depths, his voice bounced back at him, he could hear the desperation in it. He looked up at Kibbin on the other side of the chasm, a look of twisted confusion on his face. "I can't see her Kibbin, I can't see anything…EALISH!?"

"What's wrong young 'un?" Kibbin asked. No sign of alarm in his voice or on his hairy face.

Flax held up the hook he had found. "This, this is my sisters, see its identical to mine - Flea's father made her it, he told me she had one too. It's hers, she must have fallen, why else would it be here?" Flax's voice was faster and more panicked with each word. He could feel his heart beating fast in his chest and he felt like he was struggling for breath.

"What can you see Kibbin? Help me!" Flax pleaded.

Kibbin steadily dropped to his hands and knees and crawled toward the edge of his side of the chasm, stopping short of where the grass had grown over flaky rocks along the lip. He paused then looked up at Flax. Flax met his gaze with bright green-brown eyes, enhanced by the glassy tears that were forming in the corners and spreading across them as he desperately tried to blink them away.

"I see…" Kibbin began, "I see blood…" he screwed his face thoughtfully as he pointed to the cliff wall just below Flax. On the edge of one of the rocks was a dried reddish-brown smudge that Flax had missed in his rush to look as far down as he could. Neither of them could have known that this was Ealish's from when she hit her head during her fall but Flax quickly concluded that it must have been his sisters.

He could no longer hold back the tears and they fell heavily from his eyes, "Where is she Kibbin? Where is my sister?" His voice cracked as he cried out his question.

Kibbin crept even closer to the edge, as close as he dared – given how crumbly the edge was. He could still not see directly down. He laid down and inched his way to the edge until his eyes and nose hung over the side. Loose rocks fells away beneath him kicking up a small cloud of dust around his face, he coughed as the dust cleared.

Flax could hear the clicking sounds of the falling rocks reverberating back up the walls of the chasm. His eyes still searched frantically without success for any other clue as to his sister's whereabouts. He was so focused he hadn't noticed that on the other edge Kibbin had crawled back away from the edge and was now stood on the solid ground brushing dust and small pieces of rock from his wiry chest and stomach hair.

"Come on," he called.

Flax looked up, his eyes red from both the tears and the dust. He was surprised and slightly angered to see how casually Kibbin was stood and how he had just called to him. Even more so now that Kibbin used one of his stubby hands to beckon him over the chasm.

"Come on young 'un," he pointed down at the pit, "no use stayin' here, she ain't there."

-43-
TREE AS DAEED
- FLAX'S THIRD DAY ON MANNIN -

Flax cleared the Chasm with ease, landing beside Kibbin. He gripped him firmly – almost too firmly – by the shoulders.

"What do you mean she's not there? How can you be sure?"

Kibbin stepped back and released himself from Flax's grip, then declared, "She ain't there, 'cos I can see she ain't there."

Flax shook his head, trying to focus his mind, "How can you see she isn't there? I can see nothing but blackness."

"Good eyes," Kibbin shrugged as he turned and continued on the path.

Flax wanted desperately to believe him, to believe that his sister's body wasn't laying broken at the bottom of the chasm. However the same niggle of mistrust came back into his mind. He had stood at the edge and looked into it. He could not see much further into the chasm than he could reach. *Could this creature really see all the way to the depths? Why would he lie? Grub, that's why!* Flax thought. *But would he really be so callous as to say such a thing just so that he would not miss out on the chance of a meal?* Flax couldn't tell either way. He would have to trust Kibbin, after all he was still amongst The Chasms and staring into the darkness wouldn't achieve anything. He asked Kibbin, "Do you promise me she is not there?"

"Promise?" Kibbin asked.

"Yes promise, you know, do you swear?"

"Course I promise," Kibbin looked genuinely hurt at Flax's question, "not a liar!" he protested.

Immediately, all of Flax's prior concerns subsided – he realised how he had not been thinking rationally.

"I'm sorry Kibbin, I truly am. I did not mean to offend you. It's just…I thought that my sister had fallen in there…I couldn't see anything and then you just said…"

Flax's apology petered off, he knew whatever he said at this time would not change how he felt, and more importantly how he had made Kibbin feel. He placed his sister's hook in his bag and removed something else at the same time, he walked to Kibbin and put a hand gently on his shoulder.

"I really am sorry Kibbin, I hope you can forgive me?" Flax held out the last piece of cheese that he had taken from his bag as a peace offering. Kibbin looked at it momentarily then took it from Flax's hand, before he had chance to say anything Flax continued, "So if Ealish was not down there, where could she be? I don't think she climbed out of the top as her grappling hook was left there and the rope was cut."

"Sugar loaf," Kibbin said through a mouthful of cheese, "a way to the bottom at the Sugar Loaf, through the caves."

"Can you take me there Kibbin, please?"

"Course, follow me," Kibbin moved off leading the way and Flax followed behind, ashamed of his previous mistrust of his Moanee guide.

He turned his head to take one last look at the chasm into which his sister had fallen. "Please be okay Ealish," he whispered to himself.

Seven uneventful leaps later they found themselves at the gated wall that led out of The Chasms, they stepped through it and Flax felt a huge relief – knowing that he was no longer at a risk of falling to his death, unless he stepped over the cliff edge that was not too far to his right. His mind was still full of questions about what had happened to his sister; *Was that her blood? If so, was she okay? Why was the rope on her hook cut? What were the teeth marks? Where was she?* His head hurt from trying to find answers, none of which he knew or could reasonably find out in the immediate future.

He stopped and screwed his eyes tightly shut, hoping desperately to clear the bombardment of questions in his mind. He opened them again having been unsuccessful. Kibbin stood watching him from a short distance away. Flax knew what the short creature was about to ask and – in an effort to attempt to further repair the damaged trust – Flax spoke pre-emptively, "Grub?" he asked Kibbin as he sat down and took his bag from around his shoulder.

"Yummy hopper," Kibbin grinned as he strode quickly toward Flax and sat himself down next to him. The two of them sat looking along the coastline from their heightened position. Not far from where they sat, just southeast of them,

Flax saw a strange rock formation rising up from the sea. It was nearly as tall as the cliff top but was entirely separate from the cliff wall itself, the waves forced their way between the two in powerful swells. Along both the cliff side and the rock formation Flax could see sea birds and their nests, there were more than he could count. High overhead more of the birds circled, their calls carrying on the wind.

"S'the Sugar Loaf that," Kibbin announced before Flax had chance to ask. Flax produced Sid Kelly's map from his jacket pocket, he studied it for a second and found his current position. He could see the area of The Chasms was actually marked on there, rather than with writing there was just a black X drawn over the area - most likely as a warning to avoid the area all together, which unfortunately for Flax had not been an option. He used a writing stick to annotate the X with the word *chasms*, he followed the coastline on the map and found a small rock formation that he confirmed as the Sugar Loaf, again this wasn't noted so he decided to add the name to the map. He could see by studying the map that there should actually be a beach far below the cliff top they sat near. He walked cautiously toward the edge and took a quick glance over the side, sure enough a beach ran from the cove created by the Sugar Loaf and back west along the front of the cliff that acted as the southern boundary to The Chasms. From this position he could see streaks of black against the mottled greys of the cliff face, these were the fissures in the rock, The Chasms. He could see that some of these reached all the way to the beach at the base of the cliff. It lifted his spirits to see that it would be possible for somebody to exit The Chasms should they fall in and somehow survive, assuming they fell into one of the ones that led to the beach.

He looked back toward the Sugar Loaf and the cliff face next to it. There was no obvious way down to the beach from the cliff top. "Kibbin," he called, "where is the path down to the beach?"

"Inside," came the reply, "see the cave there?" Flax followed the direction of Kibbin's stubby finger, he could see a slightly darker area on the cliff face but he certainly couldn't discern it as a cave from where he was. However he trusted what Kibbin was telling him.

"You do have good eyes, don't you?"

"Yup, we all do."

Flax knew that Kibbin was referring to his kin folk, the *Moanee. They spend so much time watching and listening from beneath the shadow of the gorse forest that their senses of sight and hearing must have somehow been enhanced,* he thought.

"Kibbin, I need to get down to that beach, I need to see if my sister is down there somewhere. Can you show me the way down?"

"Hmm, never been in the caves before, not sure of the way…"

"But with your incredible sight surely you could find a way through…" Flax tried to charm him.

"Gotta stay here an' watch an' listen…" Kibbin countered.

"It would mean a lot to have a friend help me," Flax tried a different tack, he noticed Kibbin's body language change at the mention of the word friend, he capitalised on this opening and added, "plus I would catch you some more yummy hoppers…"

"S'pose I should make sure you get there safe, gotta look after our… friends." Kibbin had hesitated before he said the last word but it brought a smile to his face, which in turn put one on Flax's. Flax placed a hand on Kibbin's muscular shoulder and announced that they should get moving. Kibbin obliged and the two of them walked along the cliff path toward the Sugar Loaf. The conversation between them flowed more freely than it had at any point over the two previous days. Kibbin still answered in his short and somewhat unusual manner, but he answered, nevertheless.

Flax asked questions about the dog that his sister had been travelling with. Kibbin explained that he and the *hound* had encountered each other on a number of occasions and that the dog had been in the area since he had arrived. The dog was one of the reasons that Kibbin had found it difficult to hunt food as it would scare away the hoppers and small birds with its clumsiness when moving in the gorse forest, constantly scraping itself on the sharp barbs and yelping in pain. It was clear that this caused annoyance to Kibbin as whenever he said the word *hound* or *mutt* it was as if he had a bad taste in his mouth that he couldn't get rid of.

The thought of Ealish having found a travelling companion brought a smile to Flax's face, this smile faded as he wondered what had happened to her.

As they walked Flax kept casting his eye to the Sugar Loaf, he could see now that although it was not completely smooth or symmetrical it was almost a conical shape, the wind and waves having somehow shaped it so over time. He had always been fascinated at the power of the sea and had spent many days watching the way the waves would smash into the land around the Island forming countless unique and intriguing rock formations - his favourite of course being The Drinking Dragane at the south-eastern tip of the Island. Flax cast his eyes west across the sea in the direction of his homeland and was overjoyed to realise that from his current position he was able to see The Drinking Dragane, appearing to float on the surface of the ocean, just visible to the left of the headland on which he had spent his first night and where he had met Kibbin.

Kibbin noticed that Flax had stopped walking, "What you seen?" he asked.

"Nothing," Flax muttered without taking his eyes from the rock formation, "well not nothing, just something that reminds me of my home…well it sort of is my home…or part of it anyway."

"The Dragane stone?" Kibbin asked

"Dragane stone?" Flax repeated, he had never heard it referred to as that before but it made sense now he thought of it, "we call it the *Dragane ta giu.*"

"Drinking Dragane huh?" Kibbin cocked his head slightly to one side, "S'pose that makes sense."

"Let's move," Kibbin said, "can't keep staring at a rock."

Flax laughed aloud at Kibbin's bluntness and turned his gaze from the sea back to the path. As they neared a point where the cliff path turned from a southern direction back to the east Kibbin stopped next to a large cairn, much larger than the one Flax had slept against two nights before.

"It's here," Kibbin announced as he patted his hand on the cairn.

"What is?" Flax said, making no attempt to hide his confusion.

"The entrance, or exit, well 'tis both."

"I don't see it," Flax admitted casting his eyes over the pile of stones.

"Cos you ain't lookin'," Kibbin said with a smirk, and with that he walked around to the southern edge of the cairn and pointed to a rock almost as large as he was. Then, with impossible strength he lifted the rock to one side revealing a narrow entrance way that led down into the ground, Kibbin smirked once more at Flax and then stepped down into the entrance.

Flax had not been expecting what had just happened, he looked at the huge rock that he had just seen Kibbin lift clear. He bent his knees, gripped the rock firmly on either side with his fingers and prepared to lift it, he did not need to but it was out of pure curiosity and, if he was honest – out of competitiveness. With all his effort he extended his legs as he gripped tighter with his fingers. To his surprise and astonishment he lifted the stone with ease, in fact he had put too much effort in which meant he lifted the stone as high as his head and stumbled backwards over onto his backside, still holding the stone. It weighed next to nothing, he stood up and placed it back next to the cairn where Kibbin had put it.

"Come on then," Kibbin had poked his head back through the entrance, "hurry up!"

Flax was still staring at the stone trying to understand what had just happened.

"It's *clagh foalsey*."

Flax looked blankly at him, he knew the translation from the old tongue meant *fake rock* but he had never heard of it before.

"Never mind that," Kibbin continued, "let's go." Flax was surprised by Kibbin's newfound eagerness so he followed after him without a second thought to the rock. The entrance to the cave network was narrow, almost too narrow for Flax. Kibbin had fit through with ease but Flax had to remove his backpack, to which he had secured his father's staff, and walk through sideways whilst breathing in to be able to fit.

Once inside the cave network Flax found it to be much lighter than he had expected. A number of small holes and cracks in the cliff wall allowed enough light through that was then reflected and refracted around the caverns by a number of small pools of sea and rainwater that had found their way into the caves but not out. The rays of light travelling around the caverns cast an eerie gloom and bathed the walls in an ever-moving blueish green hue.

The pair began their descent through the cave system, naturally carved tunnels in the rock led from chamber to chamber. A number of times they found themselves at a dead end and had to retrace their steps.

As they entered one chamber, that seemed much larger than the others they had been in, they found it to be much brighter, Flax soon noticed the reason. This chamber sat close to the cliff wall and had a large opening through which the low autumnal sunlight was glaring. He walked cautiously to the edge and peered out. He couldn't be sure if it was the angle at which he was looking at it, or because he had been inside the gloomy cave system, but the sea sparkled the most magnificent shade of blue. He stood for a long moment taking it in and letting the gentle sea breeze hit his face, far below him he could hear and see the waves crashing against the rock face.

He turned back from the edge and walked toward Kibbin who was hunched over something against the wall, Flax peered over his shoulder. "What have you got there?" he asked.

"Grub," Kibbin replied, but he didn't say the word in such a way as Flax would have expected, he sounded perplexed by his find. Flax could see that Kibbin had in his hands a leather satchel bag, smaller than the one Flax carried, but it held fresh fruit, dried fish and some other edibles.

"Where is it from?" Flax asked, not expecting Kibbin to know the answer.

However he did seem to know as he replied, "Longtails."

"How do you know?" as he asked he detached his staff from his bag and held it in both hands ready to use if needed.

"Same ones I saw 'em carry," Kibbin said, as he unhooked his club from his belt and gripped it firmly in his hand. Kibbin picked up the bag with his other hand and slung it round his body. They both stood, their weapons ready in their hands as they moved to the centre of the cavern, their eyes moving to the many different tunnels cut into the walls.

Flax's foot kicked against something, a loud rattling noise echoed off the walls, somehow the noise seemed louder each time it bounced back. He looked down and found that he had walked into a pile of bones, they had been cleaned of all flesh. Amongst the bones were scraps of dirty clothing and a weapon that Flax recognised. It made his scarred forearm tingle, a memory of the pain that a small scythe just like this had inflicted on him.

"I think I've found who that bag belonged to Kibbin," Flax announced, his eyes darting left and right looking for some clue as to who or what had killed the Longtail. Against one wall he noticed another pile of bones, in a similar state to the last, a cruel curved dagger laid nearby along with another bag containing food, Flax snatched up the bag and noticed next to it the biggest feather he had ever seen in his life. It was the length of his forearm and just as wide, he picked it up and turned to Kibbin who by now was at the opposite end of the chamber stood next to a third pile of bones holding up a torn black cloak that was marked with a red circle and the skull of a rat, "*Roddanyn Doo*," Flax whispered to himself.

Kibbin noticed the feather in Flax's hand.

"Where you find that?" he demanded.

"Just next to this pile of bones here, what kind of bird do you think –"

Flax never finished his question. The chamber was temporarily cast into darkness as a large shape passed across the opening in the wall that let the light in.

As quickly as it had turned dark it was light again.

Flax looked at Kibbin, his yellow eyes were filled with fear. Kibbin spoke one word, the panic in his voice was almost tangible.

"Run!"

-44-
KIARE AS DAEED
- FLAX'S THIRD DAY ON MANNIN -

Flax ran from the cavern, Kibbin was a few strides ahead of him. He had no time to be impressed at the speed of his short companion. He had no idea what he was running from but he knew from the way Kibbin had reacted that he was running for his life. He breathed hard. His body was working overtime but his legs felt strong as a result of the training he had done on the Island. He held his staff in his right hand and in his left he still gripped tightly to the satchel he had taken from the cavern, the large feather he had left behind.

They came to a junction where their path split in three different directions, Flax noticed Kibbin slowing as he approached so he shouted from behind him, "The left one Kibbin! Go left!"

Kibbin shot down the passage to the left and the path began to climb steeply, the pair burst into one of the smaller caverns with a number of passages cut into the walls. Flax could tell that Kibbin was struggling to remember the route out in his panic, he pushed his legs hard and overtook him shouting, "Keep following me Kibbin, nearly there!"

Sweat poured down Flax's brow and stung his eyes, he shook his head to clear it away and continued on, glancing back every now and again to make sure Kibbin was still close behind. On one or two occasions he had to consciously slow his pace to prevent Kibbin falling behind on the steep uphill sprints.

His legs were starting to ache and feeling like they might seize up. *Come on Flax!* he urged himself forward. Raising his head he could see a bright shaft of daylight ahead of him and he knew that the exit was not far. He reached the narrow exit and turned to face back down the passageway, holding the staff two handed across his body in a defensive stance as he fought to catch his breath.

"You first," he gasped at Kibbin, stepping to one side to let him past and then taking up his guard position once more.

"I'm out!" Kibbin shouted from behind him.

Flax turned and passed his staff, his own bag and the Longtail satchel through the gap to Kibbin and then he squeezed through, less cautiously than before and in his haste he caught his cheek on the sharp rock. He felt the sting as the rock slashed his skin but he didn't stop to think about it.

Once through, Kibbin passed him back his possessions and lifted the *clagh foalsey* door back into place to cover up the entrance.

Flax was bent double with his hands on his knees, gasping for breath. Sweat ran down his face and into the fresh cut, it stung. He rubbed at his cheek and saw his hand was covered in a mixture of blood and sweat, he wiped it away on his jacket sleeve.

"Come on!" Kibbin shouted, "keep moving!"

At that they were off again. Running along the cliff path, which was now a gentle downhill slope, something that Flax was thankful for as it allowed him to open up his stride and stretch out his tiring legs.

The path opened up to green fields either side, the gorse forest still visible far away to the left. Stone walls lined the fields. Cold wind hit Flax in the face but it aided in his recovery from the panicked escape from the caves and he welcomed it.

He didn't know how long or how far they had been running but eventually Kibbin came to a stop next to two benches. Neither of them spoke for a long time, they leant against the benches gasping for breath. Flax removed his flask of water and drank deeply. He offered it to Kibbin who drank greedily from it before passing it back.

After a while Flax spoke. "Thank you Kibbin."

The short *Moanee* looked up at Flax with a confused look on his sweaty face, "What for?"

"When we left the caves, we were clearly still in some danger," Flax explained, "you could have easily ducked back under the gorse and left me, but you didn't, you guided me away safely. So…thank you."

A bashful look of pride spread across Kibbin's face, "S'no problem," he replied, then looked to the sky and said, "may not be safe yet though."

"Safe or not I need to rest a while," declared Flax as he sat on one of the wooden benches, "and eat," he added.

"We ate all the grub though," Kibbin said disappointedly.

"We ate all *our* grub," Flax corrected as he lifted up the Longtail satchel and pointed to the one around Kibbin's chest.

"Aha," Kibbin laughed, "very true."

The two of them sat and ate some of the food from the bags they had scavenged from the cavern. As they ate Flax took in the view, it was truly breath-taking. The benches sat on the cliff edge looking out to the east, the land ahead of them curved in and out creating a number of small coves, each with their own beach onto which the waves gently lapped. Much further east Flax could see more land where the coastline cut further south, he took out his map and studied it.

He was able to find their position, there wasn't much noted here on the map by Sid with the exception of a few scribbles. He could see that there was a larger cove further along the coast, it was hidden from view by the land ahead of him. The bay here was marked as '*Chapel Beach*', at the far end of the beach was a little annotation that simply read, '*Sid's bench*'. If the view from there was anything like the one Flax was currently looking at, then it was a bench he wanted to sit on. Flax thought so much of the view from the bench that he chose to mark its position on the map, scribbling '*Flax's Bench*' on the map with a writing stick.

He put the map away in his jacket pocket and searched through the rest of the Longtail's bag. There was still more food, so he transferred this to his own bag, other than that there was a fire striker which he didn't need but decided to keep just in case and a small piece of parchment that was folded up.

He carefully unfolded it and inspected its contents. A lump caught in his throat and a tear came to his eye when he found himself staring at Flea's face. It was a rough sketched version but it was unmistakably her, there was even the Faerie pendant hung about her neck. Below the portrait six words were scrawled:

'Take her - Do not harm her!'

Flax knew immediately that these Longtails had been part of the raiding party that had attacked the Island. They had been given pictures of Flea and specific instructions, *but how did they know what she looked like?* Maeve couldn't know, she hadn't seen her since she was a baby. Flax decided not to show this to Kibbin, he folded the parchment back up and placed the picture of his friend in his inner jacket pocket. He looked at Kibbin and it was clear he had not noticed him open the parchment, or his reaction to it. To take his mind off it he spoke.

"What were we running from Kibbin? You looked truly terrified. Did it kill those Longtails?"

"Can't be sure. Think t'was one of Foillan's lairs."

"Foillan?"

"Surely you heard of 'im?" Kibbin sounded surprised.

"Nope, you will have to enlighten me."

Kibbin explained that Foillan was a bird man, well he was *the* bird man – in that he was the only one of his kind. He had been altered by magic many, many years ago. In order to pay off a debt he had agreed to this alteration. As a result he had become immortal, or at least his body did not age. His purpose was to protect the shores of Mannin and forewarn its inhabitants against invasion from outsiders, his debt would be considered paid after one hundred years of servitude.

"Rumour is he 'as served well over a hundred now," Kibbin said.

"Should the magic not have changed him back then?" Flax asked.

"No one knows, she is the only one who does and no-one knows where she is."

"She? You mean Meave the Faerie Queen, don't you?" Flax had assumed that because magic was involved that somehow she would be involved, he was correct.

"Yup I do," Kibbin looked impressed at Flax's knowledge, as he nodded in confirmation.

"But if he is meant to protect Mannin, why should we run from him?"

"Same reason them Longtails should've. They say he went mad with rage when the spell didn't change 'im back. He couldn't find her to cure 'im. Heard he spends his days huntin' her, when he's not huntin' her, he hunts for grub. An' by grub I mean anythin' that moves."

"So, he… ate the Longtails?" Flax couldn't quite believe that someone or something could bring themselves to eat those evil twisted creatures.

"Sure seems that way," Kibbin nodded again, "an' I reckon he would've eaten us given the chance," he added.

"I have never even heard of him, how could that be? If he protects all of Mannin then surely he would fly close to our Island?"

"Don't know," shrugged Kibbin, "all I know is what I know, but I seen him. Looks like a normal man but with huge wings like a sea bird. Never got close to him. Never want to either," he added.

Flax had more questions but he presumed given Kibbin's last answer he wouldn't know the answers to them. *Bet the Traveller would know,* he thought to himself, *nice of him to warn me.*

He sat on the bench, his legs stretched out before him recovering after the unexpected run from the caves. The sun was well past its peak now and falling away behind them, bathing the sky in deep orange light that was kissed with streaks of pink and purple. The temperature had dropped but it was still pleasantly warm. He ran his fingers across the smooth wood of the bench, wondering how and why they were there, and also who had put them there? They were both identically crude in their construction; a thick plank of smoothed wood placed on top of two sections of thick tree trunk that acted as legs at either side. As his hands ran across the seat, he felt some scratches in the surface. He looked down and could see that in the wood there were marks that had been purposefully engraved, from where he sat they were upside down so he stood and faced the bench to inspect them, there were eight letters in total grouped, in pairs.

'E.C, B.G, M.L, J.R'

He wondered what they meant, he looked to the other bench to find similar markings only less of them.

'J.R, L.W'

"Hey Kibbin, what do you think these mean?" He asked without taking his eyes from the marks. There was no response, "Kibbin –" he started to call louder.

"– Shhhhh!" He was interrupted. Flax turned his head to look at Kibbin, he was off the bench and close to the cliff edge looking across the water below them. Flax followed his gaze and saw it.

From behind a small outcrop of rock rose a single plume of thick black curling smoke, rising and twisting – tarnishing the late afternoon sky.

-45-
QUEIG AS DAEED
- FLAX'S THIRD DAY ON MANNIN -

"Ealish!" Flax yelled at the top of his voice, "Ealish! I'm up here!"

Flax was struck hard from behind by something, the force of it knocked him forward to the ground.

"Keep yer bleedin' voice down young 'un!" Kibbin hissed in his ear. Flax felt him pressing down on his shoulders and pinning him to the floor.

"Okay, sorry," whispered Flax. "You didn't have to tackle me though. You could have just asked," he added as Kibbin shuffled from on top of him. He manoeuvred himself into a seated position and dusted himself down.

"No time to ask, you were shoutin' to everyone tellin' em where we are."

"But the smoke —" Flax was whispering but he stopped himself, realising it wasn't necessary. "— the smoke," he started again at a normal volume, "it must be Ealish, she must have climbed down to safety and moved round the coast."

"Nope," Kibbin said bluntly. "Don't think so."

"Why not?" Questioned Flax.

"Just don't think so."

"Well let's go down there and find out then," Flax stood, he detached his father's staff from his bag and then slung the bag around his shoulder.

"Wait," Kibbin urged.

"You don't have to come with me Kibbin, you have helped me so much already, more than I would have expected."

Kibbin looked hurt by this remark and Flax noticed it.

"I didn't mean it like that Kibbin," Flax started. "What I mean is you have already helped me more than I deserved and I cannot ask you to come down there and leave the safety of the gorse forest, to leave your post."

Kibbin seemed to accept this and turned his attention back to the smoke, "Don't think it's your sister, she's more cautious."

Flax wondered how Kibbin would know this, he had never actually met her. *But he had watched her*, Flax knew Kibbin was right. *Ealish would berate herself for leaving footprint in the mud if she didn't intend to, she wouldn't be one to start a fire in such an exposed location.*

"Maybe," said Flax, not wanting to let Kibbin know that he was most likely right. "But we have to find out."

"We?" Kibbin asked, "I'm welcome now?"

"Of course you are friend," Flax used the word *friend* intentionally, "that is, if you want to help me still?"

Kibbin didn't answer, he uncoupled his club from his belt and held it in one hand at his side as he marched away along the path. Flax passed his eyes across the benches, checking they had left nothing behind and he jogged along after Kibbin who had not stopped to wait for him.

They walked in silence for some time, Flax periodically cast his eyes down to the beach to check that the smoke was still there. "How do you think –" he started to ask but was abruptly interrupted by his short companion.

"– no talkin'!"

Flax couldn't work out from the tone of his voice whether he was still upset or if he was trying to concentrate on what possibly lay ahead of them. The path they walked dipped down into a small, wooded glen. The trees created a canopy above them that cut out most of light and cast them into a shadowy darkness in which random shafts of orange sunset broke through the gaps in the leaves like pillars of fire. The air was still in the glen and the sound of the waves on the shore could no longer be heard, in the silence Kibbin and Flax's footsteps seemed to be amplified.

Ealish wouldn't make this much noise, Flax thought to himself as he consciously tried to lighten his footsteps but with no success. He could no longer see the smoke but he kept track in his head of which direction it was in as the path wound gently from left to right through the trees that had grown clustered together in the natural shelter from the harsh winds that whipped across the moorland above.

As they descended Flax picked up the sound of running water, he welcomed the break in the silence as well as the potential opportunity to refill his water flask. He picked up his pace and overtook Kibbin who, up until this point, had been walking ahead of him. He reached the stream and checked the immediate area for any threat. Then he knelt and drank in handfuls of the cold fresh water. When he'd had his fill, he splashed more of the water over his face and into his hair, next he took his flask from his bag and filled it, before replacing it. Next to him Kibbin had been drinking too and he also filled a small flask from the bag he had taken from the cave at the Sugar Loaf.

Flax tried hard not to laugh at the sight of Kibbin with a wet face, the coarse wiry hair had been slicked down by the water and completely changed his appearance, in a comical way. He couldn't be sure if Kibbin had noticed his smirk or not but noticed that he made a conscious effort of brushing his stubby fingers through his hair and beard to try and restore his original look.

"Which way now?" Asked Flax. The path crossed the stream and climbed up an incline on the other bank but he knew the flow of the stream would lead down to the shoreline.

"Don't know," Kibbin admitted, "never been down here."

Flax sensed an uneasiness in his companion's tone.

"If we follow the path then we are climbing up, which means we will have to climb down at some point," Flax voiced aloud. "So if we follow the stream, we will already be at beach level."

"But being higher up on the cliffs might help us to plan our approach, whereas being on the beach we cannot do that." Flax continued to reason, speaking his thoughts. He looked at Kibbin hoping that he would get a decision from him, he didn't, all he did was shrug his shoulders.

Flax thought about it for a long moment. He was torn, the stream was the quickest way to the fire and potentially to his sister. But the cliffs allowed him to see if it was his sister or not, but there was no guarantee that there would be a safe way down to the beach any further along the path. He changed his mind back and forth half a dozen times. In the end he opted for speed over safety and announced, "We follow the stream to the beach." He looked at Kibbin who was clearly unsure about this suggestion, his hairy face scrunched up as if the words caused him pain.

"Don't like the beach," Kibbin said, "I'll watch from above." He pointed up the hill across the stream – and with a nimbleness that still took Flax by surprise he cleared the stream in one effortless jump. Flax had half a mind to follow after him, it would have been easier to stay in Kibbin's company. However, he knew that he had to see for himself if his sister was responsible for the smoke he had seen on the beach, and the only way he would truly know for sure was to head there. So reluctantly he watched his newfound friend shuffle steadily up the hill in the gloomy forest glen. Flax wondered what reason Kibbin had for not following him, despite the one he had given him. He knew that loyalty and bravery were in no short supply given what he had seen and learned in the last couple of days. But he also knew that Kibbin was not used to venturing into open spaces away from the comparative safety of the gorse forest. As the figure grew ever shorter in the distance Flax turned and began to follow the stream down through the glen toward the beach. He gripped his staff firmly in his right hand, not letting the bottom of it strike against the floor as he now trod more cautiously and quietly than he had before. In the quiet stillness of the glen he became all the more aware that he was alone now, he stood for a long moment and just listened.

His senses adjusted to the environment slowly but after a while he started to see and hear things he had not previously noticed. Shafts of golden light still pierced the tree canopy, small insects danced back and forth in the warm glow. The stream flowed steadily down through the glen, small waterfalls dropped into pools causing the water to bubble and froth. A gentle autumn breeze rustled the leaves. Flax could have happily stood there until dark taking in the previously underappreciated sights and sounds the glen had to offer. *I definitely need to come back to this place someday,* he told himself. He took the map out of his jacket pocket and was not surprised to see that Sid had already marked the location, next to it were the words, *'Glen Chass'*. He smiled to himself as he imagined Sid Kelly stood where he was now, taking in the sights, the sounds and the smells of the peaceful glen. Reluctantly he placed the map back in his pocket and strode off alongside the stream, following the gentle flow of the water downhill. After a few hundred paces he decided to cross over the stream, *in case it gets too wide or too deep to cross further down,* he told himself. He was now on the same side of the stream as the smoke on the beach. He hadn't been separated from Kibbin long but he wondered what his companion was doing right now.

"Probably searching for grub," Flax chuckled to himself. He looked up and he could see that he was approaching the edge of the forest, the shadows seemed brighter. The sun had still not fully set, but it wouldn't be long until dark. He pressed on, following the stream to the edge of the forest and there he waited in the shadow as he took in the scenery laid out before him.

He was crouched in an elevated position on a rock formation just above the beach. The stream flowed from the forest through a rocky outcrop over which it dropped into a deep pool on the beach below. The beach itself was not sand, it was made up of pebbles. He could tell from the tideline of seaweed and driftwood that the water wasn't at its highest but he was unable to judge if it was on its way in or out. In any case there was still beach above the tideline which meant that unless the next tide was unusually high then he would not end up stranded as he crossed the beach. Away to his left, most likely in the next cove or the one after that, the smoke still rose steadily into the sky which had now lost its deep orange colour and was that blue, almost green colour that would soon give way to darkness. He looked to the sky for the moons position, it was a half-moon that had silently risen beyond the smoke. This was good, it would give him light but not silhouette him from behind as he approached the fire. The more he thought about it, the less certain he was that his sister had lit that fire. He realised that Kibbin had the right approach. *Scout the site first approach the fire if it was safe.*

But I'm committed to the beach now, Flax thought, angry at himself for making a poor decision yet stubbornly refusing to change his plan. He waited until the last of the sun's rays had left the sky and under the soft glow of the half-moon he climbed down from the outcrop onto the pebbled beach.

His feet hit the beach and created a sound so loud he was sure that he would be heard in the next cove. He stopped and dared not move a muscle for a long moment, he didn't even want to breath for fear of giving away his position. He looked for a long time toward the direction of the smoke, there was no movement so he cautiously took a step forward. Again his footstep seemed overly loud to him, the shifting pebbles beneath his feet clicking together under his weight.

I can't go on making so much noise! he thought. He looked to his right at the high tide mark on the beach, strewn with seaweed that had been dragged up from the seabed and dumped at the change of the tide. He had come up with a plan, he timed his steps to coincide with the gentle crashing of the waves on the pebbles. But he did not move toward the fire, he moved toward the sea. After seven or eight waves – he wasn't counting – he reached the high tide mark. He stepped onto the seaweed and was relieved to find that it was thick and squashy enough to absorb the sound of his footsteps as he trod on it.

He made his way along the tideline, his staff in his hand, stepping carefully onto the soft seaweed to disguise the noise of his approach as best he could. Every few steps he would look ahead to check his progress and direction. The black smoke now somehow looked even darker against the inky blue sky. The moon still shone strong and he could see stars starting to show themselves against the dark backdrop around it.

He was over two thirds of the way along the beach and he could tell now that the tide was on its way in rather than out. The foamy waves crept ever closer to the tide line on which he walked. Looking ahead he could see that the tide line ran straight into the side of a tall rock outcrop from behind which the smoke rose, this rock formation protruded down the beach. At high tide the water would hit the rocks and cut off access to the next beach. He judged his progress against that of the incoming tide and knew it would be close as to what would reach the edge of the rock outcrop first, him or the waves. He tried to increase his speed to ensure that he reached it before the waves but he knew straight away that he was creating far more noise than he was comfortable with so he slowed his approach once more. As he crept toward the rock outcrop, he watched the tide race him. And beat him. Long before Flax reached it, the waves started to crash into the rock throwing up foam and spray that glistened as the silver moonlight passed through it. Each advancing wave that pummelled the rock made it more and more obvious that approach to the fire via the beach would not be possible, he would have to climb over the rocks.

He maintained his approach path along the tide line until he reached the rock, not far to his right the waves continued their assault, spray hit his face each time a wave hit the wall of rock. Despite the bright light that the moon had offered he now stood in darkness, the moons light blocked by the obstacle that stood between himself and the fire. He ran his hands along the wall, it was not smooth as he would have expected given the continual battering of the elements that it would have faced, far from it. The rock was craggy and rough, almost sharp in places, he would have to be careful where he put his hands and feet as he climbed.

He started to climb. He looked up and noticed the ruins of a large cube shaped structure on the top of the first rocky outcrop. He hadn't noticed this from the cliff top as he looked down, nor on his approach along the beach but his concentration had been elsewhere. He didn't pay much attention to the ruins as he knew that his intended destination was past the second outcrop of rocks. He decided to work around the outside of this small headland rather than climb over the top so as not to show out against the sky and also to avoid anyone or anything that might lurk in the ruins. As he worked around the coastline, he entered a sweeping sheltered bay. He was able to make his way across the beach, the ground was littered with pebbles but there were large flat rocks pushing up from among them on which he was able to walk and then jump from one to the next without ever walking on the loose stones. The way in which he moved reminded him of his sister making well placed foot movements as she ran. Although he was not as graceful, he slipped once or twice on the smooth surface but managed to regain his balance before falling. At the far end of the beach he approached the large rock wall that stood between him and the fire. He began to climb once more, stopping every so often to listen for any tell-tale signs of who might be near the fire. The crash of the waves hitting the beach followed by the rattle of slowly moving pebbles as the water receded created a barrier of noise through which he could hear little else. He eventually pulled himself up onto a small plateau that he had assumed would be the top, from where he might look down upon the fire. He was wrong, a further climb stood before him, then to his left something caught his eye. Flickering orange light bounced off the walls of the rock. He looked harder and focused his eyes, he realised that the light from the fire was reaching his side via a small tunnel in the rock.

He approached cautiously, the flickering light casting shadows across the wall that played tricks on his eyes, the entrance to the tunnel was low and small but he judged that he would be able to fit through it. Now that he was above the beach and further away from the waves the noise they created subsided to a constant background noise, but one over which he could hear other sounds. He heard the crackling of the fire as it spat up flames and sparks of burning wood, but above that he could hear voices. Not just one, multiple voices, multiple raspy voices that sent sensations down his spine, making the hairs stand to attention all the way down to his scarred left forearm that tingled and burned intensely.

He got down on his hands and knees and crept closer to the opening, straining to hear what was being said. He could make out the odd word but not all of it, he crept closer, the staff still gripped in his hand as he crawled forward. He accidentally knocked a loose stone with the staff, the noise it made sounded to Flax like an explosion of thunder, in reality it would be barely audible above the background noise of the fire and the waves. Still, he stopped where he was and cast his eyes around him in all directions - he then looked up and saw the short, curved blade pointing directly at his face. A pair of pale-yellow eyes glared menacingly at him and a raspy evil voice whispered with glee, "Gotcha!"

-46-
SHEY AS DAEED
- FLAX'S THIRD DAY ON MANNIN -

Flax lay on his side, his hands bound behind his back and his ankles tied tightly together. He could feel where the blood on the back of his head had dried into his hair, it pulled tightly whenever he moved his head due to the matted scab that it had formed. The wound to the back of his head had been caused by a second assailant, not the one with the dagger. Another that he had not seen sneak up behind him whilst he was preoccupied. He remembered being struck with something hard and then nothing further.

He stared at his captors sat round the fire talking in hushed tones and glancing at him every so often. He couldn't hear what was being said above the crackle of the fire and the pounding that he felt in his head. His anger filled eyes glared at them one by one. He was angry at himself for being so rushed and lax in his approach that he had been captured.

However, he was angrier at who his captors were. He counted nine of them in total – males and females. The only real way he could tell the difference between them in the ever-changing light of the fire was to listen to their voices.

"Let's just kill him, get it over with," one of the higher pitched females sneered.

"Yeah, no point draggin' it out," agreed another one, "I can do it right now." Flax saw the figure reach for a short spear next to them and pick it up in one hand.

"No, he could be worth something," interrupted another, Flax saw that this figure had his satchel bag and was rummaging through the contents of it.

"Shut up, all of you," spoke a fourth voice as a figure stood from its seated position. Flax could already tell from her height and stature that she was the leader of this group. "We take him back to *Vaaish* like we have been ordered." This Longtail wore the unmistakeable black cloak marked with the red of the *Roddanyn Doo*. As she spoke Flax felt his scar on his left forearm burn. She turned to look at him across the fire, the flames seemed to part and frame her face, her rodent features enhanced by the fire that danced in the darkness. Her yellow eyes, a completely different yellow to those of Kibbin, bore into him making no attempt to hide the malice and hatred that they held. Now that he was able to focus on her face, he could distinguish a physical difference between the male and female Longtails. Whilst her face was still angular and rat-like there was a definite femininity to her features compared to those of the males. Her eyes, even whilst filled with hate appeared slightly larger and more rounded. There was also less wiry hair on her face and her skin appeared softer.

"And if anybody touches him," she continued without breaking her gaze, "I'll kill 'em!"

She held the eye contact, as did Flax – attempting to appear as defiant as he could. "I was there," declared the Longtail. "Hell! You were all there!" She finally broke her gaze and pointed an accusing finger around the fire. "You all saw what this one's sister and father did to our kind - butchered and murdered them mercilessly, then –"

"– Murdered?! Mercilessly?" Screamed Flax in disbelief attempting to push himself up to a seated position. "You! You attacked *our* Island! We were defending ourselves!"

The she-rat leapt forward through the flames of the fire, landing directly in front of Flax just as he finished his words. He had managed to bring himself to an almost kneeling position, the cords that held his wrists and ankles bit into his skin but he ignored the pain, he did not want to show weakness in the face of his enemy.

"We did nothing to you, nothing!" spat Flax, barely able to contain the tears of anger that were starting to form in his eyes, "my father –"

"– your father got what he deserved," interrupted the Longtail. "And so will you!" She kicked him hard in the chest sending him backward to the stony floor. She turned to her group who had risen from round the fire and were lingering behind her in eager anticipation for what was to come. "Have at him," she rasped, "but don't kill him."

In a flash the group set about Flax kicking him and bringing down strikes with their clawed fists. He felt the first few blows individually but after that it was a constant barrage of violence in which he couldn't even distinguish between a kick, a punch or a strike with a stick.

Almost as quickly as it had begun it ended when the she-rat shouted, "Enough!" The other Longtails obeyed her order and stood back. She stalked towards Flax and knelt down to his level, drawing her pointed features close to his face she whispered, "I have orders to bring you in alive, but if you continue like that, I can make it a hell of a lot more painful for you than it needs to be, understand?"

Flax stared back at her, blood ran down his face and into his eyes, it was also in his mouth. He thought for a second of defiantly spitting blood in her face but he knew that would just lead to more violence. Instead he spat it out onto the stones and then returned his gaze.

"I understand."

His captors returned to their position around the fire leaving Flax off to one side, still bound tightly and now nursing his fresh wounds. He tried his best to listen to the conversation to see what information he could learn, whilst the Longtails spoke in the common tongue he quickly established that their names were like none that he had heard before, or certainly not in a language that he knew of. Some were referred to by what seemed to be nick names - Hook Tooth and One Eye. Whilst the other names he heard were clearly their given names - Diragh, Erodh and so on. He finally heard what he had been listening for, he heard her name, the female *Roddanyn Doo* - Kiragh. Flax repeated the name to himself silently a number of times to ensure that he did not forget it.

He tried to make sense of his surroundings. He was laid on the stony beach higher up from the sea than the tideline on which he had walked earlier that evening. The moon was behind him as he faced the fire. The fire sat between him and the rock outcrop on which he had climbed. He could see now on this side that the rock formation held a natural cave on this side, the cave narrowed toward the back into a small hole. This being the one that he had been listening through on the other side shortly before his capture. He had already seen one of the Longtails with his bag of possessions. Now that he looked around the group, he saw that another held in their hand Flax's knife. He used his bound hands to feel along the back of his belt confirming that the sheath was indeed empty. His sling shot he noticed was still in its small pouch on his right hip, not that it was much use at this time but it was still handy to know. He looked desperately around for his father's staff, he had not seen it yet, his eyes darted left and right up and down until he finally saw it, resting at an angle across a stone at the feet of Kiragh.

Flax stared at her across the fire once more, she didn't look at him. He tried to figure out if this was intentional or not, he had seen in her eyes before such hatred for him. Hatred that he could not understand given that Kiragh and her kind had attacked Flax's Island and not the other way round. *What could have caused her to bear such malice and ill feeling against me?* His train of thought was interrupted as something high up above the fire caught his eye for a fleeting moment. Another pair of yellow eyes, but not the sinister evil of the Longtails. No these eyes were a bright and vibrant yellow, there for a short moment, barely visible through the smoke and the heated air that rose above the flames.

Flax looked with a quiet desperation for them again, seeing nothing he began to think he had imagined them but just as he was beginning to convince himself he was seeing things he saw them once more. This time he could also make out the vague silhouette of his *Moanee* companion with whom he had parted ways before travelling down to the beach. He focused harder and could see the outline of the spiked club held loosely at Kibbin's side in one hand. As Flax's eyes became accustomed to Kibbin's location he was able to see him in greater detail, the silver moon giving just enough light to highlight his features. He was high above the Longtails and their fire and given their position in the mouth of the cave even if they looked up, they would not be able to see him on the top of the rock outcrop.

Kibbin lifted the club and brought it to rest across his body, the spiked head resting on the thick skin of his other hand, he looked at Flax and nodded. A definitive and knowing nod which Flax understood without need for any words. Flax looked back at his brave companion and gently shook his head, hoping that the movement was visible to him despite the distance and the darkness, of course he knew that Kibbin's eyesight was far superior to his and that he would be able to see him clearly.

He knew Kibbin had seen him but the short warrior's response was to raise the club from his palm and bring the spiked head down again into his hand in a menacing fashion and to nod once more. Flax shook his head again, in an exaggerated manner so that he was certain there was no mistaking it.

It was clear that Kibbin's intention was to attack the Longtails but he would be outnumbered and Flax could do nothing to help. Kibbin lifted the club up in one hand, bringing the head of it to rest against his shoulder, he started to move along the top of the rock, slowly and silently beginning his descent toward the beach and the unaware Longtails below.

"I need something to drink over here!" Flax shouted towards the fire, "hey, can you hear me? I'm thirsty, I need a drink!" His shouting had the desired effect as a couple of the Longtails stood from the fire, one of them lifted something from the ground next to them and they slowly started to walk toward him. Flax lifted his gaze once more to Kibbin who had now stood perfectly still, knowing that if one of the Longtails turned and looked up they would have a good chance of seeing him there. Once more, Flax shook his head, almost imperceptibly, but he knew that Kibbin would see it.

Kibbin dipped his head low and slowly and reluctantly shuffled back away from the beach where he sat watching the scene unfold.

The Longtails reached Flax and one of them uncorked a flask that they had picked up, "Here's your drink," he sneered as he poured a foul-smelling liquid from it into Flax's open mouth. The dark liquid instantly burned at Flax's throat causing him to cough it out, much to the amusement of his captors. They made to turn and walk back to the fire but Flax knew if they just looked up as then they would clearly see the outline of Kibbin on the cliff top, he thought quickly and called back.

"I said I need a drink you rat!" It worked, in fact three more Longtails from round the fire rose to the taunt and scurried over to where Flax lay defenceless as a torrent of blows were rained down on him with fists and feet once more.

"Enough!" called Kiragh from the fireside without even looking up, in that instant the attack stopped as quickly as it had begun. The five Longtails stood over Flax breathing heavily, congratulating each other on their work. Through a gap between them Flax was able to see the outline of Kibbin disappearing away into the blackness of the evening until he was completely out of sight, safe and gone.

-47-
SHIAGHT AS DAEED
- FLAX'S FOURTH DAY ON MANNIN -

Flax woke to the sound of waves crashing onto the pebbles, he had slept fitfully in the night having only fallen asleep when he was physically unable to keep his eyes open any longer.

As soon as his eyes had opened, he closed them once more. Feigning an ongoing sleep to allow him to assess what was going on around him.

The fire, as far as he could tell, was still burning - he could hear an intermittent crackle of flame and could still smell the smoke. He could feel the gentle warmth of the early morning sun on the back of his neck. The morning dew that had settled on his skin was starting to dry and it caused an itching sensation.

He could hear activity in the camp as the Longtails scurried around on the stony beach, there were snippets of conversation heard but not in the full context. From what he could gather they were waiting the arrival of someone or something, who or what it was he could only guess.

Silently and blindly he tried to assess the extent of the damage done to him by the two attacks he had suffered the previous evening. He focused on his body performing a mental checklist from top to bottom. His face hurt and his right eye felt as if it were swollen, he ran his tongue around the inside of his mouth and was pleased to find all his teeth were intact and that the cuts in his mouth had already started to heal through the night. His shoulders and neck ached but he told himself that could just as easily be the night he had spent sleeping on a stone beach. His wrists were still bound behind his back, the cord bindings still dug in and had caused the tips of his fingers to become slightly numb. His abdomen felt as if it were definitely bruised from the kicks and strikes he had suffered, as did areas of his legs. His ankles were secured in the same as his wrists were and there was a slight numbness in his feet.

He felt the kick into his stomach, he never saw it coming, "Wake up you!" He opened his eyes to see the Longtail he had heard called One Eye stood over him, sneering down at him. He was so close that he could smell his foul breath. Flax knew it was One Eye, his face gave away the reason for his nickname. An ugly jagged scar ran from the top of his temple, down across an open, empty eye socket and to the left corner of his mouth. Flax wondered to himself how someone could survive such a horrific injury. It made him think of his own scar that thankfully was nothing like this. The whiskers on the Longtail's face had grown through the scar tissue at awkward angles, giving the impression that his face was stitched together. "Can't sleep all day lazy," One Eye tutted sarcastically, "nearly time."

"Time for what?" asked Flax as he rolled to a sitting position, making a conscious effort not to let any pain or discomfort show on his face.

"Oh you will see," laughed One Eye as he walked back toward the fire and began to pack up some items.

Flax felt his stomach rumble, he realised he had not eaten anything since sitting at the bench the night before with Kibbin.

Kibbin? He thought to himself. He looked to the cliff top and scanned along to the right. He could see now in the morning light that the top of the rocks ran directly into the coastline where they met the main cliffs along the top of the beach. They were fairly high and they ran straight for quite some way until they gently lowered, creating the impression that they ran in a slope onto the stony beach - however Flax could not be sure if that was the case given how far away it was. He scanned back along the cliff line once more hoping to see his companion watching over him. There was no sign of him anywhere.

"Hey, you!" Flax called out to a Longtail with its back to him. The creature turned to look at him, Hook Tooth was clearly a female - and not an attractive one. If such a creature could be considered attractive. But in comparison to Kiragh there was a definite difference in appearance. Again Hook Tooth's features gave reasoning for her nickname. Of her two front protruding teeth, that were characteristic of all the Longtails, the right one had grown at an obscure angle across the front of the left one, it had also ground down on her lower teeth to a sharp point.

"What?" She spat back at Flax

"I haven't eaten anything," replied Flax.

"So?" Came a sneering reply.

"So I need to eat to stay alive, I'm fairly sure that I heard Kiragh tell you I needed to stay alive. What would your leader think if you disobeyed her?" This challenge had an effect on Hook Tooth but not the desired one. She came close to him and produced a blade, his blade that had been taken from him. She let the point of the sharp metal rest just beneath his eye and drew her face close to Flax's. In a rasping whisper she said.

"Carry on like that and I will do to you the same I did to One Eye over there. Just 'cos her daddy is King does not make her my leader; I does what I want! An' if I want to kill you, then I will! Understand?"

Flax did not answer, he silently held her stare trying to ignore the knife blade that was starting to bite into the skin on his already bruised cheek. He pondered the information that he had just learned and how he would be able to use it to his advantage. *Maybe to aid an escape?* he thought.

"They're here!" called a voice. Flax tried to look past Hook Tooth and could see another of the Longtails had climbed onto the cliff top near to where Kibbin had been the previous night. He was looking out to the sea and pointing a clawed hand.

Slowly, Hook Tooth released the pressure on the blade and turned to look in the direction that the creature was pointing. Now that she had moved he was able to see what she was looking at.

He could see on the horizon an outline of a boat pointing toward the shore, steadily growing larger. The craft was not overly large, it had a short single mast with a black sail strung from it. As it neared, he was able to make out the outline of a red rat skull on the black sail - the mark of the *Roddanyn Doo*.

Flax knew that the arrival of this boat would not be a good thing and would only make his chance of escape less likely as the boat inevitably brought with it more Longtails. He watched on as the boat approached, trying to see how many more Longtails but he was unable to tell. The boat neared a stretch of water that was flanked by angular rocks protruding above the gentle swell of the waves. He noticed that the sails were slackened off and then rolled up to the yardarm, the boat was turned broadside to the beach and an anchor was dropped from the stern.

The rocks in the sea created a natural chokepoint forcing water through a narrower gap and creating a fast-flowing current that the sailing ship would struggle to get back out through. He watched as a smaller longboat was lowered over the side, and four black shapes shimmied down ropes into it.

Whilst the sail ship remained at anchor the longboat was rowed through the chokepoint, there was a noticeable increase in its speed as it was carried through, and it continued landward until it reached the pebbly shore. Three of the black hooded *Roddanyn Doo* walked up the beach whilst the fourth remained with the boat. Hook Tooth stood and walked toward the approaching group intercepting their line of travel.

"You took your time getting here, wait until you see what we have got!" Hook Tooth declared proudly as she looked across toward Flax. The three *Roddanyn Doo* did not even slow or break their stride as they approached Hook Tooth.

"Where is she?" One of them demanded, Flax detected a tone of authority in the voice. The same authority that he had noticed in Kiragh's voice the previous night.

"She's in the cave," Hook Tooth pointed, Flax noted a definite subservience in Hook Tooth's tone and body language. A subservience that contradicted her previous claim to Flax that she would do what she wanted. As the *Roddanyn Doo* reached Hook Tooth they did not alter their path, Hook Tooth physically moved herself out of their way despite her having been stood still.

Flax assumed that there was a social division amongst the Longtails, not only were the *Roddanyn Doo* the elite guard of King Longtail - *they were the elite*. The other Longtails appeared compelled to do their bidding. The three *Roddanyn Doo* walked toward the fire at the mouth of the cave where they were met by Kiragh, they talked in low tones but the natural acoustics of the cave projected their voices to a volume at which Flax could hear most of their conversation.

"We are ready to return for a second attack Princess."

The term princess did not seem to fit with the general appearance of Kiragh thought Flax, but then again, her father was the King as Hook Tooth had let on so it was technically correct.

"No, the plan has changed," she replied, "we have a prisoner." She pointed across to Flax who quickly looked away trying to make it less obvious that he could hear them.

"Who is he?" asked one of the others.

"He is the son of the silver haired one who killed so many of ours, before my father killed him."

They think my father is dead? Thought Flax. *How can that be? Surely the King knew that the poison would not kill him?* Flax didn't have long to dwell on this thought as the conversation continued.

"This is a good omen Princess. He killed one of ours during the raid, we can return to finish our mission another time. We should take him back to *Vaaish*, to your father. He may have valuable information that will help our cause."

The thought of being taken there sent shivers through Flax that he could not describe. The image that the Traveller had portrayed of it in his story was bad enough, surely the reality of it would be even worse.

"Send a signal for the second long boat to help us return to the ship before the tide turns," Kiragh instructed the Longtail stood on the cliff top. Flax looked on as the creature made a series of exaggerated gestures with his arms and sure enough at the ship a second boat was lowered over the side, two more dark shapes slid down ropes into it.

"Prepare the prisoner for transport," Kiragh called to One Eye and another of the Longtails. They approached Flax and between them, despite their smaller height and size they managed to drag him to his knees and then partly assisted by Flax, he came to his feet.

"Walk!" One Eye instructed, pointing toward the shoreline. Flax's feet were still bound at the ankles, he looked back into One Eye's remaining eye and then down at his feet.

"Walk!" he was instructed again.

Flax attempted a step and immediately fell forward, unable to move effectively or support his own body weight, he managed rotate his body slightly so that he landed on his side rather than his face. He hit the pebbles hard sending them showering in all directions, he called out with a louder than necessary grunt of pain as he did, doing so to ensure that his fall was noticed by Kiragh and the *Roddanyn Doo*.

It was noticed. She yelled over to One Eye, "Cut his leg binds you fool! How do you expect him to walk? Or were you going to carry him?" The *Roddanyn Doo* next to her shook their heads in exaggerated disbelief. Grumbling to himself One Eye knelt at Flax's feet and took a short-bladed dagger from his belt to cut the binding around Flax's ankles. As he did this, he failed to notice that Flax used his bound hands to pick up and conceal something from the floor.

With his ankle bindings cut Flax sat up and slowly rotated each of his feet in turn, encouraging the feeling to return to them. His ankles were sore where the cords had worked their way through his skin, but it was nothing too painful given the state of the rest of his body after the beatings.

"Walk!" One Eye instructed for a third time, clearly annoyed now given the humiliation he had suffered in front of the other Longtails.

"Please just give me a minute to get my feet working," pleaded Flax, still slowly rotating his feet.

One Eye huffed and sat down on a large lump of rock, he brought a satchel that was slung over his shoulder round to the front and began to inspect the contents once more. The bag was Flax's that had been taken from him upon capture. One Eye took out the small bag of coins and held it close to his body keeping it out of sight of the others as he slowly counted them one by one.

Flax saw an opportunity and he capitalised upon it.

"I'm surprised you shared the silver," Flax declared in a low voice.

One Eye lifted his head momentarily and scowled back at Flax. "Didn't share nothing, these are all mine," he returned to counting the coins.

"Oh. Okay, I must be mistaken," said Flax, before casually adding, "just I saw her counting some of them earlier." He nodded gently towards Hook Tooth as he said this.

One Eye looked up again, he said nothing, he looked back down at the coins and hurriedly counted them again. He counted them a third time then looked up at Flax.

"You're wrong, they're all here. Thirty silver coins, see." He held them out for Flax to see.

"Thirty?" Flax lent slightly closer to One Eye and whispered, "there were fifty coins in that bag when I was captured."

"Fifty?" asked One Eye, his gaze moving between the coins and Flax.

'Fifty," whispered Flax. As he nodded he allowed a small look of concern to spread across his face, hoping to give One Eye the impression that he was genuinely trying to help him. "Saw her counting them then putting them in her pocket earlier," he added, trying to develop the situation.

His words had the desired effect. One Eye stood and stalked across the beach toward Hook Tooth, who was stood with her back towards him. One Eye broke into a run and leapt from a great distance toward the back of Hook Tooth, calling out as he did, "Thief!"

One Eye landed on Hook Tooth's back and knocked her to the floor, landing on top of her he rolled her onto her back and pinned her down. He struck her in the face with a fist and screamed "Where are they, where are the rest of them?" One Eye began to frisk at Hook Tooth's pockets looking for the coins that Flax knew he would not find, for they did not exist.

Hook Tooth took advantage of the fact that One Eye was concentrating so much on her pockets and not on her. She reached with her right hand and picked up a round pebble, she brought it crashing into her attacker's head on his blind side, he had no chance of seeing the incoming attack. It knocked him clean over and away from her. Flax was surprised to see him quickly rise to his feet, expecting that such a blow would have at least knocked him unconscious. Hook Tooth had also risen to her feet and now stalked sideways in a circular motion. She drew Flax's blade from her belt as One Eye also drew his blade.

"Time for me to take your other eye," spat Hook Tooth

"I'll take more than your eye. Nobody'll stop me this time!"

"Enough!" Came a clear and direct command from Kiragh at the shoreline who had turned to witness the aftermath of the attack.

The pair completely ignored her command and continued to circle each other.

"To the death?" Hook Tooth asked her adversary.

"To the death!" confirmed One Eye spitting on the ground.

"I said enough!" Called Kiragh once more, the impatience and anger clear in her voice this time. Still she was ignored.

Flax watched on, waiting for his next opportunity to present itself.

The two Longtails, each with a blade held in their right hand leapt at the same time toward each other, their left hands outstretched with their clawed fingers creating a secondary threat to the knives.

They collided with force and even whilst in mid-air and falling to the ground they scratched and bit and stabbed at each other, their fighting styles evenly matched in both skill and outright violence. They hit the floor and sprayed pebbles into the air, temporarily obscuring the melee.

Flax watched on and saw One Eye rise to a standing position, blood flowing from fresh wounds on his face, arms and abdomen. A look of proud triumph on his face. A look that slowly transformed to one of confusion.

On the ground lay Hook Tooth, face down, dead.

An arrow protruding from her back.

An arrow with black fletching.

- 48 -
HOGHT AS DAEED
- FLAX'S FOURTH DAY ON MANNIN -

In the brief moment of confusion that swept over the beach four things happened almost simultaneously.

The first was that One Eye was struck in the stomach by an arrow that was loosed from somewhere high up, behind Flax. He turned his head to look for the shooter. He knew already, having seen the black fletching on the arrow protruding from Hook Tooth's back, that it was his sister. He could see high on the cliff top to his right she was silhouetted in the early morning sun, her features invisible due to the bright light that haloed behind her. Bow held in one hand whilst the other was already selecting the next arrow to loose upon on the Longtails.

In that moment Flax was overwhelmed with relief, after finding her abandoned hook at The Chasms he had feared the worst, he had feared her dead and thought he would never see her again.

The second thing that happened in the confusion was that shouts of distress were heard from the water. Flax looked to his left just in time to see the second long boat capsize. Flipping its two occupants, a pair of hooded *Roddanyn Doo*, high into the air before they plunged into the cold sea. They surfaced a moment later coughing and spitting water and waving to their kin folk for help. At first glance it seemed as if the boat had simply capsized due to an error made by the occupants or a freak wave knocking the boat over.

But Flax watched as one of the two Longtails was pulled below the surface of the water by some unseen force. He knew that it was not an undercurrent given the scream of fear from the creature and the way it tried in vain to fight against it. The Longtail did not surface again. Shortly after, the second one was pulled into the depths in a similar way. He could see a number of small heads peering over the side rails of the sail ship watching the morbid spectre unfold.

The third thing that happened was that the Longtail who had been acting as lookout on the top of the rocky outcrop lifted a small bow from the ground by his feet and began shooting arrows across the beach to the perpendicular cliff top where Ealish was stood. The creature's aim was not good but the speed with which he released the arrows was effective in that it forced her to duck out of the way into cover and suppressed her attack temporarily. The Longtail noticed this and trained his bow onto the location where she had ducked down, he drew back the arrow but held it pointed at the exact location where her head would be expected to show above the cliff top first.

Flax wanted to shout out a warning to her but he was frozen still watching the events of the beach unfold in front of him. The Longtail had not shot an arrow for a few moments now and any moment Ealish would realise this and raise her head to see if it was clear for her to continue her attack. Flax looked back toward the Longtail with the bow, string still pulled taut. The creature had taken a knee to steady his aim, giving him the best chance of the arrow flying true to its mark.

To the far side of the Longtail Flax noticed a slight movement that the creature had not, this was the fourth thing that happened. The shrub that the Longtail was knelt next to seemed to move in a way that a bush would not be expected to. Flax realised what was happening. He silently urged it to happen quickly. The bush was not just a bush, well some of it was, but not all of it. The rest of it was Kibbin, he stood up to reveal his true shape and raised his club high above his head then brought it crashing down with a damaging force. The Longtail didn't have time to register what was happening before he fell dead over the side of the cliff, the arrow from the bow falling harmlessly to the floor at Kibbin's feet.

Kibbin looked down at his friend and nodded, then across the cliff top to where the female had just raised her head to make an assessment. He caught her eye and nodded again.

In the midst of all this confusion Flax made his move. He still had in his palm the sharp broken piece of stone that he had scooped up when he had purposely fallen over. He had fallen on purpose for two reasons, the first being in hope of his leg binding being released and the second in hope that he would have been able to pick up the broken stone he had seen on the beach near to him. He had been fortunate that both parts of his plan had been successful. As soon as the fight had started between Hook Tooth and One Eye he had started to manoeuvre the stone in his hands to position the jagged broken edge of the rock against the cords that held his wrists. He sawed it up and down on the rope. It was a slow process, the binding on his wrists greatly restricted his movement causing his fingers to cramp up quite quickly. As he sawed with the stone the sharp point dug into the soft skin on the underside of his forearm causing a small cut to open up. This stung but Flax pushed the pain to the back of his mind and concentrated on his escape.

As the Longtail that Kibbin had killed hit the stony beach with a sickening crack he had felt the final strand of the cord snap and his hands, whilst still individually bound, could move independently. He didn't make his move right away, instead he slowly rotated his wrists in turn and stretched out his fingers to encourage the movement to return, just as he had with his feet. He waited for his next opportunity.

There were thirteen Longtails on the beach at the start of the attack, nine of the group who had originally captured Flax and the four *Roddanyn Doo* from the longboat. The second longboat had held two more but they had never made it to shore after being attacked in the water.

Hook Tooth lay dead and One Eye was slowly dying from the arrow to the stomach, plus Kibbin had killed the look out. That left ten alive for Flax to either fight with the help of Kibbin and Ealish or to flee from. Five of these were *Roddanyn Doo*, elite warriors amongst their kin. Thankfully they were the farthest away at the moment as Kiragh and the group of three had headed to the shoreline where the remaining *Roddanyn Doo* had waited with the longboat. Around the cave and the campfire the remaining five were rushing about to collect their weapons whilst trying to figure out who or what had attacked them.

One of the five fell, struck in the chest by another black fletched arrow. The other four focused on the location that the arrow had come from, two of them shooting arrows of their own, a third with a sling, whilst the fourth took cover behind a large rock since she had no ranged weapon of her own. The *Roddanyn Doo* on the shoreline were well out of arrow range and stood in a line watching as the Longtails up the beach panicked to arrange a structured defence. They made no attempt to help them either defend or to flee to safety, they simply watched on with a morbid curiosity. Again Flax realised the truth of the social divide between Longtails and the *Roddanyn Doo*. It appeared that Kiragh and her companions had no interest in whether the four Longtails lived or died, they were certainly going to make no attempt to assist them.

Flax now had some feeling back in his hands and his feet, he scurried across the beach about halfway towards the cave, passing by Hook Tooth's body and the now dead One Eye before taking shelter behind a large rock. The Longtails did not see his approach as they were concentrating on the shooter on the cliff top. He wished he had stopped at the fallen Longtails to collect a weapon from them, he looked back toward the bodies and could see his knife on the floor between the pair. He couldn't risk moving back out into the open now though, he was conscious that he had his back to the *Roddanyn Doo* at the shoreline but a quick glance confirmed his suspicions that they had no intention of involving themselves in this fight unnecessarily. He looked around desperately for a weapon, he glanced at the floor and suddenly remembered the sling that was in the pouch on his belt. The Longtails had neglected to take this from him, it had been no use to him whilst he was bound but now a ranged weapon was just the thing he needed and he had a limitless supply of ammunition.

He took out the sling and selected a pebble from the ground, rather than using the ones he had brought with him from his Island. He lifted his head above the rock and gauged the distance. He stood and swung the sling round three times next to his head before releasing the pebble with as much force as he could manage. He had the distance but not the accuracy, his hands and wrists were still adjusting to the feeling of not being tightly bound. The small stone sailed past the head of one of the bow wielding Longtails and hit the wall of the cave with a resounding crack. The noise was enough to cause the four Longtails to turn their attention immediately toward him, the two using bows and the other with a sling of his own. The fourth still cowering in shelter behind the rock. He had to duck quickly to avoid the first arrow that came his way. The second followed shortly after, both sailed above his head. Then came the familiar sound of pebbles hitting rock as the Longtail with the sling unleashed what seemed like an endless barrage of them his way.

After a few moments the sound stopped. He crawled to the edge of the rock he was hidden behind and was able to see around the side that the two Longtails with bows had re-concentrated their efforts back at the cliffs where they had been attacked from initially. As he moved further round the rock he could see why, the Longtail who had been armed with the sling now lay dead with a black fletched arrow protruding from its neck. They had been too consumed on suppressing Flax that they had neglected the threat from the cliff top.

There was a second threat they had neglected, one that they were maybe unaware of - but soon would know about. Flax looked up and saw Kibbin moving toward the edge of the cliff, in his hands a large flat stone. He reached the edge and looked down, then lifted the stone high above his head before throwing it down with deadly accuracy. It hit one of the two bow wielding rats with a sickening thud, killing him outright. The other Longtail stopped to look at her fallen comrade.

At this point Flax expected an arrow to strike the Longtail from the cliff top, he looked over expectantly but saw the featureless silhouette stood there, bow in hand, hair blowing in the wind. For a moment his mind flashed to the image of the warrior on the hill in his vision, as quickly as the image had formed it was gone again and he found himself back in the middle of battle. Two Longtails remained, one with a bow and he decided to target this one first due to the threat it posed. He stood from behind the rock, picking up three pebbles from the ground as he did. He loaded the first pebble into his sling as he ran toward the two creatures. He swung the sling three times around in the air and let the pebble fly, it flew off to the left and hit the rock behind which the other Longtail still hid. Without a second thought to the miss he loaded and swung the second pebble. This one flew true and struck the creature directly in the side of her neck, dropping her instantly. He fought back the metallic tang that crept into his mouth from under his tongue, something he was still not able to suppress. He continued running towards the remaining Longtail as he loaded the third and final pebble. He could see that the creature had realised he was the last of his comrades and he acted quickly, he did not run towards Flax but toward one of the fallen rats.

He's going for the weapons! Flax thought as he fought hard to close the gap.

On the run he began to whirl the sling. Just as he was ready to release, his footing gave way on the loose pebbles that shifted under his weight. He began to lose his balance and knew that he would fall, in a last-ditch effort he released the stone from the sling towards the Longtail who by now had just picked up a weapon from the ground.

The stone flew through the air with force. It travelled well wide of its mark on account of Flax falling as he released it. He hit the ground hard on his right-hand side but immediately began to push himself back up to his feet and continue his run. However, when he looked ahead he found himself staring at the end of a staff - his father's staff. Holding the staff with an evil twisted grin on his face was the remaining Longtail.

He raised the staff high and snarled, "Time to die boy," he brought the staff swinging down towards Flax's head, all he could do was raise his arms, close his eyes and wait for the impact.

- 49 -
NUY AS DAEED
- FLAX'S FOURTH DAY ON MANNIN -

The staff hit Flax on his outstretched arm, he felt it - but strangely felt no pain. He expected the power of the strike to follow through and push the staff toward his head. Instead it bounced away to the side and landed on the floor.

He opened his eyes to see the Longtail laid out on the floor in front of him, clearly dead. To the side of the Longtail lay Kibbin, clearly injured. Flax looked up to the cliff top above and surmised that his friend had jumped from the top in order to save him.

He dashed to his side to assess his injuries, "Kibbin are you hurt? You saved me!"

"Course," replied the *Moanee* warrior, both answering Flax's question and confirming his statement in his usual one-word way, despite him being in obvious pain.

Flax laughed aloud, a tear of happiness and relief running down his cheek as he hugged his friend, gently of course given the pain he was in. Kibbin hugged him back with his one good arm that was not injured and then quickly pushed him away.

"No time for that yet young 'un," he declared as he pointed a short finger down the beach.

Flax turned his head to see the five *Roddanyn Doo* at the shoreline were now stalking up the beach in a *V* formation, Kiragh leading at the front armed with a short sword. Flanked by two either side, on her left one of the others carried a short spear and the other a pair of daggers with curved blades. On her right one carried a spiked club, not unlike Kibbin's. The other had a weapon unlike one Flax had ever seen, a stick with a chain attached to the end, on the other end of the chain was a small metal ball covered in vicious looking spikes.

They walked in Flax and Kibbin's direction, with purpose but without speed. They knew they had the advantage of numbers, and most likely skill with their weapons too. There was no rush, Kiragh pulled her black hood up and over her head, a moment later and in unison the other four followed suit. They created a fearful image, five messengers of death slowly approaching, weapons at the ready, yellow eyes glowing under the cover of the dark hoods.

Flax looked to the weapons on the floor around him, he still had his sling in his hand but that would be no good to him against five of them, especially head on, they would have chance to simply dodge his projectiles. He dropped the sling and quickly assessed his other options. He disregarded the bows for the same reason as the sling. A dagger lay next to one of the fallen rats, whilst he had practiced with the blade it was not his first choice. He bent low and picked up his father's staff from next to the final fallen Longtail.

"Kibbin, can you get yourself into the cave?"

"I can help you fight young 'un…" he offered back, trying to stand but then grasping his ribs in pain with his one good arm.

"I know you can friend, but I need to do this," Flax replied, not wanting to offend the brave warrior.

Flax looked back toward the slowly advancing line, he stood and walked away from the mouth of the cave where Kibbin lay, in the hope of drawing the battleground as far away from him as possible. As he walked, without warning and whilst still some distance from him the *Roddanyn Doo* to the left of Kiragh launched the short spear in his direction. It was an accurate throw and powerful too, it was only due to seeing the throw early that he was able to duck and roll along the beach to avoid it. The spear landed just beyond where he had stood, the *Roddanyn Doo* who had thrown it reached inside her cloak and produced a small, curved sickle to replace the weapon she had used. But before she had even had opportunity to grip it properly, she was struck in the chest by an arrow and collapsed to the ground dead.

The remaining *Roddanyn Doo* stopped, realising that they had strayed within range of the archer on the cliff top they quickly retreated their advance well out of her range.

Flax turned to see the silhouette of his sister on the cliff top, bow held in hand. He raised a hand to wave his thanks and recognition but found it odd that she did not reciprocate.

He could not dwell on that for now though, he turned his attention back to the four hooded creatures who had rearranged their formation and now stood in a line, equally spaced, weapons ready and watching Flax to see what he would do.

He turned to them and called out, "I do not need or want to fight you, look around, see how many are already dead here. Just take your boat and go and I will take my friend and leave. We do not have to fight."

"You are right Islander," Kiragh called back, "we do not have to fight." With that Kiragh turned her back on Flax, the three remaining *Roddanyn Doo* followed her lead and began to walk back toward the longboat on the shore.

"After all," Kiragh shouted, "we already have what we need, don't worry we will keep her nice and safe."

Flax could not be sure whether Kiragh had said this with the intention of drawing him into a fight or not but if she had, then it had worked. He gripped the staff tightly in a double handed grip, one hand over and one hand under, held diagonally across his body with the top raised higher on his left side.

He started running toward the four rodents who still had their backs toward him, seemingly oblivious to the threat he posed. He ran hard down the beach, his feet causing pebbles to spray up each time they connected with the floor. He knew they must have been aware of his approach given the sound he was making but he was not bothered.

As soon as he got within a couple of staff lengths of them, he understood his mistake, he had been drawn into a trap. At that moment the *Roddanyn Doo* turned as one and with enviable speed they spread themselves out into two pairs. Each pair then split as quickly as they had formed, one from each pair taking a great leap. They did not leap in Flax's direction but past him, landing and turning instantly. He found himself surrounded, the well-trained warriors had formed a square around him, with him in the centre able to only face one threat at a time. Instinctively he turned slowly through a full circle, holding the staff out in one hand at arm's length, hoping that the reach of the weapon would deter any immediate attack.

Unknowingly he found himself in a very similar position to that of his father the night of the Bloom Day attack. He of course had not witnessed the fight that ensued that night as he had passed out after killing the Longtail who had stabbed him in the arm.

Now, as he stood trapped in the middle of the four attackers his scarred arm tingled. Strangely he felt no fear, this surprised him, he took advantage of it. As he slowly span he focused on his four adversaries and the weapons they held.

Whilst he circled, he whispered to himself, "Sword, daggers, club, spiked chain, sword, daggers, club, spiked chain." Mentally checking each one off as he saw them. He turned full circle four or five times.

He realised that he was not in a position to attack first, nor could he continue spinning with the weapon at arm's length. He brought the staff in towards his body and took up the double handed grip again, as he did his right hand ran across the carved words in the wood.

"*Traa dy liooar*," he said softly to himself. He took a deep breath and widened his stance, crouching slightly. "*Traa dy liooar*," he said once more to himself with resolve.

He sensed the attack coming before he saw it, behind him to his left the *Roddanyn Doo* with the spiked club initiated the fight. He turned on his left heel to face the attacker who, it seemed, was moving in slow motion somehow. He held his father's staff close to his body, it felt as if it had become part of him in the moment. He took two strides toward the creature. He could see now it was a female beneath her dark hood. She held the spiked club raised high with both hands, ready to bring it down on his head. However he was able to recognise the threat and anticipate the move, he stepped neatly to one side allowing the club strike to miss him completely. Then using a sweeping motion he caught the Longtail in the back of her legs with the head of the staff, taking her feet from underneath her. Before she had even hit the ground he followed up with a second strike with the base of the staff, this hit her in the head killing her instantly. He had no time to reflect on the life he had just taken, nor did his body react in the way it had previously. He had expected to be overcome by the nausea once more, his mind and his body seemed to be working in overdrive, already preparing for the next attack.

This came immediately from his left, a male carrying the spiked chain ran toward him. The spiked ball already flailing above his head as he closed the distance to Flax. Instinctively Flax thrust the staff forward and upward into the path of the chain. The chain connected with the staff and began to wrap itself around it with the momentum that it had built up. With two hands on the staff he was able to yank the weapon from the attacker's hands leaving him unarmed. He flicked the staff to one side causing the strange weapon caught around it to fall to the ground, he quickly brought the staff back across his body in its ready position. Knowing that the *Roddanyn Doo* was unarmed and having seen how they moved he knew exactly what to expect next. The rat creature leapt just as Flax had expected. Claws forward, moving with speed and aggression. Although again, it seemed as if Flax was able to move more quickly than the creature – that was now almost suspended mid-leap. He stepped forward into the attack moving underneath and beyond the reach of the claws, staff held in both hands he pushed up toward the chest of the now defenceless creature. Exerting effort upwards and over his head he was able to use the momentum of the jump to his advantage and throw the *Roddanyn Doo* over his head causing its body to over rotate, directly into a large rock that it hit with a crunch. The rodent did not move again.

Now slightly off balance having thrown the creature backwards, Flax was able to correct his stance and prevent himself falling back only to see a dagger flying through the air toward his head. He ducked just in time to avoid it and stood quickly, facing the thrower who now held the one remaining dagger in one of his clawed hands.

Aware that Kiragh was stood somewhere to his left with a sword Flax chose to engage the dagger wielding *Roddanyn Doo* with speed rather than remain a stationary target for either of his two remaining enemies. The *Roddanyn Doo* did not expect this and the sight of Flax charging at him with the staff – golden hair blowing across a face full of controlled aggression – caused the rat to pause momentarily. This was a fatal mistake and was all Flax needed to make use of the superior range that the staff offered over the dagger. He struck the creature directly in the chest with the end of the staff and without a second thought turned a half circle on the spot, knelt down low and raised the staff horizontally above his head.

The *Roddanyn Doo* crashed to the floor at the exact same moment that Kiragh's sword blade struck the middle of Flax's staff.

The weapon shattered.

Shards of the broken sword blade flew in every direction, one of them grazing across Flax's cheek. Blood ran down his face and into the corner of his mouth.

Kiragh stood above Flax holding the broken sword handle in her hand, a look of disbelief on her face. Before she could react and slice at Flax with what remained of her weapon, he lowered the staff and struck her in the stomach. With the weapon still held horizontal, driving forwards with his legs as he straightened them. The strike bent her double and knocked her backwards onto the ground. Flax continued the motion of the attack and threw himself forward on top of her, pinning her chest with the staff.

She looked up at him with her yellow eyes full of fear and confusion, "How? How did you manage to move so fast?"

Flax didn't answer, he pressed down harder on the staff restricting her breathing further.

Still she asked through gasps, "How did you move like that?"

Still Flax didn't understand the reason for her question, he had managed to anticipate the attacks but he did not think he had moved any faster than he had in training with the Traveller. It had just seemed to him that he had been able to anticipate each attack early and therefore had more time to react.

Kiragh was now really gasping for breath, her claws reached out to scratch at Flax's face in vain. He started to feel her body going limp as the fight in her faded. As her arms began to fail on her Flax released the pressure on her chest and rolled to one side, he sat breathing heavily as the exertion of the fight caught up with him.

Kiragh rolled onto her side coughing and gasping desperately for air. For a long moment the two of them remained where they were, recovering and oblivious to the fact that they had not long since been trying to kill each other.

Kiragh spoke first, her voice hoarse and weaker than before, "That staff," she pointed a finger toward it laid at Flax's side, "it was your fathers?"

Flax said nothing, the reality of the lives that he had just taken had now hit him and it took all his strength to control the waves of nausea that were relentlessly sweeping over his whole body. He stared at a point on the ground and focused hard on it, aware of Kiragh speaking to him but unable to bring himself to answer or look at her.

"I see now how he did it, how he managed to defeat so many of us that night." She said, almost accusingly, "I see how you did it just now, how you bested us," her voice became angry now.

"You cheated!" She spoke more firmly, with anger in her voice, "your father cheated! There is magic within that weapon! How could we stand a chance in fair combat?"

Enraged at the audacity of her outburst Flax stood, shaking any feeling of nausea from his body. He lifted the staff and with a wide arcing overhead strike he brought it crashing down onto Kiragh's right leg. He heard the bone snap as the wood struck her.

"Fair combat?" He shouted. "Fair combat?! What is fair about attacking a defenceless group during a feast?! What is fair about outnumbering my father twelve to one?! What is fair about your father shooting him in the back like a coward?! And just now you outnumber me four to one, I beat you and you say that is unfair?! There is no magic afoot here, I beat you! You lost! And you say this is not fair! Look around you! Look at the bodies! This is your doing! This is you!" His voice grew steadily louder, his anger swelled with every word until by the end of his tirade he was literally spitting each word as tears of anger rolled down his face. Anger at the brazen accusations of the wicked creature that lay before him and anger at what he had been forced to do, taking lives needlessly. His rage had been so great he had not registered the scream of pain that erupted from Kiragh's throat as her knee had been shattered. Nor had he even realised that with each statement he had struck the defenceless *Roddanyn Doo* with the end of his staff, harder and harder each time.

He paused. The tip of the staff held a short distance from her throat. She had a look of pitiful acceptance on her face, she knew she was about to die and there was nothing she could do to prevent it.

Flax held his position for a long moment. Contemplating his options and internally battling with what he knew to be right and what he believed the rodent deserved. Despite all she had done and what she represented his core values won through. He could not kill an unarmed enemy no matter what the circumstances, he looked down at her shattered leg and knew that he had beaten her.

He considered taking her hostage and using her to trade with the Rat King for Flea's return. But he had no guarantee that the rodent would agree to such a trade and in any case, given the state of her leg, Flax did not think it possible for Kiragh to travel by land to *Guinn Y Vaaish*.

I could take the boat, he thought looking at the rowing boat further down the beach. But he looked beyond this to the black sailed ship sat at anchor and he quickly disregarded this as a viable option. Even as he looked to the ship now he could see that a number of small dark figures had somehow managed to salvage the second longboat that had been attacked in the water and were beginning to make their way to the beach. He did not have long. He would have to make a decision.

"Tell your father I am coming for my friend," he hissed at Kiragh who was still writhing in pain, clutching her knee.

Flax turned his back on her and with staff in hand he walked up the beach, stopping at the bodies of Hook Tooth and One Eye to collect his dagger and satchel bag and the black fletched arrows from their bodies. He noted the black symbol of The Tree burned into each arrow by his father's loving hand.

Next, he walked over to the cave where he found Kibbin sat propped up against the cave wall, clutching his arm close to his ribs. He picked up his sling and helped Kibbin to his feet and hugged him, "Come on friend, we need to move from this place."

"Course," grimaced Kibbin as he painfully shuffled along next to Flax. "You lettin' her go?" He asked, not hiding the surprise in his voice as he nodded toward Kiragh.

Flax observed the female *Roddanyn Doo* who was now pulling herself along the beach toward the shoreline, her left leg helping to push her along whilst she dragged her broken right leg.

"She knows she is beaten," replied Flax, "killing her would add nothing."

"She'd be dead, that'd be something." Kibbin offered, clearly not joking.

Flax didn't hear him though, he was staring toward the shoreline. However he was not looking at the boat of *Roddanyn Doo* that was approaching. He looked beyond it and squinted his eyes, still unable to focus on what he had seen he wiped the sweat and crusted blood from his eyes and looked once more. He was not mistaken, there sat on a flat rock staring back at him was a seal. Not just any seal, Flax could have sworn that this seal had damaged fur around its right flipper. It was the seal he had seen when crossing The Sound. Not only that but now, as he stared at it from some distance, he was sure he recognised it as the same seal that had watched him on the beach the day that the Traveller had left the Island.

Flax raised a hand and waved, he instantly felt stupid as the seal looked back at him blankly then turned its head.

"What you waving at?" asked Kibbin.

"Nothing, never mind," said Flax dismissively, feeling foolish for his actions.

"Sure," replied Kibbin, still wincing with pain, "You gonna teach me how to move as fast as you in a fight then?"

Flax was unsure what he meant by this, but it triggered Kiragh's voice in his head, how she had questioned how he moved and then said there was magic in his father's staff. He eyed the weapon that was held in his right hand, his left hand held onto Kibbin to offer him support. *Could there really be magic in this?* He asked himself. He replayed the battle in his head, perhaps it had felt like there was but he could not be sure. If there was then he certainly had no idea how he had used it or exactly what the magic had done for him.

He and Kibbin continued up the beach, toward the cliff. Behind them Kiragh was pulled into the longboat by her soldiers and was already on her way back to the sailboat.

Flax looked up to the cliff top where his sister, his rescuer had shot her bow from. He could not see her so he scanned the length of the cliff top from left to right. His eyes came to rest on her away to the right now stood on the beach having made her way down a path from the cliff top. He let go of Kibbin, ensuring he was able to support himself, then he ran across the pebbles to his sister. His head down and breathing hard after the exertion of the battle, he felt like it was taking an age to reach her. When he finally did, he looked up and saw her. He dropped to his knees on the pebbles, the staff and the arrows falling from his hand.

He wept.

- 50 -
JEIH AS DAEED

Looking up through tear filled eyes Flax could not understand.

In front of him, holding the bow was a female.

But this female was not Ealish.

The face looking back at him was much older, seventy blooms at least – maybe more. Long silver hair worn in a plait. The face was wrinkled and weathered with time; she had clearly spent a lot of time outdoors in the sea air.

Flax's mind was spinning, he had been so sure that the archer on the cliff was his sister, that she had survived the fall in The Chasms and had rescued him. It had to be her, the black fletched arrows, the bow - *they both belonged to Ealish, didn't they? So how had this female come to be in possession of them? And where was Ealish?*

Flax wanted to ask all these things and more but his voice simply would not work.

He looked into the eyes of the female, unable to hide the disappointment on his face.

He looked down at the floor, his tears fell like rain drops on the pebbles, leaving dark splashes where they landed.

The female placed a hand on his shoulder. Even through his jacket the hand felt warm. Flax looked up and held her gaze, in her eyes he saw a seriousness but also a deep kindness.

The female spoke, her accent strange yet completely understandable.

"You need to come with me Flax," this was not a request. It was an instruction. She pointed to the floor in front of him, "and bring that staff with you."

EPILOGUE

The stranger had witnessed it all.

He looked across the beach, the grey and white pebbles spoiled by the blood and the bodies of the fallen Longtails.

He had seen the grey-haired female shooting the bow from the cliff top.

The fearlessness of the stout wire-haired creature as he leapt from the cliff to save the golden-haired Islander.

He had seen the golden-haired boy defeat the elite rat warriors with blistering speed, speed that somehow seemed unnatural.

He had seen the mercy that the golden-haired boy had shown to the leader of the *Roddanyn Doo*, mercy that he was certain would not have been reciprocated.

He had seen the interaction between the golden-haired boy and the grey-haired female.

He had seen the rats' boat leave the bay and sail east.

He had seen it all.

He slipped into the water unseen. He knew he must report back what he had seen.

AFTERWORD & ACKNOWLEDGEMENTS

I had the idea to create the world of Mannin six or seven years ago whilst I was running on my favourite route – the coastal path from the Sound to Port St Mary, the same path that Flax and Ealish have adventured along in this book. I had never thought of writing a book before but I couldn't shake the idea, I became obsessed with a story that would showcase the Isle of Man, its beautiful scenery and its rich folklore. I wanted to create a world that my children, and others, could read about but then actually go and visit – Guinn Y Vaaish, The Island, The Chasms, The Sugar Loaf, the beach with the cave from the final battle – they are all real places, reimagined and embellished upon, but real, nonetheless.

The idea grew and grew in my head until one day I just started writing. I didn't tell anybody, not even my wife Lucy – and I tell her everything. I wrote the whole first draft on my iPad, touch screen – no keyboard!

When I finished it and told her, Lucy laughed at me, thinking I was joking. Once had I convinced her that I had actually written a book she became so supportive, offering editorial advice, putting up with my mind wandering mid-conversation because I was rethinking a chapter – or planning a chapter in two or three books time! So thank you for putting up with me sweetheart.

I also have to thank my sister-in-law Sarah. The book had been through a couple of self-edits before she cast an eye over it. Something I am so grateful for. Sarah's editorial advice was priceless – and actually led to me changing the names of the two main characters! It took many, many days for me to settle with Ealish and Flax but I am grateful for the advice.

The incredibly talented Meriel Puttick created the cover for this book as well as the map at the front. I am not a visually artistic person so when I asked Meriel to create me a book cover and a map I just blurted out lots of words and ideas. She quickly came up with a concept cover which we tweaked before settling on the final design, which I absolutely love, especially the outline of Mannin in the rings of the tree. With Meriel's help I have been able to see a way to carry the design on through the next books in the series.

When I decided to write The Mannin Chronicles I wanted to include some of the Manx language too, to give the story another level of depth and some authenticity – which sounds strange considering that the story is fiction but I felt that it deserved to be included. I am not a Manx speaker so I got by in the initial draft using online translators to give me an idea which terms and phrases I wanted to use.

Traa Dy Liooar was always going to be one of them, I actually wear a ring with this inscribed on, I have worn it since I was about fifteen, but I knew I couldn't put this ring in the story – a bit too LOTR! Not that this is a bad thing, I love Tolkien's stories, I just didn't want to copy. Hence the idea of the staff with the inscription – I actually made the staff in my workshop from an old Christmas Tree trunk to see how it would look, it sits in our lounge at home, I can't wait for the kids to read the book and realise that's where the idea for the staff came from.

The above is a long-winded way of getting round to thanking Ruth Keggin-Gell from Culture Vannin. I contacted Ruth and explained what I was doing, she was happy to help. I sent her a document with all my phrases, what I thought they meant, what I wanted them to mean and how I thought they sounded. How wrong I was with quite a few of them! Particularly the pronunciations! The helpful pages that you see at the front of the book are thanks to Ruth's brilliant work in seeing me right with regards to the Manx language – the old tongue.

I took a long time deliberating over the ending of the book. Whether to end it how I have or to bolt on what will now be the first couple of chapters of the next book – The Mannin Chronicles - *to be announced*. In the end I decided to stick with the ending as it is, I love a book that ends and leaves the reader with a few questions to be asked – as long as you know that they will be answered at some point. This is something that one of my favourite authors Matthew Reilly does time and time again in his Jack West Jr series, whether it be at the end of a chapter or the end of a book. They do it on TV so why not do it in book form too?

It feels strange to be typing this final paragraph as it means I am ready to go online and hit the publish button. I hope you have enjoyed reading the book, there are more to come – book two is finished in first draft form and now ready to edit. In the meantime if you are one of those people who would say, "The Isle of Man? that's somewhere I've never been but would always like to go." Then why not hop on a plane or a ferry and go explore, take a boat trip to 'The Island' – although don't be disappointed to find there is no village there, and certainly no Tree. Or walk the coastal footpath in the footsteps of Ealish and Flax. You've nothing to lose, and if you don't like it, well…there's a boat in the morning!

J. Rotchell

December 2024

Printed in Great Britain
by Amazon